FROM BIZARRE HUMOR TO SHEER HORROR,

the sixteen stories in this surprising book cover the entire range of fantasy. All are off-beat with the wry, playful, unbound-aried imagination that has gained R. A. Lafferty a steadily increasing following of delighted readers.

Stories such as *World Abounding, The Man with the Speckled Eyes, Entire and Perfect Chrysolite, Cliffs That Laughed,* and the Hugo-contending *Continued on Next Rock,* reveal Lafferty penetrating to the zany realities of the human and in-human condition.

You will move through strange worlds of personality literally splitting itself, of night-mares becoming true and preferred, of the perils of doubting and the hazards of be-lieving. And in each story you will move through the individual and beautiful styles of a master of the unexpected turn of phrase, idea and

Strange Doings

Doings

R. A. LAFFERTY

Illustrated by
JACK GAUGHAN

DAW BOOKS, INC.

DONALD A. WOLLHEIM, PUBLISHER

1301 Avenue of the Americas
New York, N. Y.   10019

Published by
THE NEW AMERICAN LIBRARY
OF CANADA LIMITED

The following stories were first published in the magazines
indicated below:

Galaxy: "All But the Words," "Aloys," "Dreamworld,"
"Rainbird," "Sodom and Gomorrah, Texas."
Copyright © 1971 UPD Corporation. Copyright
© 1961.

If: "Ride a Tin Can."
1962 Galaxy Publishing Corporation.
Copyright © 1970 UPD Corporation

The Literary Review: "The Ugly Sea."
Copyright © 1961 Fairleigh Dickinson University.

The Magazine of Fantasy and Science Fiction: "Camels
and Dromedaries, Clem," "The Man with the Speckled
Eyes," "World Abounding."
Copyright © 1961, 1964, 1971 Mercury Press, Inc.

The Magazine of Horror: "Cliffs That Laughed."
Copyright © 1968 Health Knowledge, Inc.

Orbit (6, 7): "Entire and Perfect Chrysolite," "Continued
on Next Rock."
Copyright © 1970 Damon Knight.

Quark 2: "Incased in Ancient Rind."
Copyright © 1971 Coronet Communications, Inc.

Worlds of Tomorrow: "The Transcendent Tigers."
Copyright © 1964 Galaxy Publishing Corporation.

FIRST PRINTING, APRIL, 1973

1 2 3 4 5 6 7 8 9

PRINTED IN CANADA
COVER PRINTED IN U.S.A.

The Stories

Rainbird

Were scientific firsts truly tabulated the name of the Yankee inventor, Higgston Rainbird, would surely be without peer. Yet today he is known (and only to a few specialists, at that) for an improved blacksmith's bellows in the year 1785, for a certain modification (not fundamental) in the moldboard plow about 1805, for a better (but not good) method of reefing the lanteen sail, for a chestnut roaster, for the Devil's Claw Wedge for splitting logs, and for a nutmeg grater embodying a new safety feature; this last was either in the year 1816 or 1817. He is known for such, and for no more.

Were this all that he achieved his name would still be secure. And it *is* secure, in a limited way, to those who hobby in technological history.

But the glory of which history has cheated him, or of which he cheated himself, is otherwise. In a different sense it is without parallel, absolutely unique.

For he pioneered the dynamo, the steam automobile, the steel industry, ferro-concrete construction, the internal combustion engine, electric illumination and power, the wireless, the televox, the petroleum and petro-chemical industries, monorail transportation, air travel, worldwide monitoring, fissionable power, space travel, group telepathy, political and economic balance; he built a retrogressor; and he made great advances towards corporal immortality and the apotheosis of mankind. It would seem unfair that all this is unknown of him.

Even the once solid facts—that he wired Philadelphia for light and power in 1799, Boston the following year, and New York two years later—are no longer solid. In a sense they are no longer facts.

For all this there must be an explanation; and if not that, then an account at least; and if not that, well—something anyhow.

Higgston Rainbird made a certain decision on a June afternoon in 1779 when he was quite a young man, and by this decision he confirmed his inventive bent.

He was hawking from the top of Devil's Head Mountain. He flew his falcon (actually a tercel hawk) down through the white clouds, and to him it was the highest sport in the world. The bird came back, climbing the blue air, and brought a passenger pigeon from below the clouds. And Higgston was almost perfectly happy as he hooded the hawk.

He could stay there all day and hawk from above the clouds. Or he could go down the mountain and work on his sparker in his shed. He sighed as he made the decision, for no man can have everything. There was a fascination about hawking. But there was also a fascination about the copper-strip sparker. And he went down the mountain to work on it.

Thereafter he hawked less. After several years he was forced to give it up altogether. He had chosen his life, the dedicated career of an inventor, and he stayed with it for sixty-five years.

His sparker was not a success. It would be expensive, its spark was uncertain and it had almost no advantage over flint. People could always start a fire. If not, they could borrow a brand from a neighbor. There was no market for the sparker. But it was a nice machine, hammered copper strips wrapped around iron teased with lodestone, and the thing turned with a hand crank. He never gave it up entirely. He based other things upon it; and the retrogressor of his last years could not have been built without it.

But the main thing was steam, iron, and tools. He made the finest lathes. He revolutionized smelting and mining. He brought new things to power, and started the smoke to rolling. He made mistakes, he ran into dead ends, he wasted whole decades. But one man can only do so much.

He married a shrew, Audrey, knowing that a man cannot achieve without a goad as well as a goal. But he was without issue or disciple, and this worried him.

He built a steamboat and a steamtrain. His was the first steam thresher. He cleared the forests with wood-burning giants, and designed towns. He destroyed southern slavery with a steampowered cotton picker, and power and wealth followed him.

For better or worse he brought the country up a long road, so there was hardly a custom of his boyhood that still continued. Probably no one man had ever changed a country so much in his lifetime.

He fathered a true machine-tool industry, and brought rubber from the tropics and plastic from the laboratory. He pumped petroleum, and used natural gas for illumination and steam power. He was honored and enriched; and, looking back, he had no reason to regard his life as wasted.

"Yes, I've missed so much. I wasted a lot of time. If only I could have avoided the blind alleys, I could have done many times as much. I brought machine tooling to its apex. But I neglected the finest tool of all, the mind. I used it as it is, but I had not time to study it, much less modify it. Others after me will do it all. But I rather wanted to do it all myself. Now it is too late."

He went back and worked on his old sparker and its descendents, now that he was old. He built toys along the line of it that need not always have remained toys. He made a televox, but the only practical application was that now Audrey could rail at him over a greater distance. He fired up a little steam dynamo in his house, ran wires and made it burn lights in his barn.

And he built a retrogressor.

"I would do much more along this line had I the time. But I'm pepper-bellied pretty near the end of the road. It is like finally coming to a gate and seeing a whole greater world beyond it, and being too old and feeble to enter."

He kicked a chair and broke it.

"I never even made a better chair. Never got around to it. There are so clod-hopping many things I meant to do. I have maybe pushed the country ahead a couple of decades faster than it would otherwise have gone. But what couldn't I have done if it weren't for the blind alleys! Ten years lost in one of them, twelve in another. If only there had been a way to tell the true from the false, and to leave to others what they could do, and to do myself only what nobody else could do. To see a link (however unlikely) and to go out and get it and set it in its place. Oh, the waste, the wilderness that a talent can wander in! If I had only had a mentor! If I had had a map, a clue, a hatful of clues. I was born shrewd, and I shrewdly cut a path and went a grand ways. But always there was a clearer path and a faster way that I did not see till later. As my name is Rainbird, if I had it to do over, I'd do it infinitely better."

He began to write a list of the things that he'd have done better. Then he stopped and threw away his pen in disgust.

"Never did even invent a decent ink pen. Never got around to it. Dog-eared damnation, there's so much I didn't do!"

He poured himself a jolt, but he made a face as he drank it.

"Never got around to distilling a really better whiskey.

Had some good ideas along that line, too. So many things I never did do. Well, I can't improve things by talking to myself here about it."

Then he sat and thought.

"But I burr-tailed *can* improve things by talking to myself *there* about it."

He turned on his retrogressor, and went back sixty-five years and up two thousand feet.

Higgston Rainbird was hawking from the top of Devil's Head Mountain one June afternoon in 1779. He flew his bird down through the white fleece clouds, and to him it was sport indeed. Then it came back, climbing the shimmering air, and brought a pigeon to him.

"It's fun," said the old man, "but the bird is tough, and you have a lot to do. Sit down and listen, Higgston."

"How do you know the bird is tough? Who are you, and how did an old man like you climb up here without my seeing you? And how in hellpepper did you know that my name was Higgston?"

"I ate the bird and I remember that it was tough. I am just an old man who would tell you a few things to avoid in your life, and I came up here by means of an invention of my own. And I know your name is Higgston, as it is also my name; you being named after me, or I after you, I forget which. Which one of us is the older, anyhow?"

"I had thought that you were, old man. I am a little interested in inventions myself. How does the one that carried you up here work?"

"It begins, well it begins with something like your sparker, Higgston. And as the years go by you adapt and add. But it is all tinkering with a force field till you are able to warp it a little. Now then, you are an ewer-eared galoot and not as handsome as I remembered you; but I happen to know that you have the makings of a fine man. Listen now as hard as ever you listened in your life. I doubt that I will be able to repeat. I will save you years and decades; I will tell you the best road to take over a journey which it was once said that a man could travel but once. Man, I'll pave a path for you over the hard places and strew palms before your feet."

"Talk, you addlepated old gaff. No man ever listened so hard before."

The old man talked to the young one for five hours. Not a word was wasted; they were neither of them given to wasting words. He told him that steam wasn't everything, this before he knew that it was anything. It was a giant power, but it was limited. Other powers, perhaps, were not. He instructed him to explore the possibilities of amplification and feedback, and to use always the lightest medium of transmission of power: wire rather than mule-drawn coal cart, air rather than wire, ether rather than air. He warned against time wasted in shoring up the obsolete, and of the bottomless quicksand of cliché, both of word and of thought.

He admonished him not to waste precious months in trying to devise the perfect apple corer; there will never be a perfect apple corer. He begged him not to build a battery bobsled. There would be things far swifter than a bobsled.

Let others make the new hide scrapers and tanning salts. Let others aid the carter and the candle molder and the cooper in their arts. There was need for a better hame, a better horse block, a better stile, a better whetstone. Well, let others fill those needs. If our buttonhooks, our firedogs, our whiffletrees, our bootjacks, our cheese presses are all badly designed and a disgrace, then let someone else remove that disgrace. Let others aid the cordwainer and the cobbler. Let Higgston do only the high work that nobody else would be able to do.

There would come a time when the farrier himself would disappear, as the fletcher had all but disappeared. But new trades would open for a man with an open mind.

Then the old man got specific. He showed young Higgston a design for a lathe dog that would save time. He told him how to draw, rather than hammer wire; and advised him of the virtues of mica as insulator before other material should come to hand.

"And here there are some things that you will have to take on faith," said the old man, "things of which we learn the 'what' before we fathom the 'why'."

He explained to him the shuttle armature and the self-exciting field, and commutation; and the possibilities that alternation carried to its ultimate might open up. He told him a bejammed lot of things about a confounded huge variety of subjects.

"And a little mathematics never hurt a practical man," said the old gaffer. "I was self-taught, and it slowed me down."

They hunkered down there, and the old man cyphered it all out in the dust on the top of Devil's Head Mountain. He showed him natural logarithms and rotating vectors and the calculi and such; but he didn't push it too far, as even a smart boy can learn only so much in a few minutes. He then gave him a little advice on the treatment of Audrey, knowing it would be useless, for the art of living with a shrew is a thing that cannot be explained to another.

"Now hood your hawk and go down the mountain and go to work," the old man said. And that is what young Higgston Rainbird did.

The career of the Yankee inventor, Higgston Rainbird, was meteoric. The wise men of Greece were little boys to him, the Renaissance giants had only knocked at the door but had not tried the knob. And it was unlocked all the time.

The milestones that Higgston left are breathtaking. He built a short high dam on the flank of Devil's Head Mountain, and had hydroelectric power for his own shop in that same year (1779). He had an arc light burning in Horse-Head Lighthouse in 1781. He read by true incandescent light in 1783, and lighted his native village, Knobknocker, three years later. He drove a charcoal fueled automobile in 1787, switched to a distillate of whale oil in 1789, and used true rock oil in 1790. His gasoline powered combination reaper-thresher was in commercial production in 1793, the same year that he wired Centerville for light and power. His first diesel locomotive made its trial run in 1796, in which year he also converted one of his earlier coal burning steamships to liquid fuel.

In 1799 he had wired Philadelphia for light and power, a major breakthrough, for the big cities had manfully resisted the innovations. On the night of the turn of the century he unhooded a whole clutch of new things, wireless telegraphy, the televox, radio transmission and reception, motile and audible theatrical reproductions, a machine to transmit the human voice into print, and a method of sterilizing and wrapping meat to permit its indefinite preservation at any temperature.

And in the spring of that new year he first flew a heavier-than-air vehicle.

"He has made all the basic inventions," said the many-tongued people. "Now there remains only their refinement and proper utilization."

"Horse hokey," said Higgston Rainbird. He made a rocket that could carry freight to England in thirteen minutes at seven cents a hundredweight. This was in 1805. He had fissionable power in 1813, and within four years had the price down where it could be used for desalting seawater to the eventual irrigation of five million square miles of remarkably dry land.

He built a Think Machine to work out the problems that

he was too busy to solve, and a Prediction Machine to pose him with new problems and new areas of breakthrough.

In 1821, on his birthday, he hit the moon with a marker. He bet a crony that he would be able to go up personally one year later and retrieve it. And he won the bet.

In 1830 he first put on the market his Red Ball Pipe Tobacco, an aromatic and expensive crimp cut made of Martian lichen.

In 1836 he founded the Institute for the Atmospheric Rehabilitation of Venus, for he found that place to be worse than a smokehouse. It was there that he developed that hacking cough that stayed with him till the end of his days.

He synthesized a man of his own age and disrepute who would sit drinking with him in the after-midnight hours and say, "You're so right, Higgston, so incontestably right."

His plan for the Simplification and Eventual Elimination of Government was adopted (in modified form) in 1840, a fruit of his Political and Economic Balance Institute.

Yet, for all his seemingly successful penetration of the field, he realized that man was the only truly cantankerous animal, and that Human Engineering would remain one of the never completely resolved fields.

He made a partial breakthrough in telepathy, starting with the personal knowledge that shrews are always able to read the minds of their spouses. He knew that the secret was not in sympathetic reception, but in arrogant break-in. With the polite it is forever impossible, but he disguised this discovery as politely as he could.

And he worked toward corporal immortality and the apotheosis of mankind, that cantankerous animal.

He designed a fabric that would embulk itself on a temperature drop, and thin to an airy sheen in summery weather. The weather itself he disdained to modify, but he did evolve infallible prediction of exact daily rainfall and temperature for decades in advance.

And he built a retrogressor.

One day he looked in the mirror and frowned.

"I never did get around to making a better mirror. This one is hideous. However (to consider every possibility) let us weigh the thesis that it is the image and not the mirror that is hideous."

He called up an acquaintance.

"Say, Ulois, what year is this anyhow?"

"1844."

"Are you sure?"

"Reasonably sure."

"How old am I?"

"Eighty-five, I think, Higgston."

"How long have I been an old man?"

"Quite a while, Higgston, quite a while."

Higgston Rainbird hung up rudely.

"I wonder how I ever let a thing like that slip up on me?" he said to himself. "I should have gone to work on corporal immortality a little earlier. I've bungled the whole business now."

He fiddled with his prediction machine and saw that he was to die that very year. He did not seek a finer reading.

"What a saddle-galled splay-footed situation to find myself in! I never got around to a tenth of the things I really wanted to do. Oh, I was smart enough; I just ran up too many blind alleys. Never found the answers to half the old riddles. Should have built the Prediction Machine at the beginning instead of the end. But I didn't know how to build it at the beginning. There ought to be a way to get more done. Never got any advice in my life worth taking except from that nutty old man on the mountain when I was a young man. There's a lot of things I've only started on. Well, every man doesn't hang, but every man does come to the end of his rope. I never did get around to making that rope extensible. And I can't improve things by talking to myself here about it."

He filled his pipe with Red Ball crimp cut and thought a while.

"But I hill-hopping *can* improve things by talking to myself *there* about it."

Then he turned on his retrogressor and went back and up.

Young Higgston Rainbird was hawking from the top of Devil's Head Mountain on a June afternoon in 1779. He flew his hawk down through the white clouds, and decided that he was the finest fellow in the world and master of the finest sport. If there was earth below the clouds it was far away and unimportant.

The hunting bird came back, climbing the tall air, with a pigeon from the lower regions.

"Forget the bird," said the old man, "and give a listen with those outsized ears of yours. I have a lot to tell you in a very little while, and then you must devote yourself to a concentrated life of work. Hood the bird and clip him to the stake. Is that bridle clip of your own invention? Ah yes, I remember now that it is."

"I'll just fly him down once more, old man, and then I'll have a look at what you're selling."

"No. No. Hood him at once. This is your moment of decision. That is a boyishness that you must give up. Listen to me, Higgston, and I will orient your life for you."

"I rather intended to orient it myself. How did you get up here, old man, without my seeing you? How, in fact, did you get up here at all? It's a hard climb."

"Yes, I remember that it is. I came up here on the wings of an invention of my own. Now pay attention for a few hours. It will take all your considerable wit."

"A few hours and a perfect hawking afternoon will be gone. This may be the finest day ever made."

"I also once felt that it was, but I manfully gave it up. So must you."

"Let me fly the hawk down again and I will listen to you while it is gone."

"But you will only be listening with half a mind, and the rest will be with the hawk."

But young Higgston Rainbird flew the bird down through the shining white clouds, and the old man began his rigmarole sadly. Yet it was a rang-dang-do of a spiel, a mummywhammy of admonition and exposition, and young Higgston listened entranced and almost forgot his hawk. The old man told him that he must stride half a dozen roads at once, and yet never take a wrong one; that he must do some things earlier that on the alternative had been done quite late; that he must point his technique at the Think Machine and the Prediction Machine, and at the unsolved problem of corporal immortality.

"In no other way can you really acquire elbow room, ample working time. Time runs out and life is too short if you let it take its natural course. Are you listening to me, Higgston?"

But the hawk came back, climbing the steep air, and it had a gray dove. The old man sighed at the interruption, and he knew that his project was in peril.

"Hood the hawk. It's a sport for boys. Now listen to me, you spraddling jack. I am telling you things that nobody else would ever be able to tell you! I will show you how to fly falcons to the stars, not just down to the meadows and birch groves at the foot of this mountain."

"There is no prey up there," said young Higgston.

"There *is*. Gamier prey than you ever dreamed of. Hood the bird and snaffle him."

"I'll just fly him down one more time and listen to you till he comes back."

The hawk went down through the clouds like a golden bolt of summer lightning.

Then the old man, taking the cosmos, peeled it open layer by layer like an onion, and told young Higgston how it worked. Afterwards he returned to the technological beginning and he lined out the workings of steam and petro- and electromagnetism, and explained that these simple powers must be used for a short interval in the invention of greater power. He told him of waves and resonance and airy transmission, and fission and flight and over-flight. And that none of the doors required keys, only a resolute man to turn the knob and push them open. Young Higgston was impressed.

Then the hawk came back, climbing the towering air, and it had a rainbird.

The old man had lively eyes, but now they took on a new light.

"Nobody ever gives up pleasure willingly," he said, "and there is always the sneaking feeling that the bargain may not have been perfect. This is one of the things I have missed. I haven't hawked for sixty-five years. Let me fly him this time, Higgston."

"You know how?"

"I am adept. And I once intended to make a better gauntlet for hawkers. This hasn't been improved since Nimrod's time."

"I have an idea for a better gauntlet myself, old man."

"Yes. I know what your idea is. Go ahead with it. It's practical."

"Fly him if you want to, old man."

And old Higgston flew the tercel hawk down through the gleaming clouds, and he and young Higgston watched from the top of the world. And then young Higgston Rainbird was standing alone on the top of Devil's Head Mountain, and the old man was gone.

"I wonder where he went? And where in appleknocker's heaven did he come from? Or was he ever here at all? That's a danged funny machine he came in, if he did come in it. All the wheels are on the inside. But I can use the gears from it, and the clock, and the copper wire. It must have taken weeks to hammer that much wire out that fine. I wish I'd paid more attention to what he was saying, but he poured it on a little thick. I'd have gone along with him on it if only he'd have found a good stopping place a little sooner, and hadn't been so insistent on giving up hawking. Well, I'll just hawk here till dark, and if it dawns clear I'll be up again in the morning. And Sunday, if I have a little time, I may work on my sparker or my chestnut roaster."

Higgston Rainbird lived a long and successful life. Locally he was known best as a hawker and horse racer. But as an inventor he was recognized as far as Boston.

He is still known, in a limited way, to specialists in the field and period; known as contributor to the development of the moldboard plow, as the designer of the Nonpareil Nutmeg Grater with the safety feature, for a bellows, for a sparker for starting fires (little used), and for the Devil's Claw Wedge for splitting logs.

He is known for such, and for no more.

Camels and Dromedaries, Clem

"Greeks and Armenians, Clem. Condors and buzzards."

"Samoyeds and Malemutes, Clem. Galena and molybden-ite."

Oh here, here! What kind of talk is that?

That is definitive talk. That is fundamental talk. There is no other kind of talk that will bring us to the core of this thing.

Clem Clendenning was a traveling salesman, a good one. He had cleared $35,000 the previous year. He worked for a factory in a midwestern town. The plant produced a unique product, and Clem sold it over one-third of the nation.

Things were going well with him. Then a little thing happened, and it changed his life completely.

Salesmen have devices by which they check and double-check. One thing they do when stopping at hotels in distant towns; they make sure they're registered. This sounds silly, but it isn't. A salesman will get calls from his home office and it is important that the office be able to locate him. Whenever Clem registered at a hotel he would check back after several hours to be sure that they had him entered correctly. He would call in from somewhere, and he would ask for himself. And it sometimes did happen that he was told he was not registered. At this Clem would always raise a great noise to be sure that they had him straight thereafter.

Arriving in a town this critical day, Clem had found himself ravenously hungry and tired to his depths. Both states were unusual to him. He went to a grill and ate gluttonously for an hour, so much so that people stared at him. He ate almost to the point of apoplexy. Then he taxied to the hotel, registered, and went up to his room at once. Later, not remembering whether he had even undressed or not (it was early afternoon), he threw himself onto the bed and slept, as it seemed, for hours.

But he noted that it was only a half hour later that he woke, feeling somehow deprived, as though having a great loss. He was floundering around altogether in a daze, and was once more possessed of an irrational hunger. He unpacked a little, put on a suit, and was surprised to find that it hung on him quite loosely.

He went out with the feeling that he had left something on the bed that was not quite right, and yet he had been afraid to look. He found a hearty place and had another great meal. And then (at a different place so that people would not be puzzled at him) he had still another one. He was feeling better now, but mighty queer, mighty queer.

Fearing that he might be taken seriously ill, he decided to check his bearings. He used his old trick. He found a phone and called his hotel and asked for himself.

"We will check," said the phone girl, and a little bit later she said, "Just a minute, he will be on the line in a minute."

"Oh, great green goat," he growled, "I wonder how they have me mixed up this time."

And Clem was about to raise his voice unpleasantly to be sure that they got him straight, when a voice came onto the phone.

This is the critical point.

It was his own voice.

The calling Clendenning laughed first. And then he froze. It was no trick. It was no freak. There was no doubt that it was his own voice. Clem used the dictaphone a lot and he knew the sound of his own voice.

And now he heard his own voice raised higher in all its unmistakable aspects, a great noise about open idiots who call on the phone and then stand silent without answering.

"It's me all right," Clem grumbled silently to himself. "I sure do talk rough when I'm irritated."

There was a law against harassment by telephone, the

voice on the phone said. By God, the voice on the phone said, he just noticed that his room had been rifled. He was having the call monitored right now, the voice on the phone swore. Clem knew that this was a lie, but he also recognized it as his own particular style of lying. The voice got really wooly and profane.

Then there was a change in the tone.

"Who are you?" the voice asked hollowly. "I hear you breathing scared. I know your sound. Gaaah—it's me!" And the voice on the phone was also breathing scared.

"There has to be an answer," he told himself. "I'll just go to my room and take a hot bath and try to sleep it off."

Then he roared back: "Go to my room! Am I crazy? I have just called my room. I am already there. I would not go to my room for one million one hundred and five thousand dollars."

He was trembling as though his bones were too loose for his flesh. It was funny that he had never before noticed how bony he was. But he wasn't too scared to think straight on one subject, however crooked other things might be.

"No, I wouldn't go back to that room for any sum. But I *will* do something for another sum, and I'll do it damned quick."

He ran, and he hasn't stopped running yet. That he should have another self-made flesh terrified him. He ran, but he knew where he was running for the first stage of it. He took the night plane back to his hometown, leaving bag and baggage behind.

He was at the bank when it opened in the morning. He closed out all his accounts. He turned everything into cash. This took several hours. He walked out of there with $83,000. He didn't feel like a thief, it was his own; it couldn't have belonged to his other self, could it? If there were two of them, then let there be two sets of accounts.

Now to get going fast.

He continued to feel odd. He weighed himself. In spite of his great eating lately, he had lost a hundred pounds. That's enough to make anyone feel odd. He went to New York City to lose himself in the crowd and to think about the matter.

And what was the reaction at his firm and at his home when he turned up missing? That's the second point. He didn't turn up missing. As the months went by he followed the doings of his other self. He saw his pictures in the trade papers; he was still with the same firm; he was still top salesman. He always got the hometown paper, and he sometimes found himself therein. He saw his own picture with his wife Veronica. She looked wonderful and so, he had to admit, did he. They were still on the edge of the social stuff.

"If he's me, I wonder who I am?" Clem continued to ask himself. There didn't seem to be any answer to this. There wasn't any handle to take the thing by.

Clem went to an analyst and told his story. The analyst said that Clem had wanted to escape his job, or his wife Veronica, or both. Clem insisted that this was not so; he loved his job and his wife; he got deep and fulfilling satisfaction out of both.

"You don't know Veronica or you wouldn't suggest it," he told the analyst. "She is—ah—well, if you don't know her, then hell, you don't know anything."

The analyst told him that it had been his own id talking to him on the telephone.

"How is it that my id is doing a top selling job out of a town five hundred miles from here, and I am here?" Clem wanted to know. "Other men's ids aren't so talented."

The analyst said that Clem was suffering from a *tmema* or *diairetikos* of an oddly named part of his psychic apparatus.

"Oh hell, I'm an extrovert. Things like that don't happen to people like me," Clem said.

Thereafter Clem tried to make the best of his compromised life. He was quickly well and back to normal weight. But he never talked on the telephone again in his life. He'd have died most literally if he ever heard his own voice like that again. He had no phone in any room where he lived. He wore a hearing aid which he did not need; he told people that he could not hear over the phone, and that any unlikely call that came for him would have to be taken down and relayed to him.

He had to keep an eye on his other self, so he did renew one old contact. With one firm in New York there was a man he had called on regularly; this man had a cheerful and open mind that would not be spooked by the unusual. Clem began to meet this man (Why should we lie about it? His name was Joe Zabotsky.) not at the firm, but at an after-hours place which he knew Joe frequented.

Joe heard Clem's story and believed it—after he had phoned (in Clem's presence) the other Clem, located him a thousand miles away, and ordered an additional month's supply of the unique product which they didn't really need, things being a little slow in all lines right then.

After that, Clem would get around to see Joe Zabotsky an

average of once a month, about the time he figured the other Clem had just completed his monthly New York call.

"He's changing a little bit, and so are you," Joe told Clem one evening. "Yeah, it was with him just about like with you. He did lose a lot of weight a while back, what you call the critical day, and he gained it back pretty quick just like you did. It bugs me, Clem, which of you I used to know. There are some old things between us that he recalls and you don't; there are some that you recall and he doesn't; and dammit there are some you both recall, and they happened between myself and one man only, not between myself and two men.

"But these last few months your face seems to be getting a little fuller, and his a little thinner. You still look just alike, but not quite as just-alike as you did at first."

"I know it," Clem said. "I study the analysts now since they don't do any good at studying me, and I've learned an old analyst's trick. I take an old face-on photo of myself, divide it down the center, and then complete each half with its mirror image. It gives two faces just a little bit differently. Nobody has the two sides of his face quite alike. These two different faces are supposed to indicate two different aspects of the personality. I study myself, now, and I see that I am becoming more like one of the constructions; so he must be becoming more like the other construction. He mentions that there are disturbances between Veronica and himself, does he? And neither of them quite understands what is the matter? Neither do I."

Clem lived modestly, but he began to drink more than he had. He watched, through his intermediary Joe and by other means, the doings of his other self. And he waited. This was the most peculiar deal he had ever met, but he hadn't been foxed on very many deals.

"He's no smarter than I am," Clem insisted. "But, by cracky, if he's me, he's pretty smart at that. What would he do if he were in my place? And I guess, in a way, he is."

Following his avocation of drinking and brooding and waiting, Clem frequented various little places, and one day he was in the Two-Faced Bar and Grill. This was owned and operated by Two-Face Terrel, a double-dealer and gentleman, even something of a dandy. A man had just seated himself at a dim table with Clem, had been served by Two-Face, and now the man began to talk.

"Why did Matthew have two donkeys?" the man asked.

"Matthew who?" Clem asked. "I don't know what you're talking about."

"I'm talking about 21:1—9, of course," the man said. "The other Gospels have only one donkey. Did you ever think about that?"

"No, I'd never given it a thought," Clem said.

"Well, tell me then, why does Matthew have two demoniacs?"

"What?"

"8:28—34. The other evangelists have only one crazy man."

"Maybe there was only one loony at first, and he drove the guy drinking next to him crazy."

"That's possible. Oh, you're kidding. But why does Matthew have two blind men?"

"Number of a number, where does this happen?" Clem asked.

"9:27—31, and again 20:29—34. In each case the other gospelers have only one blind man. Why does Matthew double so many things? There are other instances of it."

"Maybe he needed glasses," Clem said.

"No," the man whispered, "I think he was one of us."

"What 'us' are you talking about?" Clem asked. But already he had begun to suspect that his case was not unique. Suppose that it happened one time out of a million? There would still be several hundred such sundered persons in the country, and they would tend to congregate—in such places as the Two-Faced Bar and Grill. And there *was* something deprived or riven about almost every person who came into the place.

"And remember," the man was continuing, "the name or cognomen of one of the other Apostles was 'The Twin.' But of whom was he twin? I think there was the beginning of a group of them there already."

"He wants to see you," Joe Zabotsky told Clem when they met several months later. "So does she."

"When did he begin to suspect that there was another one of me?"

"He knew something was wrong from the first. A man doesn't lose a hundred pounds in an instant without there being something wrong. And he knew something was very wrong when all his accounts were cleaned out. These were not forgeries, and he knew it. They were not as good as good forgeries, for they were hurried and all different and very nervous. But they were all genuine signatures, he admitted that. Damn, you are a curious fellow, Clem!"

"How much does Veronica know, and how? What does she want? What does he?"

"He says that she also began to guess from the first. 'You act like you're only half a man, Clem,' she would say to him, to you, that is. She wants to see more of her husband, she says, the other half. And he wants to trade places with you, at least from time to time on a trial basis."

"I won't do it! Let him stew in it!" Then Clem called Clem a name so vile that it will not be given here.

"Take it easy, Clem," Joe remonstrated. "It's yourself you are calling that."

There was a quizzical young-old man who came sometimes into the Two-Faced Bar and Grill. They caught each other's eye this day, and the young-old began to talk.

"Is not consciousness the thing that divides man from the animals?" he asked. "But consciousness is a double thing, a seeing one's self; not only a knowing, but a knowing that one knows. So the human person is of its essence double. How this is commonly worked out in practice, I don't understand. Our present states are surely not the common thing."

"My own consciousness isn't intensified since my person is doubled," Clem said. "It's all the other way. My consciousness is weakened. I've become a creature of my own unconscious. There's something about you that I don't like, man."

"The animal is simple and single," the young-old man said. "It lacks true reflexive consciousness. But man is dual (though I don't understand the full meaning of it here), and he has at least intimations of true consciousness. And what is the next step?"

"I fathom you now," Clem said. "My father would have called you a Judas Priest."

"I don't quite call myself that. But what follows the singularity of the animal and duality of man? You recall the startling line of Chesterton?—'we trinitarians have known it is not good for God to be alone.' But was His case the same as ours? Did He do a violent double take, or triple take, when He discovered one day that there were Three of Him? Has He ever adjusted to it? Is it possible that He can?"

"Aye, you're a Judas Priest. I hate the species."

"But I am not, Mr. Clendenning. I don't understand this sundering any more than you do. It happens only one time in a million, but it has happened to us. Perhaps it would happen to God but one time in a billion billion, but it has happened. The God who is may be much rarer than any you can imagine.

"Let me explain: my other person is a very good man,

much better than when we were conjoined. He's a dean
already, and He'll be a bishop within five years. Whatever of
doubt and skepticism that was in me originally is still in the
me here present, and it is somehow intensified. I do not want
to be dour or doubting. I do not want to speak mockingly of
the great things. But the bothering things are all in the me
here. The other me is freed of them.

"Do you think that there might have been a sundered-off
Napoleon who was a bumbler at strategy and who was a
nervous little coward? Did there remain in backwoods Kentucky for many years a sundered-off Lincoln who gave full
rein to his inborn delight in the dirty story, the dirty deal, the
barefoot life, the loutishness ever growing? Was there a
sundered-off Augustine who turned ever more Manichean,
who refined more and more his arts of false logic and
fornication, who howled against reason, who joined the
cultishness of the crowd? Is there an anti-Christ—the man
who fled naked from the garden at dusk leaving his garment
behind? We know that both do not keep the garment at the
moment of sundering."

"Damned if I know, Judas Priest. Your own father-name
abomination, was there another of him? Was he better or
worse? I leave you."

"She is in town and is going to meet you tonight," Joe
Zabotsky told Clem at their next monthly meeting. "We've
got it all set up."

"No, no, not Veronica!" Clem was startled. "I'm not ready
for it."

"She is. She's a strong-minded woman, and she knows
what she wants."

"No, she doesn't, Joe. I'm afraid of it. I haven't touched a
woman since Veronica."

"Damn it, Clem, this *is* Veronica that we're talking about.
It isn't as though you weren't still married to her."

"I'm still afraid of it, Joe. I've become something unnatural now. Where am I supposed to meet her? Oh, oh, you son
of a snake! I can feel her presence. She was already in the
place when I came in. No, no, Veronica, I'm not the proper
one. It's all a case of mistaken identity."

"It sure is, Clem Clam," said the strong-minded Veronica
as she came to their table. "Come along now. You're going
to have more explaining to do than any man I ever heard
of."

"But I can't explain it, Veronica. I can't explain any of it."

"You will try real hard, Clem. We both will. Thank you, Mr. Zabotsky, for your discretion in an odd situation."

Well, it went pretty well, so well in fact there had to be a catch to it. Veronica was an unusual and desirable woman, and Clem had missed her. They did the town mildly. They used to do it once a year, but they had been apart in their present persons for several years. And yet Veronica would want to revisit "that little place we were last year, oh, but that wasn't you, was it, Clem?—that was Clem," and that kind of talk was confusing.

They dined grandly, and they talked intimately but nervously. There was real love between them, or among them, or around them somehow. They didn't understand how it had turned grotesque.

"He never quite forgave you for clearing out the accounts," Veronica said.

"But it was my money, Veronica," Clem insisted. "I earned it by the sweat of my tongue and my brain. He had nothing to do with it."

"But you're wrong, dear Clem. You worked equally for it when you were one. You should have taken only half of it."

They came back to Veronica's hotel, and one of the clerks looked at Clem suspiciously.

"Didn't you just go up, and then come down, and then go up again?" he asked.

"I have my ups and downs, but you may mean something else," Clem said.

"Now don't be nervous, dear," Veronica said. They were up in Veronica's room now, and Clem was looking around very nervously. He had jumped at a mirror, not being sure that it was.

"I am still your wife," Veronica said, "and nothing has changed, except everything. I don't know how, but I'm going to put things together again. You have to have missed me! Give now!" And she swept him off his feet as though he were a child. Clem had always loved her for her sudden strength. If you haven't been up in Veronica's arms, then you haven't been anywhere.

"Get your pumpkin-picking hands off my wife, you filthy oaf!" a voice cracked out like a bullwhip, and Veronica dropped Clem thuddingly from the surprise of it.

"Oh, Clem!" she said with exasperation, "you shouldn't have come here when I was with Clem. Now you've spoiled everything. You *can't* be jealous of each other. You're the same man. Let's all pack up and go home and make the best of it. Let people talk if they want to."

"Well, I don't know what to do," Clem said. "This isn't the way. There isn't any way at all. Nothing can ever be right with us when we are three."

"There *is* a way," Veronica said with sudden steel in her voice. "You boys will just have to get together again. I am laying down the law now. For a starter each of you lose a hundred pounds. I give you a month for it. You're both on bread and water from now on. No, come to think of it, no bread! No water either; that may be fattening, too. You're both on nothing for a month."

"We won't do it," both Clems said. "It'd kill us."

"Let it kill you then," Veronica said. "You're no good to me the way you are. You'll lose the weight. I think that will be the trigger action. Then we will all go back to Rock Island or whatever town that was and get the same hotel room where one of you rose in a daze and left the other one unconscious on the bed. We will recreate those circumstances and see if you two can't get together again."

"Veronica," Clem said, "it is physically and biologically impossible."

"Also topologically absurd."

"You should have thought of that when you came apart. All you have to do now is get together again. Do it! I'm laying down an ultimatum. There's no other way. You two will just have to get together again."

"There *is* another way," Clem said in a voice so sharp that it scared both Veronica and Clem.

"What? What is it?" they asked him.

"Veronica, you've got to divide," Clem said. "You've got to come apart."

"Oh, no. No!"

"Now you put on a hundred pounds just as fast as you can, Veronica. Clem," Clem said, "go get a dozen steaks up here for her to start on. And about thirty pounds of bone meal, whatever that is. It sounds like it might help."

"I'll do it, I'll do it," Clem cried, "and a couple of gallons of blood-pudding. Hey, I wonder where I can get that much blood-pudding this time of night?"

"Boys, are you serious? Do you think it'll work?" Veronica gasped. "I'll try anything. How do I start?"

"Think divisive thoughts," Clem shouted as he started out for the steaks and bone meal and blood-pudding.

"I don't know any," Veronica said. "Oh, yes I do! I'll think them. We'll do everything! We'll make it work."

"You have a lot going for you, Veronica," Clem said.

"You've always been a double-dealer. And your own mother always said that you were two-faced."

"Oh, I know it, I know it! We'll do everything. We'll make it work. We'll leave no stone unthrown."

"You've got to become a pair, Veronica," Clem said at one of their sessions. "Think of pairs."

"Crocodiles and alligators, Clem," she said, "frogs and toads. Eels and lampreys."

"Horses and asses, Veronica," Clem said, "elk and moose. Rabbits and hares."

"Mushrooms and toadstools, Veronica," Clem said. "Mosses and lichens. Butterflies and moths."

"Camels and dromedaries, Clem," Veronica said. "Salamanders and newts, dragonfly and damselfly."

Say, they thought about pairs by the long ton. They thought every kind of sundering and divisive thought. They plumbed the depths of psychology and biology, and called in some of the most respected quacks of the city for advice.

No people ever tried anything harder. Veronica and Clem and Clem did everything they could think of. They gave it a month. "I'll do it or bust," Veronica said.

And they came close, so close that you could feel it. Veronica weighed up a hundred pounds well within the month, and then coasted in on double brandies. It was done all but the final thing.

Pay homage to her, people! She was a valiant woman!

They both said that about her after it was over with. They would admire her as long as they lived. She had given it everything.

"I'll do it or bust," she had said.

And after they had gathered her remains together and buried her, it left a gap in their lives, in Clem's more than in Clem's, since Clem had already been deprived of her for these last several years.

And a special honor they paid her.

They set *two* headstones on her grave. One of them said 'Veronica.' And the other one said 'Veronica.'

She'd have liked that.

Continued on Next Rock

Up in the Big Lime country there is an up-thrust, a chimney
rock that is half fallen against a newer hill. It is formed of
what is sometimes called Dawson sandstone and is interlaced
with tough shale. It was formed during the glacial and recent
ages in the bottom lands of Crow Creek and Green River
when these streams (at least five times) were mighty rivers.

The chimney rock is only a little older than mankind, only
a little younger than grass. Its formation had been up-thrust
and then eroded away again, all but such harder parts as itself
and other chimneys and blocks.

A party of five persons came to this place where the chimney rock had fallen against a still newer hill. The people of
the party did not care about the deep limestone below: they
were not geologists. They *did* care about the newer hill (it
was man-made) and they did care a little about the rock
chimney; they were archeologists.

Here was time heaped up, bulging out in casing and ac-
cumulation, and not in line sequence. And here also was stri-
ated and banded time, grown tall, and then shattered and
broken.

The five party members came to the site early in the afternoon, bringing the working trailer down a dry creek bed.
They unloaded many things and made a camp there. It
wasn't really necessary to make a camp on the ground. There
was a good motel two miles away on the highway; there was
a road along the ridge above. They could have lived in com-
fort and made the trip to the site in five minutes every morning. Terrence Burdock, however, believed that one could not
get the feel of a digging unless he lived on the ground with it
day and night.

The five persons were Terrence Burdock, his wife Ethyl,
Robert Derby, and Howard Steinleser: four beautiful and
balanced people. And Magdalen Mobley, who was neither
beautiful nor balanced. But she was electric; she was special.
They rouched around in the formations a little after they had
made camp and while there was still light. All of them had

seen the formations before and had guessed that there was promise in them.

"That peculiar fluting in the broken chimney is almost like a core sample," Terrence said, "and it differs from the rest of it. It's like a lightning bolt through the whole length. It's already exposed for us. I believe we will remove the chimney entirely. It covers the perfect access for the slash in the mound, and it is the mound in which we are really interested. But we'll study the chimney first. It is so available for study."

"Oh, I can tell you everything that's in the chimney," Magdalen said crossly. "I can tell you everything that's in the mound, too."

"I wonder why we take the trouble to dig if you already know what we will find," Ethyl sounded archly.

"I wonder, too," Magdalen grumbled. "But we will need the evidence and the artifacts to show. You can't get appropriations without evidence and artifacts. Robert, go kill that deer in the brush about forty yards northeast of the chimney. We may as well have deer meat if we're living primitive."

"This isn't deer season," Robert Derby objected. "And there isn't any deer there. Or, if there is, it's down in the draw where you couldn't see it. And if there's one there, it's probably a doe."

"No, Robert, it is a two-year-old buck and a very big one. Of course it's in the draw where I can't see it. Forty yards northeast of the chimney would have to be in the draw. If I could see it, the rest of you could see it, too. Now go kill it! Are you a man or a *mus microtus?* Howard, cut poles and set up a tripod to string and dress the deer on."

"You had better try the thing, Robert," Ethyl Burdock said, "or we'll have no peace this evening."

Robert Derby took a carbine and went northeastward of the chimney, descending into the draw forty yards away. There was the high ping of the carbine shot. And, after some moments, Robert returned with a curious grin.

"You didn't miss him, Robert, you killed him," Magdalen called loudly. "You got him with a good shot through the throat and up into the brain when he tossed his head high like they do. Why didn't you bring him? Go back and get him!"

"Get him? I couldn't even lift the thing. Terrence and Howard, come with me and we'll lash it to a pole and get it here somehow."

"Oh, Robert, you're out of your beautiful mind," Magdalen

chided. "It only weighs a hundred and ninety pounds. Oh, I'll
get it."

Magdalen Mobley went and got the big buck. She brought
it back, carrying it listlessly across her shoulders and getting
herself bloodied, stopping sometimes to examine rocks and
kick them with her foot, coming on easily with her load. It
looked as if it might weigh two hundred and fifty pounds; but
if Magdalen said it weighed a hundred and ninety, that is what
it weighed.

Howard Steinleser had cut poles and made a tripod. He
knew better than not to. They strung the buck up, skinned it
off, ripped up its belly, drew it, and worked it over in an almost professional manner.

"Cook it, Ethyl," Magdalen said.

Later, as they sat on the ground around the fire and it had
turned dark, Ethyl brought the buck's brains to Magdalen,
messy and not half-cooked, believing that she was playing an
evil trick. And Magdalen ate them avidly. They were her
due. She had discovered the buck.

If you wonder how Magdalen knew what invisible things
were where, so did the other members of the party always
wonder.

"It bedevils me sometimes why I am the only one to notice
the analogy between historical geology and depth psychology," Terrence Burdock mused as they grew lightly profound
around the campfire. "The isostatic principle applies to the
mind and the under-mind as well as it does to the surface
and under-surface of the earth. The mind has its erosions and
weatherings going on along with its deposits and accumula-
tions. It also has its up-thrusts and its stresses. It floats on a
similar magma. In extreme cases it has its volcanic eruptions
and its mountain building."

"And it has its glaciations," Ethyl Burdock said, and perhaps she was looking at her husband in the dark.

"The mind has its hard sandstone, sometimes transmuted
to quartz, or half-transmuted into flint, from the drifting and
floating sand of daily events. It has its shale from the old
mud of daily ineptitudes and inertias. It has limestone out of
its more vivid experiences, for lime is the remnant of what
was once animate: and this limestone may be true marble if
it is the deposit of rich enough emotion, or even travertine if
it has bubbled sufficiently through agonized and evocative rivers of the under-mind. The mind has its sulphur and its gem-
stones—" Terrence bubbled on sufficiently, and Magdalen cut
him off.

"Say simply that we have rocks in our heads," she said. "But they're random rocks, I tell you, and the same ones keep coming back. It *isn't* the same with us as it is with the earth. The world gets new rocks all the time. But it's the same people who keep turning up, and the same minds. Damn, one of the samest of them just turned up again! I wish he'd leave me alone. The answer is still no."

Very often Magdalen said things that made no sense. Ethyl Burdock assured herself that neither her husband, nor Robert, nor Howard had slipped over to Magdalen in the dark. Ethyl was jealous of the chunky and surly girl.

"I am hoping that this will be as rich as Spiro Mound," Howard Steinleser hoped. "It could be, you know. I'm told that there was never a less prepossessing site than that, or a trickier one. I wish we had someone who had dug at Spiro."

"Oh, he dug at Spiro," Magdalen said with contempt.

"He? Who?" Terrence Burdock asked. "No one of us was at Spiro. Magdalen, you weren't even born yet when that mound was opened. What could you know about it?"

"Yeah, I remember him at Spiro," Magdalen said, "—always turning up his own things and pointing them out."

"*Were* you at Spiro?" Terrence suddenly asked a piece of the darkness. For some time, they had all been vaguely aware that there were six, and not five persons around the fire.

"Yeah, I was at Spiro," the man said. "I dig there. I dig at a lot of the digs. I dig real well, and I always know when we come to something that will be important. You give me a job."

"Who are you?" Terrence asked him. The man was pretty visible now. The flame of the fire seemed to lean toward him as if he compelled it.

"Oh, I'm just a rich old poor man who keeps following and hoping and asking. There is *one* who is worth it all forever, so I solicit that one forever. And sometimes I am other things. Two hours ago I was the deer in the draw. It is an odd thing to munch one's own flesh." And the man was munching a joint of the deer, unasked.

"Him and his damn cheap poetry!" Magdalen cried angrily.

"What's your name?" Terrence asked him.

"Manypenny. Anteros Manypenny is my name forever."

"What are you?"

"Oh, just Indian. Shawnee, Choc, Creek, Anadarko, Caddo and pre-Caddo. Lots of things."

"How could anyone be pre-Caddo?"

"Like me. I am."

"Is Anteros a Creek name?"

"No. Greek. Man, I am a going Jessie, I am one digging man! I show you tomorrow."

Man, he was one digging man! He showed them tomorrow. With a short-handled rose hoe he began the gash in the bottom of the mound, working too swiftly to be believed.

"He will smash anything that is there. He will not know what he comes to," Ethyl Burdock complained.

"Woman, I will *not* smash whatever is there," Anteros said. "You can hide a wren's egg in one cubic meter of sand. I will move all the sand in one minute. I will uncover the egg, wherever it is. And I will not crack the egg. I sense these things. I come now to a small pot of the proto-Plano period. It is broken, of course, but I do not break it. It is in six pieces and they will fit together perfectly. I tell you this beforehand. Now I reveal it."

And Anteros revealed it. There was something wrong about it even before he uncovered it. But it was surely a find, and perhaps it *was* of the proto-Plano period. The six shards came out. They were roughly cleaned and set. It was apparent that they would fit wonderfully.

"Why, it is perfect!" Ethyl exclaimed.

"It is too perfect," Howard Steinleser protested. "It was a turned pot, and who had turned pots in America without the potter's wheel? But the glyphs pressed into it do correspond to proto-Plano glyphs. It is fishy." Steinleser was in a twitchy humor today and his face was livid.

"Yes, it is the ripple and the spinosity, the fish-glyph," Anteros pointed out. "And the sun-sign is riding upon it. It is fish-god."

"It's fishy in another way." Steinleser insisted. "Nobody finds a thing like that in the first sixty seconds of a dig. And there *could not be* such a pot. I wouldn't believe it was proto-Plano unless points were found in the exact site with it."

"Oh, here," Anteros said. "One can smell the very shape of the flint points already. Two large points, one small one. Surely you get the whiff of them already? Four more hoe cuts and I come to them."

Four more hoe cuts, and Anteros *did* come to them. He uncovered two large points and one small one, spearheads and arrowhead. Lanceolate they were, with ribbon flaking. They were late Folsom, or they were proto-Plano; they were what you will.

"This cannot be," Steinleser groaned. "They're the missing chips, the transition pieces. They fill the missing place too well. I won't believe it. I'd hardly believe it if mastodon bones were found on the same level here."

"In a moment," said Anteros, beginning to use the hoe again. "Hey, those old beasts *did smell funny!* An elephant isn't in it with them. And a lot of it still clings to their bones. Will a sixth thoracic bone do? I'm pretty sure that's what it is. I don't know where the rest of the animal is. Probably somebody gnawed the thoracic here. Nine hoe cuts, and then very careful."

Nine hoe cuts; and then Anteros, using a mason's trowel, unearthed the old gnawed bone very carefully. Yes, Howard said almost angrily, it was a sixth thoracic of a mastodon. Robert Derby said it was a fifth or a sixth; it was not easy to tell.

"Leave the digging for a while, Anteros," Steinleser said. "I want to record and photograph and take a few measurements here."

Terrence Burdock and Magdalen Mobley were working at the bottom of the chimney rock, at the bottom of the fluting that ran the whole height of it like a core sample.

"Get Anteros over here and see what he can uncover in sixty seconds," Terrence offered.

"Oh, him! He'll just uncover some of his own things."

"What do you mean, his own things? Nobody could have made an intrusion here. It's hard sandstone."

"And harder flint here," Magdalen said. "I might have known it. Pass the damned thing up. I know just about what it says, anyhow."

"What it says? What do you mean? But it is marked! and it's large and dressed rough. Who'd carve in flint?"

"Somebody real stubborn, just like flint," Magdalen said. "All right then, let's have it out. Anteros! Get this out in one piece. And do it without shattering it or tumbling the whole thing down on us. He can do it, you know, Terrence. He can do things like that."

"What do you know about his doings, Magdalen? You never saw or heard about the poor man till last night."

"Oh well, I know that it'll turn out to be the same damned stuff."

Anteros did get it out without shattering it or bringing down the chimney column. A cleft with a digging bar, three sticks of the stuff and a cap, and he touched the leads to the battery when he was almost on top of the charge. The blast, it sounded as if the whole sky were falling down on them, and some of those skyblocks were quite large stones. The ancients wondered why fallen pieces of the sky should always

be dark rockstuff and never sky-blue clear stuff. The answer
is that it is only pieces of the night sky that ever fall, even
though they may sometimes be most of the daytime in falling, such is the distance. And the blast that Anteros set off
did bring down rocky hunks of the night sky even though it
was broad daylight. They brought down darker rocks than
any of which the chimney was composed.

Still, it was a small blast. The chimney tottered but did not
collapse. It settled back uneasily on its base. And the flint
block was out in the clear.

"A thousand spearheads and arrowheads could be shattered and chipped out of that hunk," Terrence marveled.
"That flint block would have been a primitive fortune for a
primitive man."

"I had several such fortunes," Anteros said dully, "and this
one I preserved and dedicated."

They had all gathered around it.

"Oh, the poor man!" Ethyl suddenly exclaimed. But she
was not looking at any of the men. She was looking at the stone.

"I wish he'd get off that kick," Magdalen sputtered angrily.
"I don't care *how* rich he is. I can pick up better stuff than
him in the alleys."

"What are the women chirping about?" Terrence asked.
"But those do look like true glyphs. Almost like Aztec, are
they not, Steinleser?"

"Nahuat-Tanoan, cousins-german to the Aztec, or should I
say cousins-yaqui?"

"Call it anything, but can you read it?"

"Probably. Give me eight or ten hours on it and I should
come up with a contingent reading of many of the glyphs.
We can hardly expect a rational rendering of the message,
however. All Nahuat-Tanoan translations so far have been
gibberish."

"And remember, Terrence, that Steinleser is a slow
reader," Magdalen said spitefully. "And he isn't very good at
interpreting *other* signs either."

Steinleser was sullen and silent. How had his face come to
bear those deep livid clawmarks today?

They moved a lot of rock and rubble that morning, took
quite a few pictures, wrote up bulky notes. There were constant finds as the divided party worked up the shag-slash in
the mound and the core-flute of the chimney. There were no
more really startling discoveries; no more turned pots of the
proto-Plano period; how could there be? There were no more
predicted and perfect points of the late Folsom, but there

were broken and unpredictable points. No other mastodon thoracic was found, but bones were uncovered of *bison latifrons*, of dire wolf, of coyote, of man. There were some anomalies in the relationship of the things discovered, but it was not as fishy as it had been in the early morning, not as fishy as when Anteros had announced and then dug out the shards of the pot, the three points, the mastodon bone. The things now were as authentic as they were expected, and yet their very profusion had still the smell of a small fish.

And that Anteros was one digging man. He moved the sand, he moved the stone, he missed nothing. And at noon he disappeared.

An hour later he reappeared in a glossy station wagon, coming out of a thicketed ravine where no one would have expected a way. He had been to town. He brought a variety of cold cuts, cheeses, relishes and pastries, a couple of cases of cold beer, and some V.O.

"I thought you were a poor man, Anteros," Terrence chided.

"I told you that I was a rich old poor man. I have nine thousand acres of grassland, I have three thousand head of cattle, I have alfalfa land and clover land and corn land and hay-grazer land——"

"Oh, knock it off!" Magdalen snapped.

"I have other things," Anteros finished sullenly.

They ate, they rested, they worked the afternoon. Magdalen worked as swiftly and solidly as did Anteros. She was young, she was stocky, she was light-burned-dark. She was not at all beautiful (Ethyl was). She could have any man there any time she wanted to (Ethyl couldn't). She was Magdalen, the often unpleasant, the mostly casual, the suddenly intense one. She was the tension of the party, the string of the bow.

"Anteros!" she called sharply just at sundown.

"The turtle?" he asked. "The turtle that is under the ledge out of the current where the backwater curls in reverse? But he is fat and happy and he has never harmed anything except for food or fun. I know you do not want me to get that turtle."

"I do! There's eighteen pounds of him. He's fat. He'll be good. Only eighty yards, where the bank crumbles down to Green River, under the lower ledge that's shale that looks like slate, two feet deep——"

"I know where he is. I will go get the fat turtle," Anteros said. "I myself am the fat turtle. I am the Green River." He went to get it.

"Oh, that damned poetry of his!" Magdalen spat when he was gone.

Anteros brought back the fat turtle. He looked as if he'd

weigh twenty-five pounds; but if Magdalen said he weighed eighteen pounds, then it was eighteen.

"Start cooking, Ethyl," Magdalen said. Magdalen was a mere undergraduate girl permitted on the digging by sheer good fortune. The others of the party were all archeologists of moment. Magdalen had no right to give orders to any-one—except her born right.

"I don't know how to cook a turtle," Ethyl complained.

"Anteros will show you how."

"The late evening smell of newly exposed excavation!" Terrence Burdock burbled as they lounged around the camp-fire a little later, full of turtle and V.O. and feeling rakishly wise. "The exposed age can be guessed by the very timbre of the smell, I believe."

"Timbre of the smell! What is your nose wired up to?" from Magdalen.

And, indeed, there was something time-evocative about the smell of the diggings: cool, at the same time musty and musky, ripe with old stratified water and compressed death. Stratified time.

"It helps if you already know what the exposed age is," said Howard Steinleser. "Here there is an anomaly. The chimney sometimes acts as if it were younger than the mound. The chim-ney cannot be young enough to include written rock, but it is."

"Archeology is made up entirely of anomalies," said Ter-rence, "rearranged to make them fit in a fluky pattern. There'd be no system to it otherwise."

"Every science is made up entirely of anomalies rear-ranged to fit," said Robert Derby. "Have you unriddled the glyph-stone, Howard?"

"Yes, pretty well. Better than I expected. Charles August can verify it, of course, when we get it back to the university. It is a nonroyal, nontribal, nonwarfare, nonhunt declaration. It does not come under any of the usual radical signs, any of the categories. It can only be categorized as uncategoried or personal. The translation will be rough."

"Rocky is the word," said Magdalen.

"On with it, Howard," Ethyl cried.

" 'You are the freedom of wild pigs in the sour-grass, and the nobility of badgers. You are the brightness of serpents and the soaring of vultures. You are passion of mesquite bushes on fire with lightning. You are serenity of toads.' "

"You've got to admit he's got a different line," said Ethyl.

"Your own love notes were less acrid, Terrence."

"What kind of thing is it, Steinleser?" Terrence questioned. "It must have a category."

"I believe Ethyl is right. It's a love poem. 'You are the water in rock cisterns and the secret spiders in that water. You are the dead coyote lying half in the stream, and you are the old entrapped dreams of the coyote's brains oozing liquid through the broken eye socket. You are the happy ravening flies about that broken socket.' "

"Oh, hold it, Steinleser," Robert Derby cried. "You can't have gotten all that from scratches on flint. What is 'entrapped dreams' in Nahuat-Tanoan glyph-writing?"

"The solid-person sign next to the hollow-person sign, both enclosed in the night sign—that has always been interpreted as the dream glyph. And here the dream glyph is enclosed in the glyph of the dead-fall trap. Yes, I believe it means entrapped dreams. To continue: 'You are the corn-worm in the dark heart of the corn, the naked small bird in the nest. You are the pustules on the sick rabbit, devouring life and flesh and turning it into your own serum. You are stars compressed into charcoal. But you cannot give, you cannot take. Once again you will be broken at the foot of the cliff, and the word will remain unsaid in your swollen and purpled tongue.' "

"A love poem, perhaps, but with a difference," said Robert Derby.

"I never was able to go his stuff, and I tried, I really tried," Magdalen moaned.

"Here is the change of person-subject shown by the canted-eye glyph linked with the self-glyph," Steinleser explained. "It is now a first-person talk. 'I own ten thousand back-loads of corn. I own gold and beans and nine buffalo horns full of watermelon seeds. I own the loincloth that the sun wore on his fourth journey across the sky. Only three loin cloths in the world are older and more valued than this. I cry out to you in a big voice like the hammering of herons (that sound-verb-particle is badly translated, the hammer being not a modern pounding hammer but a rock angling, chipping hammer) 'and the belching of buffaloes. My love is sinewy as entwined snakes, it is steadfast as the sloth, it is like a feathered arrow shot into your abdomen—such is my love. Why is my love unrequited?' "

"I challenge you, Steinleser," Terrence Burdock cut in. "What is the glyph for 'unrequited'?"

"The glyph of the extended hand—with all the fingers bent backwards. It goes on, 'I roar to you. Do not throw yourself down. You believe you are on the hanging sky bridge, but you are on the terminal cliff. I grovel before you. I am no more than dog-droppings.' "

"You'll notice he said that and not me," Magdalen burst

out. There was always a fundamental incoherence about Magdalen.

"Ah— continue, Steinleser," said Terrence. "The girl is daft, or she dreams out loud."

"That is all of the inscription, Terrence, except for a final glyph which I don't understand. Glyph writing takes a lot of room. That's all the stone would hold."

"What is the glyph that you don't understand, Howard?"

"It's the spear-thrower glyph entwined with the time-glyph. It sometimes means 'flung forward or beyond.' But what does it mean here?"

"It means 'continued,' dummy, 'continued,'" Magdalen said. "Do not fear. There'll be more stones."

"I think it's beautiful," said Ethyl Burdock, "—in its own context, of course."

"Then why don't you take him on, Ethyl, in his own context, of course?" Magdalen asked. "Myself, I don't care how many back-loads of corn he owns. I've had it."

"Take whom on, dear?" Ethyl asked. "Howard Steinleser can interpret the stones, but who can interpret our Magdalen?"

"Oh, I can read her like a rock," Terrence Burdock smiled. But he couldn't.

But it had fastened on them. It was all about them and through them: the brightness of serpents and the serenity of toads, the secret spiders in the water, the entrapped dreams oozing through the broken eye socket, the pustules of the sick rabbit, the belching of buffalo, and the arrow shot into the abdomen. And around it all was the night smell of flint and turned earth and chuckling streams, the mustiness, and the special muskiness which bears the name Nobility of Badgers.

They talked archaeology and myth talk. Then it was steep night, and the morning of the third day.

Oh, the sample digging went well. This was already a richer mound than Spiro, though the gash in it was but a small promise of things to come. And the curious twin of the mound, the broken chimney, confirmed and confounded and contradicted. There was time gone wrong in the chimney, or at least in the curious fluted core of it; the rest of it was normal enough, and sterile enough.

Anteros worked that day with a soft sullenness, and Magdalen brooded with a sort of lightning about her.

"Beads, glass beads!" Terrence Burdock exploded angrily. "All right! Who is the hoaxer in our midst? I will not tolerate this at all." Terrence had been angry of face all day. He was clawed deeply, as Steinleser had been the day before, and he was sour on the world.

"There have been glass-bead caches before, Terrence, hundreds of them," Robert Derby said softly.

"There have been hoaxers before, hundreds of them," Terrence howled. "These have 'Hong Kong Contemporary' written all over them, damned cheap glass beads sold by the pound. They have no business in a stratum of around the year seven hundred. All right, who is guilty?"

"I don't believe that any one of us is guilty, Terrence," Ethyl put in mildly. "They are found four hundred feet in from the slant surface of the mound. Why, we've cut through three hundred years of vegetable loam to get to them, and certainly the surface was eroded beyond that."

"We are scientists," said Steinleser. "We find these. Others have found such. Let us consider the improbabilities of it."

It was noon, so they ate and rested and considered the improbabilities. Anteros had brought them a great joint of white pork, and they made sandwiches and drank beer and ate pickles.

"You know," said Robert Derby, "that beyond the rank impossibility of glass beads found so many times where they *could not be found*, there is a real mystery about *all* early Indian beads, whether of bone, stone, or antler. There are millions and millions of these fine beads with pierced holes finer than any piercer ever found. There are residues, there are centers of every other Indian industry, and there is evolution of every other tool. Why have there been these millions of pierced beads, and never one piercer? There was no technique to make so fine a piercer. How were they done?"

Magdalen giggled. "Bead-spitter," she said.

"Bead-spitter! You're out of your fuzzy mind," Terrence erupted. "That's the silliest and least sophisticated of all Indian legends."

"But it *is* the legend," said Robert Derby, "the legend of more than thirty separate tribes. The Carib Indians of Cuba said that they got their beads from Bead-spitters. The Indians of Panama told Balboa the same thing. The Indians of the pueblos told the same story to Coronado. Every Indian community had an Indian who was its Bead-spitter. There are Creek and Alabama and Koasati stories of Bead-spitter; see Swanton's collections. And his stories were taken down within living memory.

"More than that, when European trade-beads were first introduced, there is one account of an Indian receiving some and saying 'I will take some to Bead-spitter. If he sees them, he can spit them too.' And that Bead-spitter did then spit them by the bushel. There was never any other Indian account of the origin of their beads. *All* were spit by a Bead-spitter."

"Really, this is very unreal," Ethyl said. Really it was.

"Hog hokey! A Bead-spitter of around the year seven hundred could not spit future beads, he could not spit cheap Hong Kong glass beads of the present time!" Terrence was very angry.

"Pardon me, yes sir, he could," said Anteros. "A Bead-spitter can spit future beads, if he faces north when he spits. That has always been known."

Terrence was angry, he fumed and poisoned the day for them, and the claw marks on his face stood out livid purple. He was angrier yet when he said that the curious dark capping rock on top of the chimney was dangerous, that it would fall and kill someone; and Anteros said that there was no such capping rock on the chimney, that Terrence's eyes were deceiving him, that Terrence should go sit in the shade and rest.

And Terrence became excessively angry when he discovered that Magdalen was trying to hide something that she had discovered in the fluted core of the chimney. It was a large and heavy shale-stone, too heavy even for Magdalen's puzzling strength. She had dragged it out of the chimney flute, tumbled it down to the bottom, and was trying to cover it with rocks and scarp.

"Robert, mark the extraction point!" Terrence called loudly. "It's quite plain yet. Magdalen, stop that! Whatever it is, it must be examined now."

"Oh, it's just more of the damned same thing! I wish he'd let me alone. With his kind of money he can get plenty of girls. Besides, it's private, Terrence. You don't have any business reading it."

"You are hysterical, Magdalen, and you may have to leave the digging site."

"I wish I could leave. I can't. I wish I could love. I can't. Why isn't it enough that I die?"

"Howard, spend the afternoon on this," Terrence ordered. "It has writing of a sort on it. If it's what I think it is, it scares me. It's too recent to be in any eroded chimney rock formation, Howard, and it comes from far below the top. Read it."

"A few hours on it and I may come up with something. I never saw anything like it, either. What do you think it is, Terrence?"

"What do you think I think it is? It's much later than the

other, and that one was impossible. I'll not be the one to confess myself crazy first."

Howard Steinleser went to work on the incised stone; and two hours before sundown they brought him another one, a gray soapstone block from higher up. Whatever this was covered with, it was not at all the same thing that covered the shale-stone.

And elsewhere things went well, too well. The old fishiness was back on it. No series of finds could be so perfect, no petrification could be so well ordered.

"Robert," Magdalen called down to Robert Derby just at sunset, "in the high meadow above the shore, about four hundred yards down, just past the old fence line—"

"—there is a badger hole, Magdalen. Now you have me doing it, seeing invisible things at a distance. And if I take a carbine and stroll down there quietly, the badger will stick his head out just as I get there (I being strongly downwind of him), and I'll blam him between the eyes. He'll be a big one, fifty pounds."

"Thirty. Bring him, Robert. You're showing a little understanding at last."

"But, Magdalen, badger is rampant meat. It's seldom eaten."

"May not the condemned girl have what she wishes for her last meal? Go get it, Robert."

Robert went. The voice of the little carbine was barely heard at that distance. Soon, Robert brought back the dead badger.

"Cook it, Ethyl," Magdalen ordered.

"Yes, I know. And if I don't know how, Anteros will show me." But Anteros was gone. Robert found him on a sundown knoll with his shoulders hunched. The old man was sobbing silently and his face seemed to be made out of dull pumice stone. But he came back to aid Ethyl in preparing the badger.

"If the first of today's stones scared you, the second should have lifted the hair right off your head, Terrence," Howard Steinleser said.

"It does, it does. All the stones are too recent to be in a chimney formation, but this last one is an insult. It isn't two hundred years old, but there's a thousand years of strata above it. What time is deposited there?"

They had eaten rampant badger meat and drunk inferior whiskey (which Anteros, who had given it to them, didn't know was inferior), and the muskiness was both inside them and around them. The campfire sometimes spit angrily with small explosions, and its glare reached high when it did so. By one such leaping glare, Terrence Burdock saw that the curious dark capping rock was once more on the top of chimney. He thought he had seen it there in the daytime; but it had not been there after he had sat in the shade and rested, and it had absolutely not been there when he climbed the chimney itself to be sure.

"Let's have the second chapter and then the third, Howard," Ethyl said. "It's neater that way."

"Yes. Well, the second chapter (the first and lowest and apparently the earliest rock we came on today) is written in a language that no one ever saw written before; and yet it's no great trouble to read it. Even Terrence guessed what it was and it scared him. It is Anadarko-Caddo hand-talk graven in stone. It is what is called the Sign Language of the Plains Indians copied down in formalized pictographs. And it *has* to be very recent, within the last three hundred years. Hand-talk was fragmentary at the first coming of the Spanish, and well developed at the first coming of the French. It was an explosive development, as such things go, worked out within a hundred years. This rock has to be younger than its *situs* but it was absolutely found in place."

"Read it, Howard, read it," Robert Derby called. Robert was feeling fine and the rest of them were gloomy tonight.

" 'I own three hundred ponies,' " Steinleser read the rock out of his memory. " 'I own two days' ride north and east and south, and one day's ride west. I give you all. I blast out with a big voice like fire in tall trees, like the explosion of crowning pine trees. I cry like closing-in wolves, like the high voice of the lion, like the hoarse scream of torn calves. Do you not destroy yourself again! You are the dew on crazy-weed in the morning. You are the swift crooked wings of the night-hawk, the dainty feet of the skunk, you are the juice of the sour squash. Why can you not take or give? I am the humpbacked bull of the high plains, I am the river itself and the stagnant pools left by the river, I am the raw earth and the rocks. Come to me, but do not come so violently as to destroy yourself.'

"Ah, that was the text of the first rock of the day, the Anadarko-Caddo hand-talk graven in stone. And final pictographs which I don't understand: a shot-arrow sign, and a boulder beyond."

" 'Continued on next rock,' of course," said Robert Derby. "Well, why *wasn't* hand-talk ever written down? The signs are simple and easily stylized and they were understood by many different tribes. It would have been natural to write it."

"Alphabetical writing was in the region *before* hand-talk was well developed," Terrence Burdock said. "In fact, it was the coming of the Spanish that gave the impetus to hand-talk. It was really developed for communication between Spanish and Indian, not between Indian and Indian. And yet, I believe, hand-talk *was* written down once; it was the beginning of the Chinese pictographs. And there also it had its beginning as communication between differing peoples. Depend on it, if all mankind had always been of a single language, there would never have been any written language developed at all. Writing always began as a bridge, and there had to be some chasm for it to bridge."

"We have one to bridge here," said Steinleser. "That whole chimney is full of rotten smoke. The highest part of it should be older than the lowest part of the mound, since the mound was built on a base eroded away from the chimney formation. But in many ways they seem to be contemporary. We must all be under a spell here. We've worked two days on this, parts of three days, and the total impossibility of the situation hasn't struck us yet.

"The old Nahutlan glyphs for Time are the Chimney glyphs. Present time is a lower part of a chimney and fire burning at the base. Past time is black smoke from a chimney, and future time is white smoke from a chimney. There was a signature glyph running through our yesterday's stone which I didn't and don't understand. It seemed to indicate something coming down out of the chimney rather than going up it."

"It really doesn't look much like a chimney," Magdalen said.

"And a maiden doesn't look much like dew on crazy-weed in the morning, Magdalen," Robert Derby said, "but we recognize these identities."

They talked a while about the impossibility of the whole business.

"There are scales on our eyes," Steinleser said. "The fluted core of the chimney is wrong. I'm not even sure the rest of the chimney is right."

"No, it isn't," said Robert Derby. "We can identify most of the strata of the chimney with known periods of the river and stream. I was above and below today. There is one stretch where the sandstone was not eroded at all, where it stands three hundred yards back from the shifted river and is

overlaid with a hundred years of loam and sod. There are
other sections where the stone is cut away variously. We can
tell when most of the chimney was laid down, we can find its
correspondences up to a few hundred years ago. But when
were the top ten feet of it laid down? There were no correspondences anywhere to that. The centuries represented by
the strata of the top of the chimney, people, those centuries
haven't happened yet."

"And when was the dark capping rock on top of it all
formed—?" Terrence began. "Ah, I'm out of my mind. It
isn't there. I'm demented."

"No more than the rest of us," said Steinleser. "I saw it
too, I thought, today. And then I didn't see it again."

"The rock-writing, it's like an old novel that I only half
remember," said Ethyl.

"Oh, that's what it is, yes," Magdalen murmured.

"But I don't remember what happened to the girl in it."

"*I* remember what happened to her, Ethyl," Magdalen
said.

"Give us the third chapter, Howard," Ethyl asked. "I want
to see how it comes out."

"First you should all have whiskey for those colds," Anteros suggested humbly.

"But none of us have colds," Ethyl objected.

"You take your own medical advice, Ethyl, and I'll take
mine," Terrence said. "I will have whiskey. My cold is not
rheum but fear-chill."

They all had whiskey. They talked a while, and some of
them dozed.

"It's late, Howard," Ethyl said after a while. "Let's have
the next chapter. Is it the last chapter? Then we'll sleep. We
have honest digging to do tomorrow."

"Our third stone, our second stone of the day just past, is
another and even later form of writing, and it has never been
seen in stone before. It is Kiowa picture writing. The Kiowas
did their out-turning spiral writing on buffalo skins dressed almost as fine as vellum. In its more sophisticated form (and
this is a copy of that) it is quite late. The Kiowa picture
writing probably did not arrive at its excellence until influenced by white artists."

"How late, Steinleser?" Robert Derby asked.

"Not more than a hundred and fifty years old. But I have
never seen it copied in stone before. It simply isn't stone-
styled. There's a lot of things around here lately that I
haven't seen before.

"Well then, to the text, or should I say the pictography?

'You fear the earth, you fear rough ground and rocks, you fear moister earth and rotting flesh, you fear the flesh itself, all flesh is rotting flesh. If you love not rotting flesh, you love not at all. You believe the bridge hanging in the sky, the bridge hung by tendrils and woody vines that diminish as they go up and up till they are no thicker than hairs. There is no sky-bridge, you cannot go up on it. Did you believe that the roots of love grow upside down? They come out of deep earth that is old flesh and brains and hearts and entrails, that is old buffalo bowels and snakes' pizzles, that is black blood and rot and moaning underground. This is old and worn-out and bloody Time, and the roots of love grow out of its gore.' "

"You seem to give remarkably detailed translations of the simple spiral pictures, Steinleser, but I begin to get in the mood of it," Terrence said.

"Ah, perhaps I cheat a little," said Steinleser.

"You lie a lot," Magdalen challenged.

"No I do not. There is some basis for every phrase I've used. It goes on: 'I own twenty-two trade rifles. I own ponies. I own Mexico silver, eight-bit pieces. I am rich in all ways. I give all to you. I cry out with big voice like a bear full of mad-weed, like a bullfrog in love, like a stallion rearing against a puma. It is the earth that calls you. I am the earth, woolier than wolves and rougher than rocks. I am the bog earth that sucks you in. You cannot give, you cannot take, you cannot love, you think there is something else, you think there is a sky-bridge you may loiter on without crashing down. I am bristled-bear earth, there is no other. You will come to me in the morning. You will come to me easy and with grace. Or you will come to me reluctant and you be shattered in every bone and member of you. You be broken by our encounter. You be shattered as by a lightning bolt striking up from the earth. I am the red calf which is in the writings. I am the rotting red earth. Live in the morning or die in the morning, but remember that love in death is better than no love at all.' "

"Oh brother! Nobody gets that stuff from such kid pictures, Steinleser," Robert Derby moaned.

"Ah well, that's the end of the spiral picture. And a Kiowa spiral pictograph ends with either an insweep or an outsweep line. This ends with an outsweep, which means—"

" 'Continued on next rock,' that's what it means," Terrence cried roughly.

"You won't find the next rocks," Magdalen said. "They're hidden, and most of the time they're not there yet, but they will go on and on. But for all that, you'll read it in the rocks tomorrow morning. I want it to be over with. Oh, I don't know what I want!"

"I believe I know what you want tonight, Magdalen," Robert Derby said.

But he didn't.

The talk trailed off, the fire burned down, they went to their sleeping sacks.

Then it was long jagged night, and the morning of the fourth day. But wait! In Nahuat-Tanoan legend, the world ends on the fourth morning. All the lives we lived or thought we lived had been but dreams of third night. The loincloth that the sun wore on the fourth day's journey was not as valuable as one has made out. It was worn for no more than an hour or so.

And, in fact, there was something terminal about fourth morning. Anteros had disappeared. Magdalen had disappeared. The chimney rock looked greatly diminished in its bulk (something had gone out of it) and much crazier in its broken height. The sun had come up a garish gray-orange color through fog. The signature-glyph of the first stone dominated the ambient. It was as if something were coming down from the chimney, a horrifying smoke; but it was only noisome morning fog.

No it wasn't. There was something else coming down from the chimney, or from the hidden sky: pebbles, stones, indescribable bits of foul oozings, the less fastidious pieces of the sky; a light, nightmare rain had begun to fall there; the chimney was apparently beginning to crumble.

"It's the damnedest thing I ever heard about," Robert Derby growled. "Do you think that Magdalen really went off with Anteros?" Derby was bitter and fumatory this morning and his face was badly clawed.

"Who is Magdalen? Who is Anteros?" Ethyl Burdock asked.

Terrence Burdock was hooting from high on the mound. "All come up," he called. "Here is a find that will make it all worthwhile. We'll have to photo and sketch and measure and record and witness. It's the finest basalt head I've ever seen, man-sized, and I suspect that there's a man-sized body attached to it. We'll soon clean it and clear it. Gah! What a weird fellow he was!"

But Howard Steinleser was studying a brightly colored something that he held in his two hands.

"What is it, Howard? What are you doing?" Derby demanded.

"Ah, I believe this is the next stone in the sequence. The writing is alphabetical but deformed—there is an element missing. I believe it is in modern English, and I will solve the deformity and see it true in a minute. The text of it seems to be—"

Rocks and stones were coming down from the chimney, and fog, amnesic and wit-stealing fog.

"Steinleser, are you all right?" Robert Derby asked with compassion. "That isn't a stone that you hold in your hand."

"It isn't a stone? I thought it was. What is it then?"

"It is the fruit of the Osage orange tree, an American moraceous. It isn't a stone, Howard." And the thing was a tough, woody, wrinkled mock-orange, as big as a small melon.

"You have to admit that the wrinkles look a little bit like writing, Robert."

"Yes, they look a little like writing, Howard. Let us go up where Terrence is bawling for us. You've read too many stones. And it isn't safe here."

"Why go up, Howard? The other thing is coming down."

It was the bristled-boar earth reaching up with a rumble. It was a lightning bolt struck upward out of the earth, and it got its prey. There was explosion and roar. The dark capping rock was jerked from the top of the chimney and slammed with terrible force to the earth, shattering with a great shock. And something else that had been on that capping rock. And the whole chimney collapsed about them.

She was broken by the encounter. She was shattered in every bone and member of her. And she was dead.

"Who—who is she?" Howard Steinleser stuttered.

"Oh God! Magdalen, of course!" Robert Derby cried.

"I remember her a little bit. Didn't understand her. She put out like an evoking moth but she wouldn't be had. Near clawed the face off me the other night when I misunderstood the signals. She believed there was a sky bridge. It's in a lot of the mythologies. But there isn't one, you know. Oh well."

"The girl is dead! Damnation! What are you doing grubbing in those stones?"

"Maybe she isn't dead in them yet, Robert. I'm going to read what's here before something happens to them. This capping rock that fell and broke, it's impossible, of course. It's a stratum that hasn't been laid down yet. I always did want to read the future and I may never get another chance."

"You fool! The girl's dead! Does nobody care? Terrence, stop bellowing about your find. Come down. The girl's dead."

"Come up, Robert and Howard," Terrence insisted. "Leave that broken stuff down there. It's worthless. But nobody ever saw anything like this."

"Do come up, men," Ethyl sang. "Oh, it's a wonderful piece! I never saw anything like it in my life."

"Ethyl, is the whole morning mad?" Robert Derby demanded as he came up to her. "She's dead. Don't you really remember her? Don't you remember Magdalen?"

"I'm not sure. Is she the girl down there? Isn't she the same girl who's been hanging around here a couple of days? She shouldn't have been playing on that high rock. I'm sorry she's dead. But just look what we're uncovering here!"

"Terrence. Don't *you* remember Magdalen?"

"The girl down there? She's a little bit like the girl that clawed the hell out of me the other night. Next time someone goes to town they might mention to the sheriff that there's a dead girl here. Robert, did you ever see a face like this one? And it digs away to reveal the shoulders. I believe there's a whole man-sized figure here. Wonderful, wonderful!"

"Terrence, you're off your head. Well, do you remember Anteros?"

"Certainly, the twin of Eros, but nobody ever made much of the symbol of unsuccessful love. Thunder! That's the name for him! It fits him perfectly. We'll call him Anteros."

Well, it *was* Anteros, lifelike in basalt stone. His face was contorted. He was sobbing soundlessly and frozenly and his shoulders were hunched with emotion. The carving was fascinating in its miserable passion, his stony love unrequited. Perhaps he was more impressive now than he would be when he was cleaned. He was earth, he was earth itself. Whatever period the carving belonged to, it was outstanding in its power.

"The live Anteros, Terrence. Don't you remember our digging man, Anteros Manypenny?"

"Sure. He didn't show up for work this morning, did he? Tell him he's fired."

"Magdalen is dead! She was one of us! Dammit, she was the main one of us!" Robert Derby cried. Terrence and Ethyl Burdock were earless to his outburst. They were busy uncovering the rest of the carving.

And down below, Howard Steinleser was studying dark broken rocks before they would disappear, studying a stratum that hadn't been laid down yet, reading a foggy future.

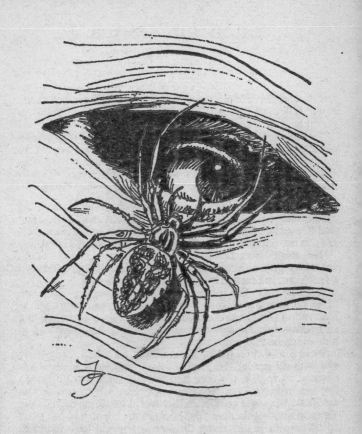

Once on Aranea

One fine spider silk, no more than 1/80,000 of an inch thick, could this bind and kill a man? He would soon know. It would be a curious death, to be done in by fine spider silk.

"—but then mine has been a curious life," Scarble muttered from a tight throat, "and it might as well have an ironic end to it. I wonder if you know, you mother-loving spiders," he called out with difficulty, "that every death is ironic. The arachnidian irony has a pretty fine edge, though."

It had begun on Aranea a week earlier. In their surveying of the planet-sized asteroids of the Cercyon Belt, their practice was (after the team had completed the Initial Base Survey) to leave a lone man on the asteroid for a short period.

The theory was that any malevolent force, which might not move against a group, could come into the open against a lone man. In practice it had given various results.

Donners said that nothing at all happened on his world when he was there alone, and that nothing had happened to him. But Donners had developed a grotesque facial tic and an oddity of speech and manner. Something had happened to him which he had not realized.

Procop had simply disappeared from his world, completely and with no residue. He couldn't have traveled a hundred kilometers on foot in the time he had, and there was no reason for him to travel even ten. He should have left traces—of the calcium which was hardly on that world at all, of cellular decomposition, of amino acids. If a gram of him had been left on that world in any form, the scanners would have found it, and they hadn't. But exploratory parties grow used to such puzzles.

Bernheim said that he had gone to pieces when left alone. He did not know whether there had been strange happenings on his world or in his head. He had straightened up only with a great effort when he saw them come back for him, he said. Bernheim had always been a man of compulsive honesty.

Marin said that it hadn't been a picnic when he was left

50

alone, but that nothing had happened there that he wouldn't be able to find an answer to if he could devote a thousand years to it. He said it was more a test of a man than of a world. But it was the test that the Party was to use for the livableness of a world.

On Aranea it was Scarble who would remain alone and make the test. On Aranea, the Spider Asteroid, there were two sorts of creatures—at first believed to be three. But two of these first apparent forms were different stages of the same species.

There were the small four-legged scutters. There were the two-legged, two-armed, upright straddling fingerlings. Finally there were the "Spiders"—actually dodecapods, the largest of them as big as a teacup. The two-legged fingerlings were the spiders, after their metamorphosis.

Bernheim was reading his report, the final bit for the Initial Base Survey:

"The basic emotion of the small quadrupeds, *Scutterae Bernheimiensis,* is subservience. They register that they are owned by the spider complex, and that they must serve it."

"So, there are two species, one slave to the other," said Marin. "It's a common pattern."

"The biped fingerlings, *Larva Arachnida Marin,* do not realize their relationship to the 'Spiders,'" Bernheim continued. "When forced into the metamorphosis, their reaction is stark consternation."

"So would mine be," said Scarble. "And what's the basic emotion of the adult spiders, the *Arachne Dodecapode Scarble?*"

"It is mother-love, lately reoriented by an intrusion and intensified many-fold."

"By what intrusion? And how intensified?" Marin asked.

"*We* are the intrusion. *We* are the intensification," Bernheim explained. "They are intensely excited only since our arrival. That murmuring and chirping of millions of them is all for us. This is maternal affection gone hysterical—*for us!*"

They exploded in the first real laughter ever heard on Aranea, and even the spiders giggled in million-voiced accord.

"Oh, those mother-loving spiders!" became their byword for their stay there, and it had to go into the report.

So it was with rare good humor that three of them (Bernheim, Marin, Donners) took off and left Scarble alone on the Spider World, himself chortling every time he thought of the maternal spiders. For companion, Scarble had only a dog named Dog, which is to say Cyon; it was a classical dog.

This would be easy. Scarble liked spiders and even looked like one—a spindly, wiry man covered with black hair almost everywhere except on the top of his head; a man who ran much to long legs and arms and had not a great amount of body to him. When he waved his arms, as he did when he talked, he gave the impression of having more than two of them. Even his humor was spiderlike.

And what was there to scare any man in the golden daylight of Aranea? Scarble had the name of not being afraid of anything; he had been diligent to give himself that name. And courage is the normal complement of the male animal everywhere. Individual exceptions are common in every species, but they are abnormal. Scarble was normal.

And, should normal courage fail, they had left him a supply of Dutch Courage, and French, Scotch, Canadian, and Kentucky; as well as a distilled-on-the-wing drink known as Rocket Red. They always left a man with a good bottled stock.

It was on this prime stock that the shadow of the coming thing first fell—and Scarble didn't recognize it. He was delighted when he woke from his first sleep on Aranea and saw the stuff as covered with cobwebs as though it had been a hundred years in a cellar. He sampled it with exceptional pleasure. Mellow! Even the Rocket Red had acquired age and potent dignity.

Then he walked all over Aranea with the dog Cyon. That whole world was covered with golden cobwebs; and it brought out the song in Scarble. Man afoot! Here was a whole echoing world to sing in! The full voice is also the normal complement of the male animal, and Scarble had a voice (a bad one) that would fill a world.

> "The Spaceman frolicked with his girl
> Though all his friends could not abide her.
> She was a pippin and a pearl,
> She was a comely twelve-legged spider."

Scarble added dozens of verses, most of them obscene, while the spider audience in its millions chirped and murmured appreciation. He sang them to the tune of 'Ganymede Saturday Night.' He sang all his ballads to that tune. It was the only tune he knew.

Marin had been wrong; it was a picnic after all. Scarble sat on the edge of one of the silken ringed spider ponds and communed with the mother-loving spiders. The cycle of them, he knew, was this:

The little biped fingerlings were born in a sort of caul. Most often the caul is only wrapped about them, and the young ones fight their way out of it and become aware. Sometimes they look as if they arrived wearing space helmets. Often the young are truly live-born, with only scraps on them of the egg they should have arrived in. The spiders had been surprised in their era of transition.

The newborn bipeds refuse the care of the adult spiders, and run wild at this stage of their being. They destroy everything of the spider nettings and handicrafts that they are able to, and the adult spiders regard them patiently with that abiding mother-love.

And sometime later, when it is time for the change, the adults drug these young, bind them, weave a silk shell around them, and then put a cap on it. Into the cap (it is the hood of the cocoon) is placed one of the small four-legged scutters, freshly killed and made putrescent in some manner. This is the whole purpose in life of the scutters, to feed the pupa form of the spiders.

The pupa spider is somnolent for a long time. Then it begins to eat of the putrescence in the hood, and to change. Four little notches grow out of each of its sides. With these it saws away the cocoon and emerges as a new being. Soon the notches will grow to full members, and the creature then takes its place as a full adult of the Nation of Spiders.

The Spiders were master engineers, and the pattern of the spider ponds built by them covered the whole world of Aranea. They controlled the waters of that world with their silken dams, weirs, levees, and hurdles. The spiders were littoral creatures and had to maintain a controllable water level.

The lakes and ponds were divided by silken barriers into small plots, some of them so completely covered by blue-green vegetation as to have the appearance of lush meadows, others adjacent to them being clear of all growth. The spiders seeded and they harvested. At some of their major dams there were anchoring cables as much as an inch in diameter. Scarble estimated that there might be as many as seven billion individual spider silks making up such a cable.

Scarble sat on the silken edge of one of the pools while the spiders in their myriads twittered about him. Then an expert crew of them performed certain rites at that pool, sweeping it, making it clearer, inviting him to drink.

"Thank you," said Scarble. He leaned into it and drank deeply. Then he stretched out to rest on the silken shore. He went to sleep.

He dreamed that it was snowing, but in a new and pleasant manner. It was not like Earth snow, and not at all like the biting snow of Priestly Planet or the blue horror that is the lethal snow on Arestor: This was warm snow, light and full of sun, snowflakes with beards on them like mote-sized comets. Scarble was being covered over by a warm snow that was half sunshine.

He awoke lazily and discovered that it was true. The spiders had been covering him with gossamer and silk, as children on a beach will cover one another with sand. They shot the silks out over him like millions of streamers of serpentine. It was a party, a ball given for him; and the spider song had now reached a point of excitement and jubilation.

Scarble tried to raise his head and found that he could not. He gave it up and lay back, deliciously lazy. This was something new in ease. Whether he was sleeping or waking it was all the same. A picnic after all, to be so pleasantly drugged—

To be what? An ugly thought came into Scarble's mind and he chased it away. It came again and sat like a little black animal on the edge of his golden dream.

Why hadn't he been able to raise his head?

He cleared his mind of the beginnings of panic.

"Here, here!" he called out. "You're covering me too deep with that damned sand. Fun's fun, but that's enough."

But it was more cohesive than sand. This might be only a noonday dream that would slide away. Well, it wasn't. It was stark afternoon reality. The spiders had him pegged down to the ground with their billion-stranded silk bonds and he could hardly move a muscle.

And the mother-loving little abominations had drugged him by whatever they had put into the inviting drinking pool. The taste in his mouth reminded him of the knock-out drops they used to pass out free as water on New Shanghai.

The spider song became more complex. There were elements of great change in it, the motifs of one world falling away and another one being born. The golden daylight of Aranea was coming to an end. Scarble had enjoyed his luxurious drugged sleep for more hours than he had believed. Completely weary of his struggle with his bonds, he dropped to sleep again; and the spiders continued to work through the night.

The first thing that Scarble saw in the morning—out of

the corner of one eye fixed in his unmoving head—was the spiders maneuvering a large golden ball towards him. They tipped it with lines from the tops of gin poles. They rolled it over and over, reset their rigging, and rolled it again.

It was the dog Cyon, dead, and cocooned in a sack of silk. The stench of it was unbearable. The dog was not only dead but decayed, almost liquid in its putrefaction, and with the high hair still on it.

Scarble was sickened by this, but he understood the nature of the happening. He was a naturalist, and he knew that anger was an unnaturalist response, and that murder and putrefaction are natural workings. But Cyon wasn't merely a dog. He was also a personal friend of Scarble.

Scarble could not turn to see what was behind his own head, but he knew that spiders had been working on something there all night. He realized now what it was: a snood, a capuchin like a friar's, the hood to be his own cocoon. He knew with horror what thing they were rolling into that hood now, and how the hood would be joined onto his own cocoon. It happened quickly.

Scarble's screams were drowned in the near liquid mass; they had a drumlike sound even to his own ears as though they were coming from under water. They merged easily with the spider music which had just the place for that screaming motif.

Then overpowering sickness sent Scarble into merciful unconsciousness after the dead and rotting dog was rolled into his face and closed in with him as their cocoons became one.

How long does it take a man to die in such circumstances? Scarble set his mind to do it as quickly as possible, but he was too tough for his own good. By second night he still could not arrive at death, but he welcomed the dark. The dog's carcass had become higher and more pungent, and the agony of Scarble took on new refinements. He was thirsty to the point of madness, and so hungry that he could eat anything—almost anything.

It frightened him that he could now understand the spider mind so clearly. The spiders worked by analogy. They believed Scarble to be an unfinished two-legged strider, come to them with his quadruped that was born for one purpose—to feed him when he went into pupa form before being metamorphosed into a giant Emperor Spider. Aye, they believed Scarble to be the Emperor Spider promised to them from the beginning of time.

The spider song was a dirge now, the passing of the old

life, the death and decay fugue. But in the complex of the dirge there were introductory passages of something much higher: the *Anastasis*, the Resurrection Song.

"You mother-loving spiders!" Scarble called out in fury. "You think I'm going to eat Cyon and then turn into a spider. You're wrong, I tell you! The biology of the thing is impossible, but how do you explain biology to spiders?"

To be dying of thirst and there no liquid to mouth except that! To be starving and there no food available but this soft putridity pressed into his face!

There was a change in the tempo of the spider song. It rose in the crescendo of transition and made Scarble angry.

"You presumptive little twelve-legged crawlers, you're getting ahead of me! Don't tell *me* what to do! Don't act as though I had already done it."

But the hours had taken their price, and Scarble had already passed through madness and into the world on the other side. He didn't know when it began, but the spiders knew of the change about third dawn. The spiders' soaring incantation rose to new heights, and Scarble was able to follow it. He was hearing tones above the range of the human ear.

Scarble began to eat of the putrefied mass—and to change. The Hallelujah Chorus of the Spider Song rose in a vast symphony.

In the Spaceman's Survival Handbook there is one instruction which some have believed to be written in humor: 'Never die till you have considered every alternative to a situation.'

Well, how does a man get out of a situation like this?

He doesn't.

Well then, how does a spider get out of a situation like this?

He grows eight more short little notches of legs, and he shuffles and saws his way out of the cocoon with them.

"It's worth a try," Scarble said. "I'll see if I've turned into a spider."

He had. He did it. It worked.

They disabilitied Scarble from the active service. He could give no intelligent account of his lone stay on Aranea. He gave out with nothing but sick quips like: "Cyon was a good dog, but only after he had become very bad," and "The Spiders tied me up and made me eat the dog, and then they turned me into a spider."

Scarble was plainly insane, but pleasantly so. And there was nothing left of the dog except curiously softened bones.

They sent Scarble back to Earth and kept him under observation. Such men were handled with sympathy. They called him the Spider Man around the wards. But after a while that sympathy ran a little thin. Earth was having her own troubles with spiders.

"I've never seen anything like them," an earthside doctor told Scarble in examining him one day, as he brushed some of that floating stuff out of his eyes. "The growths are not malignant, but they will be mighty unhandy. Since they are not malignant, I cannot remove them without your permission, Scarble. They're getting larger, you know."

"Certainly they're getting larger," Scarble maintained. "I'm quite pleased with the way they're coming along. They get to be as big as the spiders' other legs. And don't remove them! I'd as soon lose one of my other limbs as one of them. They saved my life. I couldn't have gotten out of my cocoon without them."

"You're going to have to get off this spider jag, Scarble. Have you been reading the crank reports about the spiders and have they upset you?"

"Why should they upset me, Doctor? Everything is going as smooth as—ah—spidersilk. Naturally I have my own intelligence setup on these matters. And the fact that you refer to them as 'crank reports' likewise pleases me. I'm on top of the heap, Doctor. Who else has a hundred billion soldiers ready to strike? We live in exciting times, do we not?"

"As to *that* sickness of yours, Scarble, I'll gladly leave it to your other doctor, your psycho doctor; and now it is time for you to go and see him. But I wish you'd let me remove those growths before they become larger. They're almost like other limbs."

"Quite like," said Scarble. He left the room majestically in the flowing robes which he now affected and went down the corridor to see his other doctor. The robes served a purpose. They *did* cover Scarble's afflictions, the four strange growths on each side of his body. And also:

"An Emperor always wears flowing robes," Scarble said. "You can't expect him to go dressed like a commoner."

Doctor Mosca, Scarble's other doctor, was a quiet and patient man. He was also a dull fellow who had to have simple things explained to him over and over again.

"What are you today, Scarble?" Doctor Mosca asked again as he brushed some of the floating stuff away.

"Why, I'm the Emperor of the Dodecapod Spiders of Aranea," Scarble said pleasantly. "I explain that to you every day, doctor, but you don't seem to remember. I am also Prefect Extraordinary to the Aranea Spiders of the Dispersal. And I am Proconsul to the Spiders of Earth."

"Scarble, I'll be plain with you. Your planet probe experience (whatever it was) has unhitched your mind. And you have somehow connected whatever happened on Aranea to the recent spider incidents on Earth. I will admit that some of these incidents are peculiar and almost insane—"

"No, no, Doctor, not insane. They are absolutely reasonable—according to the Higher Reason. They are organized and directed and strictly on schedule. To call the incidents insane would be almost like calling me insane."

"Mr. Scarble, we don't keep you here for your pool-shooting ability, though you're good at that. We keep you here because you're very sick—mentally. Now listen to me carefully: You are a man, and not a spider."

"I'm glad you think so, doctor. Our high council decided that it would be better if I retained the basic man-appearance until our present military operation is completed. It should be completed today."

"Scarble, you've got to get hold of yourself!" Doctor Mosca insisted. He brushed heaps of the accumulated silkstuff off his desk. "You are a man, and an intelligent man. We have to get you off this insane spider jag of yours. And it's not my department, but somebody had better get the world off its jag, too. Every year has its own peculiar sort of nuttiness, but the Spider Incidents have become downright silly. Do you know that, with the recent astronomical increases of the spiders—"

"That may be an unconscious pun," Scarble interrupted.

"—that it is estimated there are now a hundred billion spiders in this country alone."

"Multiply that figure by a thousand if you wish," Scarble said. "Last night was the Night of the Great Hatching, and the young ones grow to effective size in hours, all stages of them quickly now. The time is at hand. I give the word now!"

"Great thumping thunder!" Doctor Mosca howled. "I'm bitten badly! Another spider bite."

"Not just another bite," Scarble said. "That was the critical bite. I'm sincerely sorry for the pain: but, with so many people to impregnate, I could not equip all my creatures with painless probes. It eases off now, though, doesn't it? The injection contains a narcotic and a soporific."

It did. Doctor Mosca drowsed. He half-dreamed that it was snowing, but in a new and pleasant manner. It was warm snow, light and full of sun, flakes with beards on them like mote-sized comets.

The suddenly appearing spiders were covering Doctor Mosca with gossamer and silk, as children will cover each other with sand on a beach. And they were covering many millions of others, all stung and sunk into pleasant lethargy and drowsiness, with billions of streamers of serpentine silk.

It was deliciously lazy for Doctor Mosca to lie back in the chair and hear that demented Scarble drone on that he was no longer a man—(Doctor Mosca found that he could no longer move his head: there was something odd about that)—that Scarble was no longer a man, whatever his appearance, that he was really the Emperor of the Dodecapod Spiders of Aranea, and of all Spiders everywhere.

Sodom and Gomorrah, Texas

Manuel shouldn't have been employed as a census taker. He wasn't qualified. He couldn't read a map. He didn't know what a map was. And he only grinned when they told him that North was at the top. He knew better.

But he did write a nice round hand—like a boy's hand. He did know Spanish, and enough English. For the sector that was assigned to him, he would not need a map. He knew it better than anyone else, certainly better than any mapmaker.

Besides, he was poor and needed the work.

They instructed him and sent him out. Or they thought that they had instructed him. They couldn't be sure.

"Count everyone? All right. Fill them all in? I need more papers."

"We will give you more papers if you need more, Manuel, but there aren't so many in your sector."

"Lots of them, *lobos, tejones, zorros,* even people."

"People only, Manuel. Do not take the animals. How would you write them up? They have no names."

"Oh, yes. All have names. Might as well take them all."

"Only people, Manuel."

"Mulos?"

"No."

"Conejos?"

"No, Manuel, no."

"No trouble. Might as well take them all."

"Only people—God give me strength!—only people, Manuel."

"How about little people?"

"Children, yes, that has been explained to you."

"Little people. Not children. Little people."

"If they are people, take them."

"How big they have to be?"

"It doesn't make any difference how big they are. If they are people, take them."

Manuel took Mula and went. His sector was the Santa Magdalena—a scarp of baldheaded and desolate mountains, steep but not high, and so torrid in the afternoons that it was said that the old lava sometimes began to writhe and flow again from the sun's heat alone.

In the Center Valley, there were five thousand acres of slag and glassified rock from some forgotten old blast that had melted the hills and destroyed their mantle, reducing all to a terrible flatness. This was Sodom—strewn with low-lying ghosts as of people and objects, formed when the granite bubbled like water.

Away from the dead center, the ravines were body-deep in chapparal, and the mountains stood gray-green in old cactus. The stunted trees were lower than the giant bushes and yuccas.

Manuel went with Mula—a round easy man and a spare gaunt mule. Mula was a mule, but there were other inhabitants of the Santa Magdalena whose genus was less certain.

Yet even about Mula there was an ancestral oddity. Her paternal grandfather had been a goat. Manuel once told Mr. Marshal about this, but Marshal had not accepted it.

"She is a mule," he said. "Therefore, her father was a jack. Therefore his father was also a jack, a donkey. It could not be any other way, Manuel."

Manuel often wondered about this, for he had raised the whole strain of animals and he remembered who had been with whom.

"A donkey! A jack! Two feet tall, and with a beard and horns! I always thought he was a goat."

Manuel and Mula stopped at noon on Lost Soul Creek. There would be no travel in the hot afternoon. But Manuel

had a job to do and he did it. He took the forms from one of
the packs that he had unslung from Mula and counted out
nine of them. He wrote down all the data on nine people. He
knew all there was to know about them—their nativities and
their antecedents. He knew that there were only nine regular
people in the nine hundred square miles of the Santa Magdalena.

But he was systematic, so he checked the list over again
and again. There seemed to be somebody missing. Oh yes,
himself. He got another form and filled out all the data on
himself.

Now—in one way of looking at it—his part in the census
was finished. If only he had looked at it that way, he would
have saved worry and trouble for everyone, and also ten
thousand lives. But the instructions they had given him here
were ambiguous, for all that they had tried to make them
clear.

So very early the next morning, Manuel rose and cooked
beans and said, "Might as well take them all."

He called Mula from the thorn patch where she was graz-
ing and gave her salt and loaded her again. Then they went
to take the rest of the census—but in fear. There was a clear
duty to get the job done, but there was also a dread of it that
the superiors did not understand. There was reason also why
Mula was loaded with packs of census forms till she could
hardly walk.

Manuel prayed out loud as they climbed the purgatorial
scarp above Lost Soul Creek "—*ruega por nosotros peca-
dores ahora*"—the very gulches stood angry and stark in the
hot early morning—"*y en la hora de nuestra muerte.*"

Three days later an incredible dwarf staggered into the
outskirts of High Plains, Texas. He was followed by a dying
wolf-sized animal that did not look like a wolf.

A lady called the police to save the pair from rock-
throwing kids who would have killed them; and the two as
yet unclassified things were taken to the station house.

The dwarf was three feet high—a skeleton stretched over
with brown-burnt leather. The other was an uncanine looking
dog-sized beast so full of burs and thorns that it might have
been a porcupine. But it was more a nightmare replica of a
shrunken mule.

The midget was mad. The animal had more presence of
mind; she lay down quietly and died. That was all she could
do considering the state she was in.

"Who is census chief now?" asked the mad midget. "Is Mr. Marshal's little boy the census chief?"

"Mr. Marshal is, yes. Who are you? How do you know of Marshal? And what is that which you are pulling out of your pants—if they are pants?"

"Census list. Names of everyone in town. I had to steal it."

"It looks like microfilm—the writing is so small. And the roll goes on and on. There must be a million names here."

"Little bit more, little bit more. I get two bits a name."

They got Marshal there. He was very busy, but he came. He had been given a deadline by the mayor and the citizens' group. He had to produce a population of ten thousand persons for High Plains, Texas. This was difficult, for there weren't that many people in the town. He had been working hard on it, though. But he came when the police called him.

"You Marshal's little boy?" the mad midget asked him. "You look just like your father."

"That voice—I should know that voice even if it's cracked to pieces," said Marshal. "That *has* to be Manuel's voice."

"Sure, I'm Manuel, just like when I left thirty-five years ago."

"You can't be Manuel—shrunk three feet and two hundred pounds and aged a million."

"You look here at my census slip, Mr. Marshal. It says I'm Manuel. And here are nine more of the regular people, and one million of the little people. I couldn't get the little ones on the regular forms. I had to steal their list."

"You can't be Manuel," said Marshal.

"He can't be Manuel," said the big policemen and the little policemen.

"Maybe not then. I thought I was. Who am I then? Let's look at the other papers to see which one I am."

"No, you can't be any of them either, Manuel. And you surely can't be Manuel."

"Give him a name anyhow and get him counted," said the head of the citizens' group. "We got to get to that ten thousand mark."

"Tell us what happened, Manuel—if you are—which you aren't—but tell us."

"After I counted the regular people, I went to count the little people. I took a spade and spaded the top off their town to get in. But they put an *encanto* on me and made me and Mula run a treadmill for thirty-five years."

"Where was this, Manuel?"

"At the Little People Town—*Nuevo Danae*. But after

thirty-five years, the *encanto* wore off, and Mula and I stole the list of names and ran away."

"But where did you really get this list of so many names written so small, Manuel?",

"Suffering saddle sores, Marshal, don't ask the little bug so many questions! You got a million names in your hand. Certify them! Send them in! There's enough of us right here to pass a resolution. We declare that place annexed forthwith. This will make High Plains the biggest town in Texas."

So Marshal certified the names and sent them in to Washington. This gave High Plains the largest percent increase of any city in the nation—but it was challenged. There were some soreheads in Houston who said that it wasn't possible—that High Plains had nowhere near that many people and that there must have been a miscount.

In the days that the argument was going on, they cleaned up and fed Manuel—if it were he—and tried to get from him a cogent story.

"How do you know it was thirty-five years, Manuel?"

"On the treadmill, it seemed like thirty-five years."

"It could have been only about three days."

"How come I'm so old then?"

"We don't know that Manuel. We sure don't know that. How big were these people?"

"Who knows. A finger long, maybe two."

"And what is their town?"

"It's an old prairie dog town that they fixed up. You have to dig down with a spade to get to the streets."

"Maybe they really were prairie dogs, Manuel. Maybe the heat got you and you only dreamed that they were little people."

"Prairie dogs can't write as good as on that list," said Manuel. "Prairie dogs can't write hardly at all."

"That's true. The list is hard to explain. And such odd names on it, too."

"Where is Mula? I don't see Mula since I came back."

"Mula just lay down and died, Manuel."

"Gave me the slip. Why didn't I think of that? I'll do it too. I'm too worn out for anything else."

"Before you do, Manuel, just a couple of last questions."

"Make them real fast then. I'm on my way."

"Did you know the little people were there before?"

"Oh sure. Everybody in the Santa Magdalena see them. Eight, nine people know they are there. 'Who wants to be laughed at?' they say. They never talked about it."

"And, Manuel, how do we get to the place? Can you show us on a map?"

Manuel made a grimace and died quietly. He didn't understand those maps, and he took the easy way out. They buried him—not knowing for sure whether he was Manuel or not. There wasn't much of him to bury.

It was the same night—very late, and after he had been asleep—that Marshal was awakened by the ring of an authoritative voice. He was being harangued by a four-inch-tall man on his bedside table—a man of dominating presence and acid voice.

"Come out of that cot, you clown! Give me your name and station!"

"I'm Marshal, and I suspect that you're a late pig sandwich. I shouldn't eat so late."

"Say 'Sir' when you reply to me! I am no pig sandwich and I do not commonly call on fools. Get on your feet, you clog!" Wondering, Marshal did.

"I want the list that was stolen. Don't gape. Get it! Don't stall, don't stutter. Get me that tax list! It isn't words I want from you."

"Listen, you cicada," said Marshal with his last bravery, "I'll take you and—"

"You will not! You will notice that you are now paralyzed from the neck down. I suspect that you were always so from there up. Where is it?"

"S—sent it to Washington."

"You bug-eyed behemoth! Do you realize what a trip that will be? You grandfather of inanities, it will be a pleasure to destroy you."

"I don't know what you are," said Marshal. "I don't believe you even belong on the world."

"Not belong on the world? We *own* the world. We can show written title to the world. Can you?"

"I doubt it. Where did you get the title?"

"We got it from a promoter of sorts, a con man really. I have to admit that we were taken, but we were in a spot and needed a world. He said that the larger bifurcates were too stupid to be a nuisance. We should have known that the stupider the creature the more of a nuisance it is."

"I have decided the same thing about the smaller the creature. We may have to fumigate that old mountain mess."

"Oh, you can't harm us. We're too powerful. But we can obliterate you in an instant."

"Hah!" exploded Marshal.

"Say 'hah, sir' when you address me. Do you know the place in the mountain that is called Sodom?"

"I know the place. It was caused by a large meteor."

"It was caused by one of these," said the small creature, and what he held up was the size of a grain of sand. "There was another city of you bug-eyed beasts there," continued the small martinet. "You wouldn't know about it. It's been a few hundred years. We decided it was too close. Now I have decided that you are too close."

"A thing that size couldn't crack a walnut," said Marshal.

"You floundering fop, it will blast this town flat."

"And if it does, what will happen to you?"

"Nothing. I don't even blink for things like that. I haven't time to explain it to you, you gaping goof. I have to get to Washington."

It may be that Marshal did not believe himself quite awake. He certainly didn't take the threat seriously enough. For, in a manner still not understood, the little man did trigger it off.

When the final count was in, High Plains did *not* have the highest percentage gain in the Nation. Actually it showed the sharpest decline of any town—from 7313 to nothing. It is believed that High Plains was destroyed by a giant meteor. But there are eight, nine people in the Santa Magdalena who know what really happened, and they won't tell.

They were going to make a forest preserve out of the place, except that it has no trees worthy of the name. Now it is proposed to make it the Sodom and Gomorrah State Park from the two mysterious scenes of desolation there just seven miles apart.

It is an interesting place, as wild a region as you will ever find, and is recommended for the man who has seen everything.

The Man with the Speckled Eyes

In those days there had been a clique of six men who controlled it all. Any new thing went to one of them—or it went nowhere. Discovery and invention cannot be allowed to break out all over the lot.

These six men did not work in particular harmony. They were called the clique because they were set apart from others by their influence; and because of their names, which were: Claridge, Loric, Immermann, Quinn, Umholtz, and Easter.

Now the six men were reduced to two. On successive days, Claridge, Loric, Immermann, and Quinn had disappeared—and they had done it pretty thoroughly. In each case, somebody had to know something about their disappearance; and in each case, that somebody refused to tell.

Claridge's man, Gueranger, had been with Claridge at the time of the disappearance or shortly before. He admitted that much. But nothing intelligent could be got from him.

"The truth of it is that I don't know the truth of it," Gueranger insisted. "Yes, I was there, but I don't know what happened."

"Don't you know what you saw?" asked the investigator.

"No, I don't. That's the whole point of the matter: I will not accept, and will not tell, what I saw. Certainly I know that I'm held on suspicion of murder. But where is the body? You find it—anywhere—in any shape and I'll sure sleep better."

In the second case, Ringer and Mayhall both seemed to know something of the disappearance of their employer, Loric. The three of them had walked in the plaza at evening. Only two of them had come back—and they much shaken.

"I know what I seemed to see," Ringer ventured, "and I will not tell it. I'm not stubborn and I'm not sensitive to laughter, but I've sealed the whole thing off in a corner of my mind and I won't disturb it. I've hopes of hanging on to some pieces of my reason, and to open this again would set me back."

"Loric?" Mayhall grunted. "I guess the damned fool swallowed himself. He's sure gone completely. Yes, I was with him, and I won't say any nearer than that what happened."

"I simply will not explain," said Immermann's advisor, Hebert. "He is gone, and I do not believe he will be back. No. If it was a hoax, I wasn't in on it, and I don't understand it. Do I believe that he wished to disappear for a private reason? Did he—wherever he has gone—go willingly? No, gentlemen, *he did not go willingly!* I never saw a man so reluctant to go."

"I will *not* say what happened to Mr. Quinn," said Pacheco, Quinn's assistant. "Of course I know that he was an important man—the most important in the world to me. You say that you will have answers out of me one way or the other? Then you'll have nothing but babbling out of a crazy man.

"Why, yes, I suppose that you can hang me for murder. I don't know how those things are worked. It seems extreme, however. I thought there was a Latin phrase involved, about a body being required. Lay off now, fellows. I'm cracking up, I tell you."

The investigators didn't lay off, but so far they had got nothing out of any of the witnesses. The four disappearances had to be as one, and the witnesses were certainly of a pattern.

"Are Extraterrestrials Kidnapping Our Top Talent?" the news banners read.

"Oh, hell," said Umholtz in his cluttered office. "Hell," said Easter in his clean one. They both knew that they were not men of any particular talent, and that the four men who had disappeared were not. They were shufflers and dealers in talent, that is all. In popular idea, they were responsible for the inventions they marketed. But off-Earth people—bent on such showy kidnappings—would have picked off seminal geniuses and not talent brokers.

Four gone, two to go. Would the next one be Umholtz or Easter? Umholtz felt that it would be himself. He and his assistant, Planter, were worrying about it together when Shartel the aide came in to them.

"There's *one* to see you, Mr. Umholtz," said Shartel with diffidence, for he was only half the bulk of his employer.

"An inventor?" Umholtz always sneered with his eyebrows when he spoke that word, although inventors were the only stock he dealt in.

"Who else comes to see us, Mr. Umholtz? This one may be worth investigating, though probably not for any invention he has."

"A crackie? What does he have?"

"A crackie from end to end, and he won't say what he has."

"We're not scanning clients these days, Shartel. I explain that to you every ten minutes. We're spending all our time worrying about the disappearances. Creative worry, Planter here calls it, and I don't appreciate his humor. I haven't time for a crackie today."

"He got to see Claridge, Loric, Immermann, and Quinn—all a couple of hours before their disappearance."

"All inventors make the same rounds. There's nobody else they can go to. And weren't there a couple of others who saw them all?"

"The others have all been checked out clean. This is the last one. The authorities have been looking for him and have left word to call if he showed. I'll ring them as soon as he's in here. There's a slim chance that he knows something, but he sure doesn't look it."

"Send him in, Shartel. Has he a name?"

"Haycock. And he looks as though he had slept in one."

Haycock didn't really have hay in his hair—that was only the color and lay of it. He had blue eyes with happy, dangerous gold specks in them, and a friendly and humorous sneer. He looked rather an impudent comedian, but inventors come in all sizes. He had something of the back-country hayseed in him. But also something of the panther.

"I have here what may turn out to be a most useful device," Haycock began. "Good. You have sent the underlings away. I never talk in their presence. They're inclined to laugh at me. I am offering you the opportunity to get in on the top floor with my device, Mr. Umholtz."

"Haycock, you have the aspect of a man entranced by one of the four basic fallacies. If so, you are wasting my time. But I want to question you on a side issue. Is it true that you visited all four of them—Claridge, Loric, Immermann, and Quinn—on the days of their disappearances?"

"Sounds like their names. Four blind bats! None of them could see my invention at first. All of them laughed at it. Forget those fools, Umholtz. You can grow new fools, but what I have here is unique. It is the impossible invention."

"By the impossible inventor, from the looks of you. I hold up four fingers, and one is it. Tell it in one word, Haycock!"

"Anti-grav."

"Fourth finger. It's not even the season for anti-grav, Haycock. These things go in cycles. We get most of the anti-gravs in early winter. All right, I give you four seconds to demonstrate. Raise that table off the floor with your device."

"It's barely possible that I could raise it, Umholtz, but not in four seconds. It would take several hours; instant demonstration is out. It's a pretty erratic piece of machinery, though I've had good luck on my last several attempts. It isn't really very impressive, and a lot of what I tell you you'll have to take on faith."

"Haven't any, Haycock. Even a charlatan can usually put on a good show. Why the two pieces? One looks like a fishing tackle box, and the other like a sheaf of paper."

"The papers are the mathematics of it, Umholtz. Look at the equations carefully and you'll be convinced without a demonstration."

"All right. I pride myself on the speed I bring to spotting these basic errors, Haycock. They seem very commonplace equations, and then they break off when it's plain that you're getting nowhere. What happened to the bottom of these sheets?"

"Oh, my little boy ate that part of them. Just go ahead and you'll pick up the continuity again. Ah, you're at the end of it and you laugh! Yes, is it not funny how simple every great truth is?"

"I've seen them all, Haycock, and this is one of the most transparent. The only thing wrong with it is that it won't work and it's as full of holes as a seine."

"But it does work part of the time, Umholtz, and we'll fill up the holes till it's practical. Well, is it a deal? It'll take a couple of years; but if you'll start plenty of money rolling, I'll get on with the project in a big way. Why do you roll your eyes like that, Umholtz? Is there a history of apoplexy in your family?"

"I will be all right in a moment, Haycock. I am afflicted by inventors, but I recover quickly. Let us set the gadget aside for the moment. Do you know where the four now-celebrated men have gone?"

"Papers said it was as if they had disappeared from the Earth. I imagine they sent a reporter or someone to check on it."

"Take Claridge, for instance," said Umholtz, "Did he seem disturbed when you last saw him?"

"I think he was the little one. He was kind of boggle-eyed, just like you were a minute ago. Kind of mad at me for wasting his time. Well pig's pants! I wasted my time, too! Blind as a bat, that man. Don't think he was convinced that my thing would work till maybe right at the end. Now let's get back to my instrument. It will do a variety of jobs. Even you can see where it would be useful."

"It would be, if it worked, and it won't. Your piece of mathematics is childish, Haycock."

"Might be. I don't express myself well in that medium. But my machine does work. It creates negative gravity. That is, it works quite a bit of the time."

Umholtz laughed. He shouldn't have, but he didn't know. And he did have an ugly sort of laugh.

"You laugh at me!" Haycock howled out. Gold fire popped from his eyes and he was angry. The hayseed began to look like the panther. He touched his machine, and it responded with a sympathetic *ping!* to the anger of its master.

Umholtz was having fun with the now-blazing inventor.

"What do you do, Haycockandbull, turn that machine on and point it at something?" he guffawed. Umholtz enjoyed deriding a fellow.

"You hopeless hulk! I turned it on a minute ago when you laughed at me. It's working on you now. You'll be convinced in the end," Haycock threatened.

"Do you not know, Haycock, that anti-grav is the standing joke in our profession? But they still come in with it, and they all have that same look in their eyes."

"Umholtz, you lie! Nobody else ever had this look in his eye!"

That was true. The gold specks in the blue eyes glinted in a mad way. The eyes did not focus properly. It seemed to Umholtz that Haycock did not look at him, but through him and beyond. The man might well be a maniac—the sort of maniac who could somehow be involved in the four disappearances. Never mind, they were coming for him. They'd be here any minute.

"Anti-grav is a violation of the laws of mass and energy," Umholtz needled.

"To change the signature of a mass from plus to minus is not a violation of any law I recognize," said Haycock evenly. "It is no good for you to justify now, Umholtz, or to find excuses. It is no use to plead for your life. Are you deaf as well as blind and stupid? I told you plainly that the demonstration had already begun. You were all a stubborn lot, but I convinced all four of them in the end, and I'll convince you. I tell you, Umholtz, that entrenched stupidity makes me mad, and when I get mad I sure do get mean. I've cancelled you out, you open idiot! Umholtz, I'll send you away screaming!"

"Rather I'll send you away in that act," Umholtz purred, for the men in black were now into the room, and they laid legal hands on Haycock.

"Take him away," Umholtz grunted out. "He's fishier than Edward's Ichthyology."

Haycock didn't go away screaming, but he went roaring and fighting. That man was very mean, and those gold specks in his eyes were really sulphur.

Say, they couldn't get a thing out of that fellow. Haycock was an odd one, but that was all. They went over him from the beginning. He was known in his own neighborhood for his unsuccessful inventions and for his towering temper, but he hadn't any bodies lying around, and he hadn't been anywhere near any of the four men at the time of their disappearances.

He was a crackie from end to end, but he hadn't a handle they could get hold of.

"I am not ghoulish," Umholtz said to his men Planter and Shartel, "but the disappearance of four of my five competitors has opened up some pretty obvious opportunities for me. Oh, other men will be designated to replace them, but it'll be a long time before they get that sharp."

"What did the crackie have this afternoon, Mr. Umholtz?" Planter asked him.

"It isn't worth mentioning. One of the oldest and silliest."

The three of them were walking in the park in the evening.

"I suddenly feel odd," said Umholtz and he placed one hand on his head and the other on his paunch. "Something I ate for supper didn't agree with me."

"It's the worry," said Planter. "The disappearances have upset you. With the thought that you might be next on the list, there has been a great weight on you."

"I really feel as though a great weight has been lifted off me," said Umholtz, "but I don't like the feeling. I'm light-headed."

"The walk will do you good," Planter told him. "You look well to me. I've never seen you move with so light a step."

"No, no, I'm sick," Umholtz moaned, and he began to look up in the air as though fearful of an attack from that sector. "My feet don't track right. There's a lightness in me. My stomach is turning inside out. Lord, but it would be a long way to fall!"

Umholtz flopped his way forward, his feet slipping on the grass as though he had lost traction. He got hold of a tree—a small elm.

"I'm starting to go!" he howled in real terror.

He put a bear hug around the tree, locking on to it with both arms and legs. "Great dancing dogfish, don't let me fall," he sobbed. "How did I ever get so high up?"

"Umholtz, you are six inches from the ground," Planter told him. "The man's gone mad, Shartel. Let's pry his legs loose first. When we get his feet on the ground he may get over his mania about falling."

"Fools! Fools! You'll let me fall all the way down," Umholtz screamed, but he was looking upward, and his face was flushed as though all the blood had run to his head.

"He was right," Umholtz sniffled wetly in an interlude from his screaming and sobbing. "I'm finally convinced."

"There's one leg loose, Shartel," said Planter as he worked on Umholtz, "but for some reason it seems pretty difficult to hold it to the ground. Now the other leg, and we'll set him down on his feet. Whoops! What's wrong? You're going up with him, Shartel!"

Shartel did go up with him at first, for Umholtz was much the heavier man. But Shartel broke away and fell a dozen feet down to the grass.

Umholtz grabbed a precarious lodging in the tree top, but he was shearing off fronds and branches and going fast.

"For God's sake, get me up from here!" Umholtz screamed, hanging upward from the topmost branch. He was like a tethered balloon tugging at its mooring.

"Throw a rope down to me! Do something!" he sobbed upsidedownly from the tree top. "I'll fall all the way, and I can't even see the bottom."

The topmost branch broke, and Umholtz fell off the world.

He fell upward into the evening sky, his scream dropping in pitch as he accelerated. He fell end over end, diminishing till he was only a dot in the sky. Then he was gone.

"What will we tell people—what—what can we say—however explain—how explain what we seen seem—" Shartel rattled, the bones in his body shaking like poker dice in a toss box.

"You tell your lie and I'll tell mine," Planter grumbled. "I'm crazy, but I'm not crazy enough to have seen that."

Of the clique, only Easter was left. He was the most evenminded of the bunch and the least inclined to worry. It had been a peculiar series of events that had devoured his competitors, but he hadn't been able to base any theory on the disappearances. If he continued, he would be next.

"I may try a little worrying myself," he mused. "A man of my sort shouldn't neglect any field of cogitation. I'll give it a try. It should come easy for me today."

So Easter worried, but he didn't do it well. It isn't easy if you haven't the lifetime habit of it.

Then a man came in to him unannounced.

This was a man with hay-colored hair, with blue eyes with happy dangerous gold specks in them, a man with a friendly and humorous sneer. He had something of the hayseed in him. But also something of the panther.

"I have here what may turn out to be a most useful device," Haycock began.

All but the Words

The IDT Project had been going on for a dozen years with no real advance toward its ends. It would have been abandoned long before except for its collateral discoveries in other fields. The accidental offshoots that it had produced were well worth the considerable expense of the Project.

The Project had assigned to it one great mind and several very good minds; no other project at that time could say as much. The great mind was that of Gregory Smirnov, and his greatness lay in his instant perception of the possibilities of an idea. He always knew whether an idea or a notion had a spark in it. He discerned where the flightiest, most apparent idiocy carried the ultimate spark, and where the most brilliant and most plausible thesis did not. He played his colleagues like a hand of cards, and he scored every possible point with them.

The several very good minds associated with the Project were those of: Charles Cogsworth, the inventor of the Recapitulation Correlator, as well as the Cerebral Scanner; Aloysius Shiplap, who had been associated with the late Cecil Corn in the experiment which ended Corn's life—which may have been a dead end and may have been an opening door; the stiff-necked Gerald Glasser, the designer of the E.P. Locator; Valery Mok, a woman of vivid eido-creation whose mind had put Cogsworth into a state of shock when he first went into it with his scanner.

Also associated with the Project was Energine Eimer. Although she had a good mind by ordinary standards, she was not in the class with the others; for it was really an understatement to speak of them as having very good minds. Energine herself was flighty to seeming idiocy, but Smirnov had detected that from her might come the ultimate spark.

The purpose of the IDT Project was to devise an Instant

Distant Translation device, which might be either mechanical or psychic, or something of an entirely different aspect. It was to reach and establish rapport with a distant—a very distant—mind, any mind anywhere beyond the pale. It would have to combine and go far beyond such tools as were already available.

Extrasensory Perception, now that it was known to be but another aspect of simple sensory perception and of disappointing limitations, was one very inadequate tool. The translation devices themselves would be adequate for ordinary work. They could now interpret roughly the thought processes of earthworms and ferns and even crystals. They could record and even verbalize the apprehensions of metals under stress and, to an extent, the group consciousness of gathering thunderheads. Any language, terrestrial or distant, could be given a cogent interpretation. But something more was required.

It was the six hundred and twelfth weekly progress meeting of the group.

"Energine," said Gregory Smirnov, "it has just come to me how you are different from the rest of us."

"In one way she's different from the rest, except myself," said Valery, "but I'm not sure that you've ever noticed that difference."

"I've known about the difference of the sexes for a long time, Valery," said Smirnov. "I was a precocious child and an early reader of biology. In my own life I have relegated the implications of the difference to a minor corner. There is little enough time in even a long life to do the work I have set for myself, and the ramifications of the sex complex are time-consuming. No, the difference is that Energine likes to talk to people."

"Does not almost everyone?" asked Shiplap.

"Many do, but none of us on the Project except Energine," said Smirnov. "We are not the sort of people who like people, and we talk to them as little as possible. Mostly we talk to ourselves, even when we are nominally talking to others. There is an inhibition in the—ah—cultivated minds. We are a withdrawn bunch, and we tend to become more so as we follow our specialties and our studies. That is the irony of it."

"Where is the irony?" asked Cogsworth.

"We are trying to talk to 'people' over cosmic distances, and we do not even like to talk to people near at hand. We do not like to talk to people at all. We aren't the ones for the job. Mostly we are bored with people."

"Then who are the ones for the job?" asked Glasser. "Logorrhea is rampant in the world. We could find a billion low folks who love to talk to other low folks."

"Possibly those we will ultimately contact will also be low folks," said Smirnov. "It is likely that the lowest common denominator of the Universe will be both low and common. Rapport is what we want, and we don't have it. We can study the dragonfly, but are we ever really concerned with the dragonfly's concern for his family? We don't really like the monstrous miniatures. We've no sympathy with the terrified arrogance of the arachnid; how can we have sympathy for really *strange* creatures? How can we talk to an alien if we don't even like to talk to our own kind?"

"I have a landlady who even talks to bugs," said Glasser. "Shall I get her? She'd droodle to a vole on a planet just as well if we pointed her that way. And you believe that she would be better than ourselves who have all the techniques and information?"

"We have Energine," said Smirnov. "She has the techniques, such as we all have. And she likes to talk to people. She might just be able to break us out of our restriction."

"Then why hasn't she done it?" asked Valery. "She's had as much time on the senders and scanners as any of us, and no more luck."

"Because she hasn't let herself go. She has been constrained to use our own approach and formulae. Energine, let yourself go and talk to those people! Now! Tonight! Talk to them!"

"I will, I will. But how? You mean just like I talk? I've thought of that, but I didn't think you'd allow it. I bet those folks have gotten awful bored with our salutations and mathematical symbols. A circle is a circle, and a square is a square, and so are we. Hey—me third planet out. Who you?—I bet they think we're nutty to use that kind of stuff.

"I'll get hold of one of them tonight and tell him all about the new Indonesian restaurant I found. Maybe he found a new restaurant up there and can tell me some of the dishes. Whoever he is I bet he likes to eat, too."

"Energine, do you still belong to a Lonely Hearts Club?"

"Why, I belong to all of them! Just let me read you one letter I got this morning. Why, it's the nicest letter—"

"Spare us! Protect us! Earth swallow us!" cried Glasser.

"That, Glasser, is an illustration of what is holding us back," said Smirnov. "We don't like to talk to people and we don't like to listen to people. It may be that they have been talking to us for a long time and we were not in tune to listen."

"Well then, you will surely listen, Mr. Smirnov," cried Energine. "This is a letter from Eugene upstate—"

"No, as a matter of fact I will not listen," said Smirnov. "I am now too old to develop a sympathy for the vital things of life. But what I want you to do, Energine, is to let yourself go; to talk, to send, just as if you were writing to one of your lonely hearts people. Go all the way out, girl. If it doesn't work, only the stars will laugh at you."

"Oh, I never minded being laughed at. It shows that people are having fun. I'll tell him about Charley; that's just to make him jealous. You don't know about Charley? Let me read you—well, never mind then. This might be the first extraterrestrial lonely hearts club. I could be president."

"Yes, you could be president of it, Energine. Now, the first live blip you get on the scanner, you just let yourself go with all you've got. Send him one of those lonely hearts letters. Make it lavender."

"Purple. Oh, I will, I will."

And that evening on the scanner Energine picked up either a minor blip or a minor malfunction; it was always impossible to tell which. Those little egg-shaped anomalies—they looked egg-shaped, they sounded egg-shaped, they broke into egg-shaped sine curves—were the only evidence of the sort of target they were seeking. Energine let herself go on the sender.

"Dear Albert—since I must call you something and I am sure that your name is very like that—I will try quite hard to reach you, and I beg that you answer me. Your name in the Project now becomes Albert-(Tentative). To others you are only an egg-shaped anomaly, but you are more than that to me.

"This is the first essay to the establishment of a stellar lonely hearts club, and it just *has* to be a success. In the lonely hearts clubs we write in love and affection to those we would like to know, and we would like to know everyone.

"I will tell you about our world, and you tell me about yours. I hope that we can get very close together. There is an ecstasy on me when I can grow very close to another. I believe that the only thing of any importance on this world is love. Is not that the only thing of importance on yours?

"I had another picture of Charley today. He is not as handsome a man as he was in the first picture that he sent. I do not believe that the first picture was even a picture of Charley. But sometimes the first picture that I send is not a picture of me, either. Do you want to see a picture of me? I will send one as soon as I find out how.

"I went to a Mexican restaurant last night. They had roast kid stuffed with almonds and sauced all over with burnt brown sugar. And they had those little flat pancake things that taste like cardboard. I love them. I wonder if you enjoy eating as much as I do.

"Albert, please answer me with anything at all, and we will begin to establish rapport. I feel that we could grow very close together. Albert, I will treasure your answers with those of Fred and Harold and Richard—that one turned out badly but he *did* write nice letters—and Selby and Roger and Norbert. Do you also save old letters? Answer me. I will stay right here till morning, and if I do not hear from you by then I will wait again tomorrow evening and every evening. Signed—Energine."

She waited, but she didn't have to wait as long as she had feared. It was only about an hour till the response began to come through. The first sign of it was the dimming of the lights and the vibration of the building as the auxiliary generators cut in, for the translation device seemed to be laboring under a heavy, unaccustomed load. But the machine had amazing resources. It could translate anything, anything.

Then the answer came.

"Energine," came the answer. "That call letter? That name? That world? That people? That what?

"Jubilation here to learn that there is friendly life on your world. Your world previously ignored as little bit sick. You know sick? Word *sick*? Possibly first word mutually understanding.

"Comprehending all your communication except the words. What is lonely? What is hearts? What is club? What is grow very close together? What is a Charley? What is picture? What is Mexican? What is kid? What is little flat pancake thing? What is cardboard? What is a Fred and Harold and other entities?

"Word *love* understood intuitively. Explain mechanics of thing with you. Extreme variation in different sectors. In ecstasy of symbiosis which one swallow who?

"Yes, answer, answer, answer, whatever that means. What is Selby? What is Norbert? What means wait right here? What means morning? Rapport also understood intuitively. We be so completely. We how many? You group or integer? Send how to roast kid stuffed. What is roast kid stuffed? Delirious interest here in subject, sure to increase when we know what subject consist of. Also love you already passionately. What is passionately? What is already?—

                    KGG3LP*Y UU—Albert-(Tentative)."

He had answered. Albert-(Tentative) had answered. He had understood all of her communication except the words. They were in perfect rapport.

The translation device shuddered and groaned after the effort. Then it panted softly and fell to sibilant silence. The building was quiet and the night gathered lovely about it.

The first and most difficult step of the IDT Project had been achieved after twelve years. The rest would follow. Others would venture where Energine had pioneered. The glad news of the achievement was given to the world.

The matter and exact wording of the two messages were not, however, given to the world. These remained classified. In the early contacts with aliens there are always details which will seem incongruous to the unlearned.

Others tried the feat with some success, and Energine repeated it again and again. The rapport grew. Soon Albert Tentative began to understand some of the words as well as the feelings of the messages. Small misunderstandings were gradually set right, as one from Albert—

"You ask if we can be sure that we are of opposite sex? How not opposite? With us are five sexes. Everybody partake of several, so everybody a little opposite. This make for clarity. Surely you drollery when you say there only two on your world.

"You wish to see me but say it is impossible. Why in kss@#rr*WQ"—'mild profanity'.—Trans. note—"it not possible? Travel no problem with us. It problem with you? You want me—I be there. Like in little verse we find in Block Massive Cultural Transmission Corpus from your world, 'Brush your tooth, say your prayer, go to sleep, I be there.' What *brush?* What *tooth?* What *prayer?* What *sleep?* What it mean, understanding that great poetry not always to be taken literally? Profound poetry from your world having great appeal here. Also Aristotle Joke Book and fragments of Sport Page Statistic Epic Cycle. Decline in your civilization, huh? No .400 hitters for years.

"Who I see buy stock on exchange? Always looking for sound investment. All difficulties erased when we see each other. Albert Tentative."

"He is coming to see me," said Energine dreamily.

"It is possibly a translation error," cautioned Smirnov. "Perhaps there has been omitted a phrase such as 'What

mean come see me?' You know it would be impossible that
he should come. Our Block Massive Cultural Transmission
will not be digested by them all at once. I am pleased at the
success it has already had."

"He is coming to see me," said Energine.

"No, no, girl. That couldn't be. You are deluded, but I can
never tell you how much I appreciate what you have done."

"He is coming to see me."

"No, he is not. It is completely out of the question."

He came to see her.

It was known that he had arrived, that something had arrived. Instruments of a dozen sorts had recorded him. "Albert Tentative arrives" was the glad word, but where was he,
what was he? He seemed to be invisible and inaudible. But
for the evidence of the instruments there were some who
would have doubted the arrival of Albert in the world.

"I want a week off," said Energine to Gregory Smirnov.
"No, I want a year off. Albert and I have so much to say to
each other that we will never get it all said. And we're going
to get married if we can figure out how to go about it. I
really need some private advice on that. But look, just look!"

"A very beautiful and odd ring, Energine. Did he give it to
you?"

"Did he give what to me?"

The ring was a sort of furry metal. It glowed and it
changed colors. It circled the chubby little finger of Energine,
and she held it up to her cheek.

"I had no idea that anything could be so wonderful," she
raptured. "We're so happy together. We went to the new Syr-
ian restaurant last night and had camel purée. It's so cute
the way he eats it."

"How, Energine?"

"Gets right down in the bowl."

"Ah—Energine—let's get to the point. Where is Albert
Tentative? It's important that we see him and examine him.
Where is he?"

"Why, right here, Mr. Smirnov. Did you ever see anyone
like him?"

"No, I never did, mainly because I can't see him at all."

"Can't you see him? Why, I never suspected that. You
mean that I'm the only one who can see him?"

"Patience, Patience, thou universal regent, do not desert
me now! What does he look like, Energine?"

"Why, he's round and shining and furry, and he changes
color."

"Energine, the ring he gave you—"

"Mr. Smirnov, that is no ring. That is my Albert. Oh, Albert, he thought you were a ring. How funny!"

Albert Tentative was of great interest for about three weeks. There was first of all the epic press conference that Gregory Smirnov set up for him as soon as the method of plugging Albert in and giving him amplification was discovered. It might be said that there was first and last of all the epic press conference.

It was a success, let there be no doubt of that. It was a total success. There were those who came to wonder if the success was not too total.

There was resentment at first that foreign correspondents were not alerted and given a chance to attend it. Some came anyhow to see what they could pick up after it was over with, and found that it was not over with. Albert was still talking when they got there; he had been talking for a week.

Albert was a fine talker, now that he knew the words. The pidgin of the translation device had been that of the device, not of Albert. He answered all questions completely, oh how completely! He went into a spate and answered questions that had never been asked, and the newsmen and personages listened to him in relays, fascinated.

After a week of standing by, Energine—whose finger Albert had long since abandoned for many others—said that she thought she would go out to get something to eat. She looked dazed. She did not come back.

Albert answered the questions of the Chinese and the Arabs. He answered the questions of all the newsmen of Earth. He also had a Block Massive Cultural Transmission Corpus which he wanted to communicate. He recited the Epic Gilmish in which is comprised all wisdom. That took him thirty hours, perhaps not too long a period to be given to a work that comprises all wisdom. But the listeners were of flesh and blood, and nobody knew what Albert was.

Gregory Smirnov stayed with it two weeks and then walked out. He shouldn't have done it as he was the host, but there was a weakness in the great man that manifested itself here. He went to see the President of the Republic.

"Suggest Project's discontinuance," he said to the President.

"But Mr. Smirnov, is not the Project a colossal success?"

"Quite."

"But you have now established rapport with a completely alien being for the first time."

"Unfortunately. And perhaps not alien enough."

"Possibly you yourself are burnt out by your great labors on the Project."

"Possibly."

"I would be unwilling to abandon the Project now that it has proved such an outstanding success. Perhaps we should transfer the operation to another group. Could you suggest another group that might be able to handle it?"

"Enfield's Automations."

"An excellent suggestion. They're a bunch of comers. We will take steps for the transfer of authority."

"Good-by," said Smirnov, and left.

"Did you notice that he seemed very short-spoken today?" the President asked one of his aides when Smirnov had left.

Albert Tentative was a great success for about three weeks. Then the Project was turned over to Enfield's Automations, and the whole thing went on automatic. Albert is still talking.

It was some time later that Gregory Smirnov met Valery Mok on the street.

"Well?" he asked her.

"I, yes. You, I hope. News?"

"Of the bunch? Cogsworth dead. Shiplap mad. Glasser vanished."

"Energine?"

"Nun."

"Which?"

"Contemplative. Not talk, you know."

"Their address?"

"Here."

"Thanks."

Smirnov went to have a glossotomy performed on himself, as well as an intricate operation on the ears. So they all arranged their lives.

In their final solution they all owed much to Albert Tentative. For in his recitation of the Epic Gilmish he had omitted nothing, not even the remarkable five-hour speech on the medicinal value of silence.

The Transcendent Tigers

This was the birthday of Carnadine Thompson. She was seven years old. Thereby she left her childhood behind her, and came into the fullness of her powers. This was her own phrase, and her own idea of the importance of the milestone.

There were others, mostly adult, who thought that she was a peculiarly backward little girl in some ways, though precocious in others.

She received for her birthday four presents: a hollow, white rubber ball, a green plastic frog, a red cap and a little wire puzzle.

She immediately tore the plastic frog apart, considering it a child's toy. So much for that.

She put on the cap, saying that it had been sent by her Genie as a symbol of her authority. In fact none of them knew who had sent her the red cap. The cap is important. If it weren't important, it wouldn't be mentioned.

Carnadine quickly worked the wire puzzle, and then unworked it again. Then she did something with the hollow, white rubber ball that made her mother's eyes pop out. Nor did they pop all the way in again when Carnadine undid it and made it as it was before.

Geraldine Thompson had been looking pop-eyed for a long time. Her husband had commented on it, and she had been to the doctor for it. No medical reason was found, but the actual reason was some of the antics of her daughter Carnadine.

"I wonder if you noticed the small wire puzzle that I gave to my daughter," said Tyburn Thompson to his neighbor, H. Horn.

"Only to note that it probably cost less than a quarter," said Horn, "and to marvel again at the canny way you have with coin. I wouldn't call you stingy, Tyburn. I've never believed in the virtues of understatement. You have a talent for making stingy people seem benevolent."

"I know. Many people misunderstand me. But consider that wire puzzle. It's a very simple-appearing puzzle, but it's twenty-four centuries old. It is unworkable, of course, so it should keep Carnadine occupied for some time. She has an excess of energy. This is one of the oldest of the unworkable puzzles."

"But, Tyburn, she just worked it," said his wife Geraldine.

"It is one of the nine impossible apparatus puzzles listed by Anaximandros in the fifth century before the common era," continued Tyburn. "And do you know, in all the centuries since then, there have been only two added to the list."

"Carnadine," said her mother, "let me see you work that again."

Carnadine worked it again.

"The reason it is unworkable," said Tyburn, "though apparent to me as a design engineer, may not be so readily apparent to you. It has to do with odds and evens of lays. Many of the unworkable classic puzzles are cordage puzzles, as is this actually. It is a wire miniature of a cordage puzzle. It is said that this is the construction of the Gordian knot. The same, however, is said of two other early cordage puzzles."

"But she just worked it, Tyburn, twice," said the wife.

"Stop chattering, Geraldine. I am explaining something to Horn. Men have spent years on the puzzle, the Engineering Mind and the recognition of patent impossibility being less prevalent in past centuries. And this, I believe, is the best of all the impossible ones. It is misleading. It looks as though there would surely be a way to do it."

"I just believe that I could do it, Tyburn," said Horn.

"No, you could not. You're a stubborn man, and it'd drive you crazy. It's quite impossible. You would have to take it into another dimension to work it, and then bring it back."

Carnadine once more did something with the hollow rubber ball.

"How did you make the rubber ball turn red and then white again, Carnadine?" her mother asked her.

"Turned it inside out. It's red on the inside."

"But how did you turn it inside out without tearing it?"

"It'd spoil it to tear it, mama."

"But it's impossible to turn it inside out without tearing it."

"Not if you have a red cap it isn't."

"Dear, how do you work the puzzle that your father says can't be worked?"

"Like this."

"Oh, yes. I mean, how does it happen that you can work it when nobody else could ever work it before?"

"There has to be a first time for everything, mama."

"Maybe, but there has to be a first-class explanation to go with that first time."

"It's on account of the red cap. With this cap I can do anything."

So Carnadine Thompson in the fullness of her powers, and in her red cap, went out to find the rest of the Bengal Tigers. This was the most exclusive society in the world. It had only one full member, herself, and three contingent or defective members, her little brother Eustace, Fatty Frost, and Peewee Horn. Children all three of them, the oldest not within three months of her age.

The Bengal Tigers was not well known to the world at large, having been founded only the day before. Carnadine Thompson was made First Stripe for life. There were no other offices.

Yet, for a combination of reasons, the Bengal Tigers now became the most important society in the world. The new power was already in being. It was only a question of what form it would take, but it seemed to show a peculiar affiliation for this esoteric society.

Clement Chardin, writing in *Bulletin de la Société Parahistorique Française*, expressed a novel idea:

> It is no longer a question whether there be transcendent powers. These have now come so near to us that the aura of them ruffles our very hair. We are the objects of a visitation. The Power to Move Mountains and Worlds is at hand. The Actuality of the Visitation is proved, though the methods of the detection cannot now be revealed.
>
> The question is only whether there is any individual or group with the assurance to grasp that Power. It will not be given lightly. It will not come to the craven or contabescent. There is the sad possibility that there may be none ready in the World to receive the Power. This may not be the first Visitation, but it may well be the last. But the Power, whatever its form and essence (it is real, its presence had been detected by fine instrumentation), the Power, the Visitation may pass us by as unworthy.

This parenthetical for those who might not have read it in the journal.

That which struck just West of Kearney, Nebraska, was an elemental force. The shock of it was heard around the world, and its suction flattened farmhouses and barns for miles.

The area of the destruction was an almost perfect circle

about two miles in diameter, so just over two thousand acres were destroyed. The first reports said that it was like no disaster ever known. Later reports said that it was like every disaster ever known; and it did have points of resemblance to all.

There was the great crater as though a meteorite had struck; there was the intense heat and the contamination as though it had been of fissionable origin; there was an after-flow of lava and the great ash clouds as though it were the super volcanic explosion of another Krakatoa. There was the sudden silence of perhaps two seconds actually, and perhaps two hours as to human response. And then the noise of all sorts.

The early reports said that the hole was three miles deep. That was said simply to have a figure and to avoid panic. It was not known how deep the hole was.

But it was very much more than three miles—before the earthquake had begun to fill and mask it—before the hot magma had oozed up from its bottom to fill those first miles. It was still very much more than three miles deep after the rapid gushing had declined to a slow waxlike flowing.

Had anyone heard the preceding rush, or seen a meteor or any other flying object? No. There hadn't been a sound, but there had been something pitched a little higher than sound.

There hadn't been a meteor or a flying ball. But there had been what some called a giant shaft of light, and others a sheen of metal: a thing too big to be believed, and gone too soon to be remembered.

One farmer said that it was like the point of a giant needle quickly becoming more than a mile thick, and a hundred thousand miles long.

Did he know how to judge distances? Certainly, he said, I know how to judge distances. It is ninety yards to that tree; it is seven hundred yards to that windmill. That crow is flying at right onto eighty yards above the earth, though most would guess him higher. And that train whistle is coming from a distance of five and one-quarter miles.

But did he know how to judge great distances? Did he know how far was a hundred thousand miles? Certainly, he said, a great distance is easier to judge than a small one. And that sudden bright shaft was one hundred thousand miles long.

The farmer was the only one who offered any figures. Few had seen the thing at all. And all who had seen it maintained that it had lasted only a fraction of a second.

"There should be something to take the minds of the people from the unexplained happening near Kearney, Nebraska," said a group of advisors who had national status. "It will not be good for too much notice to be taken of this event until we have an explanation of it."

Fortunately something did take the minds of the people off the unexplained happenings near Kearney. What took their minds from the unusual happenings in Nebraska were the happenings at or near Hanksville, Utah, Crumpton, Maryland, Locust Bayou, Arkansas, and Pope City, Georgia. All of these sudden destructions were absolutely similar in type and vague in origin. National panic now went into the second stage, and it was nearly as important to halt it as to solve the disasters themselves.

And what in turn took the minds of the people off these disasters were the further disasters at Highmore, South Dakota, Lower Gilmore, New Hampshire, Cherryfork, Ohio, and Rowesville, South Carolina.

And what took the minds of the people off these later disasters were still further disasters at—but this could go on and on.

And it did.

So with the cataclysmic disasters erupting over the country like a rash, there wasn't a large audience for the academic discussions about the New Potential of Mankind. There were those, concerned about the current catastrophes, who said that Mankind might not last long enough to receive the New Potential—or anything else.

But Winkers observed from the Long Viewpoint—paying no more attention to the destructions than if they had been a string of firecrackers, such not being his field:

It is paradoxical that we know so much and yet so little about the Power Immanent in the World: the Visitation, the Poyavlenie, as it is now called internationally.

It has been detected, but in ways twice removed. An earlier statement that it had been detected by instrumentation is inaccurate. It has not been detected by instrumentation, but by para-instrumentation. This is the infant science of gathering data from patterns of failure of instruments, and of making deductions from those failure patterns. What our finest instruments fail to detect is at least as important as what they do detect. In some cases it is more so. The patterns of failure when confronted with the thesis of the Visitation have been varied, but they have not been random.

There appears to be a validity to the deductions from the patterns.

The characteristics of the Power, the Visitation, as projected by these methods (and always considered in the Oeg-Hornbostel framework) is that it is *Aculeiform, Homodynamous, Homochiral*, and (here the intelligence reels with disbelief, yet I assure the lector that I am deadly serious) *Homoeoteleutic.*

For there is a Verbal Element to it, incredible as it seems. This raises old ghosts. It is almost as if we hear the returning whisper of primitive magic or fetish. It is as if we were dealing with the *Logos*—the word that was before the world. But where are we to find the logic of the *Logos?*

Truly the most puzzling aspect of all is this Verbal Element detected in it, even if thus remotely. Should we believe that the Power operates homeopathically through some sort of witches' rhyming chant? That might be an extreme conclusion, since we know it only by an implication. But when we consider all the foregoing in the light of Laudermilk's Hypothesis, we are tempted to a bit of unscientific apprehension.

How powerful is the Power? We do not know. We cannot equate it in dynes. We can only compare effect with effect, and here the difference is so great that comparison fails. We can consider the effect of the Titter-Stumpf Theory, or of the Krogman-Keil Projection on Instrumentation and Para-instrumentation. And we humbly murmur "very powerful indeed."

Carnadine Thompson had begun to read the newspapers avidly. This was unexpected, since reading was her weak point. She had had so much trouble with the story of the Kitten and the Bell in the First Reader that her mother had come to believe that she had no verbal facility at all. This had been belied a moment later when Carnadine had torn the offending pages out of the Reader and told her mother and the world just what they could do with that kitten, and told it with great verbal facility. But it seemed that for reading Carnadine had no talent.

But now she read everything she could find about the new disasters that had struck the country—read it out loud in a ringing voice in which the names of the destroyed places were like clanging bells.

"How come you can read the paper so well, Carnadine?" her mother asked her. "How do you know how to say the names?"

"Oh, it's no great trick, mama. You just tie into the stuff and let go. Crumpton! Locust Bayou! Pope City! Cherryfork! Rowesville!"

"But how can you read all those hard names in the paper when you couldn't even read the story about the little kitten?"

"Mama, with things going the way they are, I think there's a pretty good chance that that damned kitten will get what's coming to her."

Far out, very far out, there was a conversation.

This was on a giant world of extreme sophistication and nondependence on matter. It was such a world as those on which Laudermilk's Hypothesis was built. That such a world existed, even in a contingent sense, was a triumph for Laudermilk.

"Then you have invested one?" asked Sphaeros, an ancient rotundity of that advanced world.

"I have invested one," said Acu, the eager young sharpie, and bowed his forehead to the floor. The expression was figurative, since there was neither forehead nor floor on that world.

"And you are certain that you have invested the correct one?"

"You toy with me. Naturally I am not certain. Every investiture may not be successful, and every seed may not grow. One learns by experience, and this is my first experience on such a mission.

"I examined much of that world before I found this person. I thought first that it would be among the masters of the contrapuntal worlds—for even there they have such and masters of such. But none of these persons—called by themselves actors and impresarios and promotors and hacks—none of these qualified. None had the calm assurance that is the first requisite. What assurance they had was of another sort, and not valid. Also, their contrapuntal worlds were not true creations in our sense—not really worlds at all."

"Then where did you look?" asked Sphaeros.

"I looked to the heads of the apparatus. On retarded worlds there is often an apparatus or 'government.' On that world there were many. But the leaders of these—though most showed an avidity for power—did not show the calm assurance that should go with it. Their assurance, if it could be called such, was of an hysterical sort. Also, most of them were venal persons, so I rejected them."

"And then?"

"Then I explored remote possibilities. Those who employ in their work a certain power over another species—jockeys, swineherds, beekeepers, snake-charmers. But with them I didn't find what I looked for—the perfect assurance of the truly superior being."

"And then, Acu?"

"Then I went into instruments, not trusting my own judgment. I set the Calm Assurance Indicator on automatic and cruised about that world. And on that whole world I found only one person with perfect assurance—one impervious to doubt of any kind and totally impervious to self-doubt. On this one I made the investiture and conferred the concept of great Power and Sharpness."

"You have made a mistake. Fortunately it is not a great mistake as it is not a great world. You were too anxious to make a good showing on your first attempt. When nothing can be found, you should leave that world alone. On very many of them nothing can be found. Assurance is not the only quality that makes up this competence; it is simply the quality for which we look first on alien spheres.

"The one on whom you made the Investiture, though full of assurance, was not full of other qualities equally important. It was in fact a pupa form, a child of the species, known locally as a kid. Well, it's done and cannot be undone. Fortunately such power conferred carries its own safety factor. The worst it can do is destroy its own world and seal it off safely from others. You made the Investiture correctly?"

"Yes. I left the Red Cap, the symbol of authority and power. There was instant acceptance and comprehension."

"Now we'll do the big towns," screamed Carnadine Thompson in the clubhouse of the Bengal Tigers.

"Peas and Beans—
New Orleans!"

She jabbed the needle into New Orleans on the map, and the great shaft a hundred thousand miles long came down into the middle of the Crescent City.

A needle? Not a pin? No. No. Pins won't work. They're of base metal. Needles! Needles!

"Candy store—
Baltimore," howled Carnadine and jabbed in another needle, and the old city was destroyed. But there was never a place that screamed so loudly over its own destruction or hated so much to go.

"Fatty's full of bolonio—
San Antonio."

And Carnadine stuck it in with full assurance of her powers, red cap atilt, eyes full of green fire. There were some of
us who liked that place and wished that it could have been
spared.

"Eustace is a sisty—
Corpus Christi."

"I know one," said Eustace, and he clapped the red cap on
his own head:

"Eggs and Batter—
Cincinnater."

He rhymed and jabbed, manfully but badly.

"That didn't rhyme very good," said Carnadine. "I bet you
botched it."

He did. It wasn't a clean-cut holocaust at all. It was like a
clumsy, bloody, grinding job—not what you'd like.

"Eustace, go in the house and get the big world map," ordered Carnadine, "and some more needles. We don't want
to run out of things."

"Peewee is a sapolis—
Minneapolis."

"Let me do one," pleaded Peewee, and he snatched the red
cap:

"Hopping Froggo—
Chicago."

"I do wish that you people would let me handle this," said
Carnadine. "That was awful."

It was. It was horrible. That giant needle didn't go in clean
at all. It buckled great chunks of land and tore a ragged gap.
Nothing pretty, nothing round about it. It was plain brutal
destruction.

If you don't personally go for this stuff, then pick a high
place near a town that nobody can find a rhyme for, and go
there fast. But if you can't get out of town in the next two
minutes, then forget it. It will be too late.

Carnadine plunged ahead:

"What the hecktady—
Schenectady."

That was one of the roundest and cleanest holes of all.

"Flour and Crisco—
San Francisco."

That was a good one. It got all the people at once, and
then set up tidal waves and earthquakes all over everywhere.

"Knife and Fork—

World Abounding

How many habitable worlds there are depends on the meaning given to 'habitable' and to 'world.' 'Habitable without special equipment and conditioning' is the usual restriction on the first. 'Of no mean size' and 'of no extreme distance' are two common conditions of the second. Thus Roulettenwelt and Kentron-Kosmon are really asteroids, too small to be worlds. But how about Hokey Planet and such? And how about the distant traveler's-tale worlds?

Butler lists only seventeen habitable worlds, limiting them to the fair-sized and generally hospitable worlds of Sol and of the Centauri Suns. So all these were closely grouped. The early notion that double or triple sums would not have planets because of their irregularity had been an erroneous estimate, fortunately.

Thus, revolving around Sol there is only Gaea (Earth). Around the Sun Proxima (the Grian Sun) are Kentauron-Mikron, Camiroi, Astrobe, and Dahae. Around the Sun Alpha are Skandia, Pudibundia, Analos, and the equivalently-named twins with such different superior fauna, Proavitus and Paravata; and Skokumchuck (the Shelni Planet). Around the sun Beta are the three trader planets, Emporion, Apateon, and Kleptis; tricky places, it is said. But if you think the Traders are tricky, how about the other three Beta Planets? There are Aphthonia (also called World Abounding), Bellota (Butler lists this as a Planet, though there are larger bodies listed as asteroids: he says, however, that Bellota in its present creation is much larger than its size of record, a puzzling statement), and Aranea (or the Spider Planet).

These latter three are habitable by all definition, but they are generally uninhabited, each for its own unclear reason. It was to clear up the reason and impediment concerning Aphthonia or World Abounding that a party was now in descending hover.

"We are on this mission because of one phrase, repeated by leaders of five different parties, and maintained in the face of vigorous courts martial," Fairbridge Exendine, the singling leader, said with a sort of hooked wonder. "I have never been able to get that phrase out of my mind. 'You'd never believe it' was the phrase, and the men of the five parties, of the more than twenty parties in fact, would not elaborate on it much."

"I hardly believe it either," Judy Brindlesby said, "and I haven't been there yet. It almost jumps at you. There is certainly no other world that presents so pleasant an appearance from medium hover. The continent named Aegea and the howling beauty of those oceans and seas that invade it so deeply! The river named Festinatio, the largest *clear* river on any world! The volcano named Misericors! Why should a river be named 'I hurry' and a volcano be named the 'merciful'?"

"It was John Chancel who named them," Rushmore Planda said with that curious reverence which all use in speaking of the great explorer. "And it was he who first said that this was the finest world ever, and that it should be left alone to be just that."

World Abounding had been visited by the great John Chancel just fifty years before. He had been the first Gaea man on very many of the worlds. It was John Chancel who said that only men should go to work on World Abounding, that it was no place to raise a family. Later he repented even of this and said that nobody at all should go there.

Chancel had stated that World Abounding was the most generous and fertile world ever, and that its very generosity would blow one's mind. It was his opinion that this was the Hasty Planet of the earliest travelers' tales, and that there was something very much too hasty about it. And he said that the most famous product of World Abounding should never be used at more than one-thousandth strength.

Gorgos, the magic animal and plant hormone (it wasn't that, but such was the popular explanation of it), came from World Abounding. Cut it a thousand times and it still was the magic growth-trigger. Ah, why cut it at all though? Why not take it at the full where it abounded in its fullness? To be spooked off by too much of a good thing was childish. "Let us examine it as scientists and adults," Fairbridge said as they came into lower hover, "as balanced persons who know what we are about."

The seven balanced persons who knew what they were about were Fairbridge Exendine, the canny commander; the Brindlesbys, Judy and Hilary; the Plandas, Erma and Rushmore; the Kerwins, Lisetta and Blase. They were three couples and one remarkable singling, a superior microcosm.

They came down easily and safely from low hover as twenty-two parties had come down before (twenty-three if one counts the solo voyage of John Chancel). They were pleasantly staggered by the sudden green power of that place. There was no need of any caution: Nobody of any party had ever suffered even slight injury or sickness on World Abounding. They found such generosity as would gladden any mind and body. It would be difficult, initially, to be scientists and adult about World Abounding.

Well, revel in the joy then. Afterwards, analyze it all minutely, but without losing any of that joyousness. *Do not complain too strenuously about a stacked deck if it is all stacked in your favor.*

They were on the Terraces—"which aren't mentioned by John Chancel at all," Erma Planda said with a toss of her whole golden body, "and it is only gradually that members of the other parties begin to mention them. Could the Terraces have grown up in fifty standard years?"

The Terraces formed a great elongated, stepped plateau, overcome with its own lushness. From the great green broad height of the hover-craft landing, the Terraces tumbled down seventy meters in more than twenty giant steps to the plain. This was all between the volcano and the river, and the Terraces had shoved out into the river to produce gracious rapids with their musical foam.

"Yes, the Terraces have apparently grown in fifty years, or have been spewed out by the volcano named Merciful," Fairbridge said. "Chancel described the plain between the volcano and the river and he didn't mention the Terraces at all. He set up a spire for monument in the middle of the plain, and where is it now? I believe that it is engulfed in the Terraces, and I intend to find it. I also intend to find why some of the latter parties refer to the Terraces as the Graves. No member of any party died here. All returned. I have a sudden exuberance come over me and I'll start my digging now."

And Fairbridge Exendine had already set the earth-augers to cutting down into the Terraces.

"I have my own new exuberance," Judy Brindlesby shouted like a whole covey of trumpets. "Hilary, my clay-headed hero, we will make luscious life together all day and all night."

Judy was large, but surpassingly shapely and graceful, like a hover-craft. Her brindled black-red hair was so weighty and enveloping that a lesser woman could hardly have carried it; and it seemed to be growing by the minute, like the grass there. One couldn't actually quite see the World Abounding grass grow, but one could hear it; it made a pleasant squeaking sound. And there was a hint of quick music about Judy's heavy hair that indicated that it was growing and growing.

"Yes, it is volcanic ash," Rushmore Planda was saying as he joined Fairbridge at the earth-augers. "It is quite airy ash." The volcanic ash was chalky white to pearl gray. Then it had a streak of green in it, and another.

"You are through the first stratum, Fairbridge," Rushmore said, "and into a layer of compressed vegetation that hasn't even rotted yet. This is the vegetation that was recently the top of the second stratum; very recently, I believe. This is a curious pile of Terraces."

"Oh, it's a holy pyramid," Erma Planda told them all, "and the Volcano built it especially for the holy people, ourselves. John Chancel said that he always felt himself to be a holy man when he first set foot on a good new world. I feel myself to be a holy woman now."

"Do not stuff yourself, holy woman," her man Rushmore told her. "Chancel preached temperance in all things. Do you have to eat everything you see? Do you have to eat *all* of everything you see?"

"Yes, I have to, I have to! And was it not the great John Chancel, he who first warned against this place, who said that there was no possibility of poisoning on World Abounding? Oh, and he said that there was no possibility of over-indulgence here either. He stated that the essence Gorgos has no limits, but that it pretends that it has. Everything that can be chewed or swallowed here is safe to eat or drink. There is no insect or animal that bites, nor worm that gnaws, nor moth that harms. There'll be no extreme heat or cold. The nineteen-day polar tumble combined with the diurnal rotation keeps the air breezy and invigorating. Invigorating, yes, yes, extremely so. More than invigorating. It's a pretty horny world, actually. Rather a rambunctious feeling it gives one. More than that, it—"

"What has happened to all you girl-folk?" the leader Fairbridge asked, rather puzzled and almost alarmed. "I have never seen you so wild-eyed and charged."

"Poor Fairbridge," Judy Brindlesby needled him. "Never mind, Fairbridge, I'll *get* you a girl. I'll get you one within a standard month. I promise you."

"Impossible, sweet Judy, unless you slay your own mate.

We're to be here for a long year, or until we solve the problem, and nobody else will touch down. Where would you get me a girl?"

"That I don't know. But the very rocks are singing to me, 'You'll get a girl, Judy, you'll get a girl for old Fairbridge within a month.' "

"Gorgos is not merely a magic animal-and-plant hormone," Rushmore Planda was speaking with a suddenly improved, new and magnificent voice. "It's a way of life, I see that now. It will impose its own shape on my wife, however much she stuffs herself. It will impose its shape on everything. It is a new pace and a new sort of life."

"It may be that its pace is too fast," Fairbridge warned.

"Makes no difference. There can't be any other pace here. Get the song of those romping birds there! It's the same beat that Gaea lunatics, treated with Gorgos, begin to sing with as soon as their sure cure begins. Get the whole stimulating, pleasant, almost drunken smell of this planet! Here is not so much the uncanny feel of things seen before, but of things smelled before. All great smells (Can one speak of great smells? Yes, one can.) have a reminiscent element, but with *this* it is reminiscent of a future. There is a pleasurable mustiness here, that's sure, but it isn't of past time: it's of future time, long waiting, and now beginning to unfold suddenly."

"You men are drunk on only the expectation of wine," Lisetta Kerwin said. "But the one thing I remember from the journal of the great John Chancel was the recipe for making morning wine in nine minutes on World Abounding. And I've already started it. Time's arunning."

Lisetta was crushing purple fruit into a high calathus or basket made by pulling the inner corolla out of a giant flower bloom.

"It would be chemically possible to make a potable fruit alcohol in nine minutes," Blase Kerwin said, "but it wouldn't be wine. It wouldn't have the bouquet. It wouldn't have the—but it has it. I smell that it has already, and it grows. Here, here, let me swig that—"

"No, no, it isn't ready," Lisetta protested. "It still moves itself, it lends its color to the cup, it bites like a serpent."

"Look out, serpent and wife, I'll bite back. Have at you!" And Blase Kerwin took a huge draught from the green cup. He turned a bit green himself, but cheerfully so. He lost his voice, and he did a little dance on one foot while he grasped his throat with both hands, but he was quite pleased about it all. There are some things too good to wait for.

"A little patience," Lisetta said. "Four minutes yet."

Blase still hadn't his speech back but he could howl his high pleasure over the breathtaking encounter. And soon, quite soon, they were all lushy over the singing, heady stuff. It was very difficult to be scientific and adult about World Abounding.

So they probed the world very unscientifically and kiddishly, except Fairbridge and Rushmore, who still probed the levels of the Terraces. The three ladies especially were happy maniacs and they were all over that abundant land. They caught and rode huge gangling animals. After all, on the world of Chancel and others, everything was harmless. They wrestled with big starfish in the river named Festinatio. They ate the snap-off tails of huge lizards and sent them away bawling and running on their two hind legs. Never mind; the big lizards could regrow their snap-off tails.

"Those five party leaders who wrote 'You'd never believe it,' do you think they were laughing when they wrote it?" Judy Brindlesby exploded the question when she clambered once again back up to the diggings.

"One of them, I believe, wrote in laughter, Judy," Fairbridge said. "And one of them, I know for certain, wrote in absolute horror. I don't know about the other three."

"Fairbridge, I suggest that we clear out a square about five meters on a side and excavate the whole top level of it," Rushmore Planda said. "I believe that there is more mystery buried here than we have met in all our lives."

"All right, we will do that," Fairbridge agreed. "The least we can do is see what is right under our feet."

"But not there!" Judy trumpeted at them. "Dig here where the people are."

"What people, Judy?" Fairbridge asked her patiently. "All the people who have ever been on this world have been accounted for."

"Not till we account for them they haven't. How do I know what people they are till you dig them up? Dig carefully, though. They are real people here. You call yourselves diggers and you don't even know where the people are buried."

"We dig where you say, Judy. You are a people-witcher in your several ways."

"But don't dig all the time. You're missing it. Life is being lived today and tonight." And she was off again, leaping down the three-meter steps of the Terraces.

"I don't know what she means," Fairbridge said as he set the excavators to work and then adjusted them to 'Slow and Careful.' "I hardly ever know what she means."

"I believe that I know what she means, Fairbridge," Rushmore said in an eerie voice with a scarce human chuckle in it.

So the excavators excavated, moving the light volcanic ash that was below the vegetation. There was real mystery in the ash that was turned up. That stuff was not completely dead.

"One thing I like about it here is the size of the party," Fairbridge mumbled as he sensed something near and put the excavators on 'Very Slow.' "Seven. That's right, that's just right. That's just how many persons should be on a world. More than that is a crowd. But a man cannot live pleasantly alone. What do you think about that, Rushmore? Isn't seven about right? Rushmore?

"He's gone. The party isn't seven now. It's one, me. I'm alone. I suspect that they have chosen the better part, though. Yes, I know what Judy meant, and it does come in very strongly here. But it isn't just with them; it's coming up from the very ground here. I'll dig on."

Fairbridge dug down till he came to the people.

It was night. Ancilla, the smaller moon, was overhead; Matrona, the larger moon, had just arisen. Fairbridge went to find the three couples of the party.

"They all have the new exuberance on them and they make luscious life together all day and all night. But I have to tell them what I have found."

It would be easiest to find Judy Brindlesby, the liveliest of them all. Wherever she was, any man would know it by special sensing. Fairbridge's special sensing led him to a river meadow and into a high brake of reeds that still squeaked from sudden new growth. Judy lay there with her clay-headed hero and husband Hilary.

It was magnificent Judy stretched on her back in giggling slumber. Hilary, chuckling with pleasure, lay atop her and was cutting her hair with great shears: cutting her incredible hair, cutting her superabundant hair, cutting the *mountains* of her hair. He had sheared off great heaps of it, possibly twenty kilograms of it, and she still had more than she'd had that afternoon.

"You are almost completely hidden in the reeds, Hilary," Fairbridge said then. "I'd never have found you, except that any man can sense Judy's presence."

"Hullo, Fairbridge," Hilary grunted pleasantly. "The reeds weren't here when we lay down. They've grown up since. Everything that touches her grows, and she is enlivened wherever she touches this ground. Look at her hair, Fairbridge.

She's in accord with it here. Gorgos or whatever the growth element is, she's with it. So am I."

"I dug down to people in the Terraces, Hilary."

"Yes. Judy said there would be people there."

Fairbridge and Hilary went and took Rushmore from the sleeping arms of Erma in the blue-stem hills. And they met Lisetta and Blase Kerwin coming out of the orchards.

"Lisetta says that you have dug down to people," Blase cried vividly. "Oh, for the love of abundant Aphthonia, let's go see what this is about!"

"I've dug down to people, yes," Fairbridge said, "but how could Lisetta know it?"

They climbed up the tall Terraces and came to the open shaft.

"We will remove the rest of the volcanic dust and crust from about them," Fairbridge said. "And when old Beta Sun comes up, we can get a good look at them."

"Oh, this is fine enough light for it," Lisetta said. "Aren't they nice people, though. So friendly. We will get acquainted with them before the brighter light is on them. It's best to become acquainted with good people in dim light first, especially when they've been through an odd experience. Then they'll brighten up with the light."

There were twelve of the people there, twelve adults. They were seated, apparently, on stone benches around a stone table. The details would be known when the rest of the volcanic dust had been cleared away and when Beta sun was risen. The twelve were got up in a gala and festive way. They had sat eating and drinking when it came over them, *but they had not been taken by surprise*. It was a selective volcanic thrust that had covered them. It came only onto the Terraces that had become a shoulder of the volcano. The people needn't have been there; and they needn't have sat and waited while it covered them. The surrounding plains hadn't been covered by the volcanic thrust.

"Why, they're pleasantly dead, and not at all decayed," Lisetta cried. "They are really such nice people. Don't they seem so to the rest of you? There is something almost familiar about a few of them—as if I had met them before."

"How long?" Fairbridge asked Hilary Brindlesby.

"Two years, maybe. They haven't been dead longer than that."

"You're crazy, Hilary. You are the tissue man of this party. Take tissue samples."

"I will, of course. But they've been dead for about two years."

"Then they were alive when the Whiteoak party was here."

"Likely."

"Then why didn't Commander Harry Whiteoak mention them?"

"Whiteoak was one of those, Fairbridge, who used the phrase 'You'd never believe it,'" Rushmore Planda cut in. "Maybe he figured that covered it all."

"But who are they?" Fairbridge persisted. "Every person of every expedition has been accounted for. These are our own sort of people, but they aren't people of the Whiteoak party. I've met all the Whiteoaks, and all came back."

"Aren't they of the Whiteoak party, Fairbridge?" Blase asked with an air of discovery. "You'd better pray that the light doesn't get any better, man. You're near spooked now. There's a couple of ghosts there: an ear, a brow, a jaw slope. And that lady there, isn't she a little like another lady we met, enough like her to be a sister or daughter? I tell you that there are strong resemblances to several of the Whiteoak people here."

"You're crazy. The Whiteoaks were here for only six standard months. If they met these mysterious people, why didn't they give an account of it?"

They didn't do much more with it till daylight. They moved some of the volcanic filler and uncovered to a little more depth.

"Can you prop under this level and leave these people here, and then excavate the layer under them?" Lisetta Kerwin asked.

"We can, but why?" Fairbridge inquired. Fairbridge was jumpy. He didn't seem to appreciate how nice it was to come onto such a nice group of people.

"Oh, I think that these people picked a spot that had been picked time and time again before them."

Along about daylight, Judy Brindlesby and Erma Planda, with a variety of noises, came up to the others on the Terraces.

"Folks, are we ever sick!" Judy sounded out. "I'm sicker than Erma, though. I go further into things than she does. Don't you wish you were sick the way we are, Lisetta?"

"But I am, I am," Lisetta said, "and it didn't take me all night to find out. It's fun, isn't it?"

"Sure it is. I never had so much fun being sick in my life." And Judy retched funfully.

It was a little unusual that all three ladies should show the first signs of pregnancy at the same time. It was odd that they should all have morning sickness. Oddest of all was their being so delighted with their sickness. There was something about World Abounding that seemed to make all experience, even nausea, a happy experience.

And the dead people in the Terraces——

"They are the happiest-looking dead people I ever did see," Erma Planda declared. "I will have to know what they are so happy about. They would tell me if I had the proper ears to listen. It's hard to hear when it comes to you that way. What, dear? What are you saying?"

"I wasn't saying anything, Erma," Rushmore told her.

"Wasn't talking to you, Rushmore," Erma said with a flick of her golden body. "What, dear? I can't quite make it out." And Erma Planda thumped her body as if to get better reception.

"Your ears aren't in your belly, Erma," Rushmore reminded her.

"Oh well, maybe some of them are. No, I just get it a little at a time what they are so happy about."

The happy dead people had been preserved by the volcanic fill, and perhaps by the essence Gorgos or some other substance of World Abounding. They didn't feel dead. They were rather waxy to the touch; they were about as warm as the air, and they hadn't any clamminess; there was even a slight resiliency to them which is usually a property of live flesh and not of dead flesh. They were clad in the light native garments of World Abounding. They were, in some manner hard to reconcile, kindred to the members of the Whiteoak expedition. They were beautiful and mysterious people, but they didn't mean to be mysterious. They'd have told you anything you wanted to know if only proper accord might be established between dead tongue and live ear.

But was there not something a little bit too glib about the impressions that all these new explorers received from the dead folks? Yes, a little too glib here and there, but how could anyone be blamed for that?

"Just a minute, nevertheless," Lisetta Kerwin was saying both to the dead people and to the live. "We all say, or we all think, that you, our good friends here, are clad in the light native garments of World Abounding. Our good commander, Fairbridge, in fact, has just scribbled those very words in his notebook. But how did we know what the light native garments of World Abounding should look like since we never saw any of them before? And since there has never been, for the record, any human native on World Abounding, never been any human being born here, hasn't this all a fishy smell? Or has it? For I recall now that the fish of World Abounding have a pleasant fruity smell. Well, take your time, folks. Being dead, you are in no hurry, and I am not; but tell us about it when you get to it."

They sank a second shaft beside the first. They ran reinforcing timbers under the place of the pleasant dead people so that they would not be disturbed or collapsed. They dug the second shaft down through the volcanic fill to the next level of vegetation. There was an unexpected thing: it had been dug before. They were excavating an old excavation.

They cleared the space below the dead people (and it showed every sign of having been cleared before); they came, as they had weirdly known that they must come to such, to another clutch of dead people. They had been expecting just that, but they were stunned by it even more than by the first discovery or first report.

"How many times, do you think?" Fairbridge asked them all in real wonder.

"I guess twenty-two times," Hilary squinted. "There are, in all, twenty-two levels to the Terraces."

"Would a colossal joker, a demonical joker, a supernal joker, a godly joker, even an ungodly joker pull the same joke twenty-two times in a row? Wouldn't it begin to pall even on him after twenty-two times of it?"

"Not a bit of it," Erma said. "Whoever he is, he still thinks thunder is funny, and he's pulled the thunder joke billions and billions of times. And he laughs every time. Listen for the giggle sometimes; it comes around the edge of every thunder."

Slight differences only this time. The dead people of the second level numbered eleven adults. They had been dead a little longer than the first, but they hadn't been dead for more than four or five years. They were as well-preserved and as happy-seeming as the upper gentry. They added a bit to the mystery.

Fairbridge and his folks and his excavators continued to excavate, about one level a day. All the shafts that they dug now had already been dug out several times before. At the fifth level down they came to the tip of the spire or steeple that John Chancel had built as monument on the plain between the volcano and the river. They knew that it was older than the Terraces, that it went all the way down to the flat land; they also knew that it was only fifty years old.

There were sixteen of the gracious and pleasantly dead

people on this level. They had made a circular stone table around the tip of the spire where it came through the lower Terrace. They had wined and dined themselves there while they waited for the volcano named Merciful to cover them up. But who were these people, so beautiful and so pleasant and so dead, arranged on levels several years apart?

"The mystery gets deeper all the time," Fairbridge said weightily.

"Yes, it gets about three meters deeper every day," Hilary grinned. "Anybody got any strange stories to add to this?"

"Yes, I've a strange one," Judy told them. "I know that it seems pretty short notice, and I had no idea that it could be so far along, and I'm sure that it's completely impossible, but my time is upon me right now."

They all gaped at her.

"I said Right Now, Hilary," Judy told her husband in an almost tight voice, "and I mean right now."

Well, Judy was large (though shapely and graceful as a hover-craft), and the issue would apparently be quite small. But all of them had scientific eyes, trained to notice things large and small, and none of them had noticed that it would be so soon with Judy.

There was no trouble, of course. Hilary himself was a doctor. So was Blase. So, come to think of it, was Lisetta Kerwin. But Lisetta herself was feeling a bit imminent.

No trouble, though. On World Abounding everything happens easily and pleasantly and naturally. Judy Brindlesby, easily and pleasantly, gave birth to a very small girl.

Well, it was less ugly than most babies, less a red lump and more of a formed thing. And quite small. There was a spate of words from all of them, but no words could convey the unusual formliness of the very little girl.

"She is really pretty, and I never thought I'd say that about a baby, even my own," Hilary bleated proudly. "She is so small and so perfect. She is the least lass I ever saw."

"She is wonderful, she is beautiful, there has never been anyone like her," Judy was chanting in ecstasy, "She is perfect, she shines like a star, she sparkles like an ocean, she is the most enchanting ever, she is—"

"Oh, cool it, mother, cool it," the Least Lass said.

2

Fairbridge Exendine reacted in absolute horror to this, and he remained in a state of horrified rejection. The others, however, accepted it pretty gracefully. Explanations were called for, of course. Well then, let us seek the explanations.

"There has to be an answer to the Case of the Precocious Little Girl," Rushmore said. "Does anyone have an answer?"

"She's yours, Judy," Erma said. "You tell us if we heard what we thought we heard."

"Oh, I thought she talked quite plain enough, and I'm sure you heard what she said. But why should you ask me about it when she is right here? How did you learn to talk, dear?" Judy asked her little daughter, the Least Lass.

"Five days in the belly of a chatterbox and I shouldn't have learned talk?" the Least Lass asked with fine irony for one so young. So the explanation was simple enough: the little girl had learned to talk from her mother.

But Fairbridge Exendine was still gray-faced with horror. And she didn't belong to that singling at all. Why should he be so affected by this?

"Do you know that you are the first human child ever born on World Abounding?" Judy asked her child a little later.

"Oh, mother, I'm sure you're mistaken," Least Lass said. "I was under the impression that I was the two hundred and first."

"Can you walk?" Blase Kerwin asked the little girl a little later yet.

"Oh, I doubt it very much," she said. "It will be a standard hour before I even attempt it. It may be a standard day before I do it perfectly."

But Fairbridge Exendine had gone back to his digging now. He was in new horror of the mystery of the excavations, but he was still more in horror of the little girl.

Yet she was the prettiest child that anyone had ever seen—so far.

"Anything that we do is always anticlimactic to whatever Judy does," Erma Planda said with mock complaint. Erma, with her golden body and her greater beauty, wasn't really jealous of Judy Brindlesby. Neither was Lisetta Kerwin, with her finer features and her quicker intelligence. Both knew that Judy would always anticipate them in everything. She had certainly done it in this, though by no more than a couple of hours.

"Well, it's surely a puzzle," Rushmore Planda was talking pleasantly that day or the next. "We are all human persons. And the gestation period for humans is more than five days."

"Don't—don't talk about it," Fairbridge stuttered. "Dig—dig, man."

"Of course it's possible that the three conceptions took place nine months ago. That's the logical thing to believe, but a little illogic bug keeps croaking to me 'You know better than that.' And all three of the children say that they were in the bellies for only five days. There was certainly an extraordinary enlivening in all of us that first night here, except in you, Fairbridge."

"Don't—damn—talk about it. Dig—damn—dig."

"This is a miracle world, of course, and it is full of miracle substances. Nevertheless, I believe that the Miracle Master is a little grotesque in this trick. I love my own small son beyond telling, yet I feel that there is something in him that is not of myself and is not of Erma. Part of his parentage is World Abounding."

"Don't—don't talk crazy. None—none of this has happened. Dig—dig, man."

There was never a more frightened, more nervous man than Fairbridge. He buried himself in the digging work to get away from it; he'd buried himself nearly forty-five meters deep in the excavating work by this time. Oh, that man was edgy!

"I imagine that the same thing happens on Gaea," Rushmore was rambling on. "We were, for most of the centuries, so close to it that we couldn't see that the planet was the third parent in every conception. We saw it only a little when we came to Camiroi and Dahae and Analos: a twenty-day shorter gestation period in the one case, a twelve-day longer one in another. We were a long time guessing that there is no such thing as biology without environment. But who could have guessed that World Abounding would be so extreme?"

"Don't—don't talk about it," Fairbridge begged. "Thirty days, dam—dammit, and four—fourteen of them gone already. Dig, dig."

"What thirty days, Fairbridge? Is there a thirty-day period mentioned of our expedition? I don't know of it. Fairbridge, man, you only dig because you're afraid to wonder. Whoever saw children grow so much in nine days? But then there are trees here that grow twenty meters high in one day. And look at the way the hair grows on Judy Brindlesby, and she a human! Not that the children aren't human, not that they aren't even two-thirds earth-human.

"Fairbridge, those are the three smartest children that anybody ever saw. When I was their age (oh, damn, I don't mean nine days old, I mean their apparent age of nine or ten years old), when I was their age I wasn't anything like as sharp as they are, and I was rated smart. And who ever saw such handsome people anywhere? They're on a par with the dead people here in the Terraces. Do you believe that they're of the same genesis?"

"D—dig, man, or drop dead, but don't—don't talk about it. It isn't there. It hasn't happened."

"Erma thinks that the children have rapport with the dead people here in the Terraces. After all, they are one-third blood kindred. They all have one common parent, World Abounding. Erma also thinks that all three children are coming to their puberty period now. She believes that the pubescent manifestations here will be much stronger, much more purposive, much more communal than anything on Gaea or Camiroi or Dahae. The useless and vestigial poltergeistic manifestations of Gaea-Earth will not compare with them at all, she believes. Was there ever such frustrating failure in communicating as the whole poltergeist business?

"Erma believes that the manifestations here will go even beyond the three-angel paradoxes of the pubescents on Kentauron-Mikron. And why should these things not go beyond? We had premonitions of such wonderful weirdnesses even on our own world. My mate Erma believes that these puberty insights (the volcano is a part and person of these insights) will begin very soon. Two more days; three at the most."

"D—dig, man. Don't—don't think."

Coming of age on World Abounding is a closed subject. It is not closed in the sense of being all secret or restricted, but in being a thing closed upon itself. From its very beginning it is conscious of its resolution.

Least Lass Brindlesby, Heros Planda, and Kora Kerwin were paradoxical children. It seems foolish to speak of relaxed intensity, of foolish sagacity, of placid hysteria, of happy morbidity, of lively death-desire. The children had all these qualities and others just as contradictory. They were at all times in close wordless communication with their parents and with all other persons present, and they were at the same time total aliens. The children were puzzling, but they themselves certainly weren't puzzled: they were always quite clear as to their own aims and activities. They had no more doubt of their direction than the arc of a circle has.

Lisetta Kerwin worried a little that she might have a retarded daughter. It was not that the girl was slow about things, just that she was different about things. Should a nineteen-day-old girl be called retarded because she dislikes reading? Kora could read, most of the time. Whenever her intuitions cocked their ears with a little interest she could go right to the heart of any text. But mostly all three of the children disliked the reading business.

Hilary Brindlesby scolded the children because they showed no sign of the scientific approach or method. But the scientific approach with its systematic study would not have brought them along nearly as fast as they did go. They all had the intuitive approach and it brought them rapidly to a great body of knowledge.

The children were well acquainted with the dead people in the Terraces (Fairbridge, in his horror-filled distracting work, had excavated almost all the Terrace levels now). The children named the names of all the dead people and told of their intricate relationships. Lisetta Kerwin recorded all this from the children. It tied in remarkably with the surnames of the people of the various expeditions.

"You can't really communicate with the dead people of the Terraces," Blase Kerwin told his daughter Kora. "It is just a bit of flamboyant imagination that you all seem to have."

"Oh, they say pretty much the same thing about you and us, father," Kora said. "They tell us that we can't really communicate with such stuffy folks as you who weren't even born on World Abounding. We do communicate with you, though; a little bit, sometimes."

And then one evening, Heros Planda and Kora Kerwin said that they were married.

"Isn't twenty-two days old a little young to marry?" Rushmore Planda asked his son.

"No, I don't believe so, father," Heros said. "It is the regular age on World Abounding."

"Who married you?" Lisetta Kerwin asked. After all, it had to be somebody who had done it, and there were no human persons on the world except those of the party.

"We don't know his name," Kora said. "We call him Marrying Sam in fun, but lots of the Terrace people have called him that too. We might suppose that that is his name now."

"He isn't a human person? Then what species does he belong to?"

"He doesn't belong to any species, mother, since he is the only one of his kind. The Volcano says that Marrying Sam is his—the Volcano's—dog. He doesn't look like a dog, as I intuit dogs, though. He can't very well look like anything else, since he is the only one of his kind."

"I see," Lisetta Kerwin said, but she saw it a little cockeyed. She was vaguely disappointed. She had always wanted a grand wedding for her daughter, if she had ever had a daughter. And now the daughter and the wedding had come so close together that something seemed lacking. She didn't know that it had been a very grand wedding, with elementals such as a Volcano and an Ocean participating; she didn't even know that she had participated, along with everything else on World Abounding.

"I thought you would be pleased, mother, that we had married and regularized our relationship," Kora suggested hopefully.

"Of course I'm pleased. It's just that you seem so young."

Actually, the wedding celebration was not yet completed. Part of it was tangled with an event that involved almost all of them that night. It was similar to the mysterious carnal happenings of the first night of the party on World Abounding.

It was another of those extraordinary enlivening events. It got them. It got Erma Planda of the golden body, and Judy Brindlesby of the sometime incredible hair. It got Lisetta Kerwin of the now shattered serenity; it got Rushmore and Hilary and Blase.

Perhaps it had been thought that connubial passion happened without regard to place or planet. Such is not the case. And the case on World Abounding was very different from the case on Gaea or Camiroi or Dahae. There was a pleasantness at all times on World Abounding, there was a constant passion of a sort, an almost pantheistic communion of all things together. But there was something else that came on much stronger at special times, that was triggered by special events without an exact time arriving, that was wild and rampant and blood- and seed-pungent.

It was the rutting season.

Ah, we deck it out better than that. It was a night, or a day and a night, of powerful interior poetry and music, of personal affirmation, of physical and moral and psychic overflowing, of aesthetic burgeoning. It was clear crystal passion.

But let us not deck it out so nice that we won't know it. It was the horniest business ever, and it went on all night and all day and all night.

Hilary and Judy Brindlesby: he had the length and the strength: she had the fullness and the abundance. They made such laughing love that it sounded like chuckling thunder in the reed-brakes. Even the birds and the coneys took up the cadence of it.

Rushmore and Erma Planda: he of the buffalo bulk and the impression of swooping Moses-horns on his head; she of the golden body and the emerald eyes. "They should take the two of us for models," Erma had said on that memorable time twenty-seven nights before. "Nobody has ever done it as we have. We should give lessons."

And then Blase and Lisetta Kerwin—no one will ever know just how it was with them. They had a thing that was too good to share (except in the planet-sharing aspect of it), that was too good to tell about, that was too good even to hint at. But, after such pleasures, they seemed the most pleasured of all the couples.

But Kora and Heros were at home in this. World Abounding was really a third flesh of their union in a way that it couldn't be for the others. They held their own pleasures atop the volcanic Terraces, not in the reeds or the blue-stem hills or the orchards as the World-Gaea couples did.

World Abounding is the most passionate of worlds, with the possible exception of Kleptis of the Trader Planets where the rapacity in all things is so towering. The Miracle-Maker of legend and fact on World Abounding was always shocked and bewildered by such coming together as that of Heros and Kora, even though it was a licit relationship and done in the licit manner. It was the depth and violence of it that was beyond law, that almost made the Miracle-Maker doubt that he had made such an indomitable thing as this.

Really, it was the Abounding Time, the name-thing of the world.

The only discordant (ill-fitting, but not completely unpleasant) elements in the thunderous season-time of World Abounding were Fairbridge Exendine and Least Lass Brindlesby.

"Now I am an old maid out of joint with the time," Least Lass said as she wandered on the hills of her home. Both the smaller moon Ancilla and the larger moon Matrona were a-shine. "My proper mate is unready and unbelieving. My third parent, World Abounding, who is also the third lover of our love, is not sufficiently penetrating. Father of Planets, help us! You gave us here the special instruction 'What you do, do quickly,' yet it isn't with us as with other places. Answer me, answer me right now!"

Least Lass threw angry rocks at the sky when she was not answered right now. But there is no time for slow answers on World Abounding.

And Fairbridge (still in the horror that would never leave him, but now touched by something both brighter and deeper) could only bark harshly to himself, "I am a human man. These things cannot be, have not been, must not be allowed to be. They are all hallucination, and this is an hallucinatory world. The monster-child remains monstrous, breathtakingly monstrous. It would be the only love I had ever had, if it could have been, if the cause of it were real. How could a human man mate with an imagination, how with a monster, be she a demon or an angel?"

It did not come to these two incongruities, in proper season, as it came to the other persons there.

By second morning, the partaking couples were in a state of dazzling exhaustion. But they knew that they were well fruited, fruited forever. Then there came the several days of golden desuetude. Even the letdowns on World Abounding were wonderful.

All the folks sympathized, of course, with the passion-impounded Fairbridge and with the lost-in-a-maze Least Lass. The case of Fairbridge and Least Lass was comical with the sort of cloud-high comedy that is found on World Abounding. There was everything ludicrous about it. There was a poignancy and a real agony about it also, but the betting was that these qualities would give way. You drive the sharp poignancy staff into the ground of World Abounding and it will grow green leaves on it before you can blink; yes, and grotesque blooms like monkey faces. But it won't lose any of its sharpness when it blooms.

Fairbridge Exendine was a rough-featured man, in no way handsome. He missed being clumsy only by the overriding power of his movements. He had always been a singling. He could hardly be called a woman-hater, since he was infinitely courteous and respecting to women, but he must be set down as a woman-avoider. Either he had been burned badly once, or the singling nature was in his roots and bones.

He was an abrupt man with a harsh sound to him. There was seldom in itself anything harsh about his acts or his words; the harshness was in the shell of him, in the rind that wrapped him up.

And Least Lass Brindlesby:—Fairbridge believed that she wasn't real; and she was. She had been the most beautiful child that anyone had ever seen for no more than an hour or two; until the birth of the children Kora and Heros those twenty-four days ago. She was still of almost perfect beauty; she could only be faulted for a certain heartiness bursting out, too big to be contained in the beauty. She wasn't really the Least Lass anymore; she was as large as her mother; she was bigger than either Kora or Heros. She had a shapeliness and grace superior even to that of her mother, for she was born on World Abounding.

But she looked like Fairbridge Exendine, for all her elegant beauty and for all his craggy ugliness. She looked like him as a daughter will look like a father, as a wife may sometimes come to look like a husband. She had 'grown towards him' in the World Abounding phrase, and all such growths here had to be very swift.

She had a great deal of humor, this girl Least Lass, and she needed it. She was not of flimsy growth: none of the children (children no longer) were. On some worlds and quasi-worlds of rapid growth, there is a defect of quality. The quick-grown tree-sized things will really be no more than giant weeds; the quick-grown creatures will not have much to them. On World Abounding that wasn't so. The quick-grown plants and creatures here were fine-grained and intricate and complete. The persons were so, and especially Least Lass.

She was no weed. Weeds have no humor (except the Aphthonia Sneezeweed, of course). But Least Lass sometimes pursued Fairbridge with humor that would make one shiver.

"My good man holds me in horror," she'd say. "He likes me really, but he believes that I am unnatural, and he has a real horror for the unnatural. Oh, I will turn him ash-gray and I will turn him fruit-purple! I will turn him swollen blood-black. I'll give him all the seven horrors, and I love him. Fairbridge, Fairbridge, even the rocks are laughing at your horror and your plight, and mine is the rockiest laugh of them all."

Ah, the rocks laughed like clattering hyenas at the poor distraught man.

Sometimes, Least Lass cried a little, though. There is a quick gushiness about tears on World Abounding, a voluminousness that would drown the world if continued more than a short instant. She cried a cupful there one day, actually filled a big blue crystal cup with her tears. Then, in a swift change of mood, she set it at Fairbridge's place at the dinner. And when he, puzzled, tasted it and sputtered, the composite laughter of all assembled nearby shattered his spirit. (Tears on World Abounding are quite pungent, more than just salty.)

Fairbridge Exendine then did a strange thing. He covered the cup with a nap, then wrapped it in a towel and carried it away to his singling quarters to preserve it just as it was.

Then Least Lass cried at least another cupful on the

ground. But that was only a matter of seconds. She was always the sunniest girl ever, immediately after tears.

Things wound themselves up in the thirty-first day of the expedition on World Abounding. It was a clear and exuberant day. Both the Grian sun and the Alpha sun could be seen like bright stars in the daylight sky. This is always a good sign. And the Beta sun itself was pleasantly scorching. A good strong day.

We cannot know just how it happened. The fields themselves announced that there was a special and privileged rutting time, not for all, only for a select two. The sand squeaked oestrius sounds. Kora had talked to the Volcano and to the one-of-a-kind subcreature called Marrying Sam, and had learned that the ceremony itself had been a rather stilted one. There was something of very deep emotion cloaked over with layers of rock hard reserve, world deep passion covered with a careful crust. The volcano was familiar with such things in his own person, and explained that such surface covering is often necessary to very deep people.

Then, somewhere on World Abounding, Fairbridge and Least Lass and the Planet itself had their private experience (an orgy, actually, but their privacy extends even to the selection of the word); they had their time of it, and it may have been a high old time. The others could admire from a distance, and from secondary evidence; but they had no direct evidence, only the planetary resonances and the ghostly reports.

When it was over with, the day and the night of it, when the whole double Nation of those folks was together again, Fairbridge still had that look of horror (it would never leave him). But now it was only one element of many. It was one part of a look or a play more properly named *The Comedy of Horror;* and this was but a portion of a whole assembly of deep comedies: *The Comedy of Soul Agony, the Comedy of Quick Growth* (one new furrow in the Fairbridge face represented the almost pun that 'quick' here means 'alive,' means it specially on World Abounding), the *Comedies of World Ending, of Love Transcending,* or *Death and Deep Burial.*

Fairbridge hadn't been loosed of any of his own agonies, but at least he had learned that they were funny.

And Least Lass had a look of almost total happiness, it being understood that almost-total happiness is often a shaggy clown-looking thing, with at least a slight touch of insanity, and a more than slight touch of death's-head. Quite a gay girl she was and would always be: she had been born knowing that death is open at both ends.

The end of the world, the end of a discrete culture comes quickly. Lisetta Kerwin worried about a certain impossibility here.

(Four children had been born on the same day; then, two days later, a fifth. That made eight persons of the half nation, the World Abounding Nation; and, of course, there were still the seven persons of the World-Gaea Nation.)

"We have been here for just thirty-six days," Lisetta worried, "and we have more than doubled our population. What if there should be (What is the phrase they used back in the Era of Wonderful Nonsense?) a People Explosion?"

"You know that is impossible, mother," Kora said. "World Abounding sets its own lines, as is the habit of worlds."

"Yes, it is quite impossible, grandmother," Chara Kerwin, the newborn daughter of Kora, said. "This is all there will be for this particular world. I myself, and those of my generation, will not experience it all directly. We will experience part of it by sharing. Our present numbers are our final numbers. It is less than some worlds have, I know, so we must make up for it by being as vital as we can be."

"But, in another twenty days or so," Lisetta protested, "there will be another passion period, and then—"

"No, there will not be," Kora tried to explain. "To do a thing more than once, to do a thing more than twice (twice is sometimes necessary when there is an intersection of two worlds), that is to become repetitious, and to be repetitious is the unforgivable sin. Touch stone, mother, kick sand, knock wood (as you report is said on Gaea), and pray that it may never happen to any of us."

"But of course it will happen, children, and it will become an increasingly compounded happening. Consider how many there will be in even one year——"

"A year!" Chara shrilled from the arms of Kora her mother. "Has anyone ever lived for a year?"

"I don't know," Kora puzzled. "Has anyone? Have you, mother?"

"Yes, I'm afraid that I have," Lisetta admitted. But why should she be apologetic at having lived more than one year?

"I had no idea, mother," Kora mumbled in half-embarrassment. "I guess this is the reason for the gaps in our communication, however hard we try to close them."

Then, for a long while (by local standards), it was all an easygoing time on World Abounding. It was a period of action packed leisure (though not all will be able to understand this); it was crammed full of events, the outcomings and incomings of a new maturing fruitful culture. There was not room in the concentrated leisured hours of any of them to experience it all directly; each one must simultaneously live in the mind and body of everyone to be able to contain it all. There was the unhurried rapidity of thought and act and enjoyment. There was little difference in the day and night hours: sleep and wakefulness were merged; dreaming and experience were intermingled. The fulfilled persons would sometimes sleep while walking or even running, especially those of the full World Abounding generations.

"Are we awake or sleeping?" Least Lass asked her lover one day, or night.

"That I do not know," Fairbridge said, or thought, in whatever state he was in. "But we are together. May the Planet Plucker grant that we be always together."

"We are together," Least Lass agreed, "and yet I am climbing and leaping on the north ridges of the Volcano Misericors, and I am sound asleep. And you are swimming in the estuary of the River Festinatio, very deep below the surface where it is ocean water below the running water, and you also are asleep. Give me your hand. There! On a false level of reality it might seem that my hand was closed on the meaty bloom of a rock crocus, but that rock crocus is a part of yourself. It might seem, to an observer of no understanding, that your own hand has closed on an Aphthonia Blue-Fish (the Blue-Fish himself is such an observer and he believes this), but that Blue-Fish is really myself with the scales still on his eyes and on his whole fishness. But the scales have fallen from our own eyes a little bit so that we may see reality. Grip my hand very hard."

They gripped hands very hard. They were together.

Ceramic flutes! The flutes were one signature of the present World Abounding culture. They have a tone of their own that cannot be touched by either wooden or brass horns. This light, hard, airy ceramic is made from the deposits of windblown loess from the ocher hills, from the limey mud of the plashes of the River Festinatio, from the ash and the pumice of the Volcano Misericors. This makes a ceramic like no other; there will always be old tunes nesting in every horn and pipe of it.

There were also green-wood clarinets with tendrils still growing on them; aeolian stringed boxes that played themselves in harmonic to whistling; snakeskin drums; hammered electrum trumpets (what a rich sound they had!); and honey-wood violins.

Such orchestration as was employed was of a natural sort. Usually it was the whistling coneys (who are very early risers) who would set the aeolian strings to going: then the several nations of birds would begin to intone; the people, whether waking or sleeping, would soon come in with their composite solos. Or sometimes it was one of the persons who began a music.

"Think a tune, father," Heros Planda might call. And his father Rushmore, afternoon dreaming somewhere in the blue-stem hills, would think of one. Heros would begin to blow a few notes of it, though he might be several kilometers distant from his father. It might be taken up then by boom-birds or by surfacing riverfish with their quick sounding that was between a whistle and a bark. There was a lot of music in this World Abounding culture, but it was never formal and never forced.

There was a sculpture culture, though Fairbridge warned that it was a dangerous thing. World Abounding was so plastic a place, he said, that one might create more than he had intended by the most simple shaping or free-cutting. "Half the things alive here have no business being alive," he said. "One is not to trust the stones, especially not trust any stones of the Volcano."

Nevertheless, the sculpture culture, done in high and low relief, or in the free or the round, was mostly on the south face of that trustless volcano. Whenever the Volcano exuded a new flow-wall during the night, all the people would be at the bright and soft surface in the morning, before it had cooled. These flow-walls were of mingled colors, of bright jagged colors sometimes, or soft colors at other times, then again of shouting colors: it was a very varied and chemical Volcano and it bled like rock rainbows.

Usually the Volcano himself set the motif for a sculpture-mass. He could do good and powerful work in the rough. He could form out large intimations of creatures and people and events. But he was like a geniused artist who had only stubs, no hands. It was the human persons who had to do all the fine and finishing work of the almost living murals.

The performed dramas of this culture fell into a half-dozen cycles. They were mostly variations or continuations of things done by groups of the dead Terrace peoples, or by primordials before them. They were always part of an endless continuity. Here they might be in scene five of act four hundred of one of the Volcano cycles. Earlier acts had been performed by earlier peoples, by the primordials, by Aphthonian bears, by characters or manifestations which had had no life of their own outside of the dramas.

Poetry wasn't a separate act here. The people of World Abundant *were* poetry, they lived poetry, they ate poetry, they drank it out of cups. All the persons were in rime with each other, so they had no need of the sound of it.

Eating was an art. No two meals on World Abounding had ever been the same. Every one of them was a banquet, beyond duplication, beyond imitation.

So it went on for a long while (by local standards); it went along for near three standard months. All the persons of the native World Abounding generations now appeared to be about the same age, this in spite of the fact that some of them were parents of others of them.

3

"We have done absolutely everything," Chara Kerwin said one day. "Some of us, or other of us, or all of us have done everything. Now we will wind it up wonderfully. Is it not a stunning thing to have done everything?"

"But you haven't done everything, you bumptious child," Lisetta told her. "You haven't borne children, as your mother has, as myself your grandmother has."

"But I have. I have borne myself, I have borne my mother Kora, I have borne you, my grandmother Lisetta, I have borne every person ever birthed on World Abounding or elsewhere. What we do not do as individuals, we do in common. All of our nation has now done everything, as I have. So we will wind it up."

All eight of the gilded youths of the World Abounding nation came at the same time to the realization that they had done everything. They called it back and forth, they echoed the information from the blue-stem hills to the orchards to the mountains. They all came together full of the information. They assembled on the top of the Terraces. They sat down at table there, and demanded that the elder World-Gaea nation should serve them.

"Out-do yourselves!" Least Lass Exendine called to all those elders. "Give us a banquet better than any you ever invented before. But you may not share it with us. It is for ourselves only. Serve us. And eat ashes yourselves."

So the oldsters, those who had not been born on World Abounding, served the assembled younglings, and did it with delight. There seemed to be a wonderful windup fermenting for all of them.

The Comedy of Horror, perhaps, showed a little stronger than it had recently on the face and form of Fairbridge, but it was still only one of that complex of deep comedies. Fairbridge had a very stark and terrible intuition now. He had a horrifying premonition of the real substance of those twin Comedies of World Ending and of Love Transcending. But even horror is a subject of comedy of World Abounding, and it is supposed to have that jagged edge to it.

"Bring all our things, bring all our artifacts," Chara ordered when they were still deep in the wining and dining. "Bring all our instruments and robes and plaques and free sculptures. Pile up enough food for a dozen banquets. Bring our green shroud-robes."

"It may be that you have not really done everything," Fairbridge said once in white agony while all the things were being piled up. "Let us think if there is not something left that you haven't done."

"No, no, good father, good husband, good lover, good ancestor, good descendant, good Fairbridge mine," Least Lass was saying, "we have done everything. We have done everything that could be in your mind, for plumbing the Fairbridge mind to its total depth is one of the many things we have done. And if there is some thing that we really have not done, then we will do it after we are dead. We do all sorts of communicating things in our sleep. Well, we will also do them in our deaths, as do the other dead people living in the Terraces. Fairbridge, my passion, my patsy, my toy, my love, go tell the Volcano that it is time."

"How should I talk to a Volcano?" Fairbridge asked.

"Why, you will speak to it directly, Fairbridge. Is it not a Gaea proverb that a man may talk to a volcano just as a beggar may talk to a horse or a cat to a king?"

"And I should say *what* to the Volcano?"

"Simply tell him that it is time."

Fairbridge Exendine climbed up from the Terraces onto the steep eastern slope of the Volcano Misericors. He climbed clear to the cone. The cone was a ragged laughing mouth; the whole face was a distorted laugh. One eye of that face was far down the north slope, and the other eye was over in the blue-stem hills. The ears were sundered off somewhere; the brow was exploded; the jaw was shattered all over the scree slopes. It was a fine merry face that the Volcano had, even though it was a little disjointed and disparate.

Something overly glandular about this Volcano, though. Ah, it was great-glanded. The Gorgos gland that supplied all of World Abounding was a part of this Volcano.

"Are you sure that it is as funny as all that?" Fairbridge gruffed at this open-mawed mountain. "It strains my idea of the comic a little. It could stand some revision."

They both were silent for a little while.

"Ah, the young persons told me to tell you that it is time," Fairbridge said glumly. The Volcano belched a bit of fire. There was something of cruel laugh in that sound: a snort, really. Fairbridge suspected that the Volcano was more animal than man.

Then the Volcano became somewhat raucous, foul-mouthed ("that quip is my own, my last," Fairbridge said in his throat), rumbling and roaring, smoky and sulphurous, scorching, sooty. Fairbridge left it in its own passion.

He came down towards the shouldering Terraces again. All the World-Gaea people were calling him to come to the plain below where the hover-craft was at the ready. He ignored them. He continued to the high Terraces and to the native generations of World Abounding. It was like hot snakes hissing at his heels as he went, pouring streams of lava. The air had become like a furnace, like a forge with bellows puffing.

The river Festinatio had become quite excited. It palpitated in running shivers of waves. It was a-leap with all its fishy fauna, with all its bold turtles and squids. The Volcano always invaded the river at the climax of its eruptions: each successive Terrace ran further into the River. Nobody should have been surprised at the excitement of the River, nobody who had watched or taken part in the dramas of the Volcano cycles.

Fairbridge came down to the death-edge young people on the Terraces.

"You must not be here with us," Heros told him. "There is no way that you can earn that right. We are completed, but you are not."

Fairbridge threw himself down on the Terraces, however, and the ground of the Terraces had already begun to smoke.

"You cannot stay here, my other love, my other life," Least Lass told him. But he lay at her feet. He embraced her ankles.

"Shall we allow them to stay on the Terraces and be burned to death and buried with ashes?" Judy Brindlesby asked uneasily on the land below.

"Yes. We must allow it," Hilary said.

"But there is a whole world that will not be covered. Only the Terraces will be covered and burned."

"Yes."

"They sit there eating and drinking, and already we can smell the scorched flesh of their feet. They are all so young, and they could live so long and so happy anywhere else on this world."

"We don't know that they could live any longer. We don't understand it."

"But they are our children."

"Yes."

"Shall I feed you scraps from the table as though you were a dog at my feet?" Least Lass asked Fairbridge. "Go at once now. You have no business dying here. Go with them. They come in great danger and pain to themselves to get you."

Rushmore Planda and Blase Kerwin came and dragged Fairbridge off the top of the smoking Terraces and down the slopes where lava and ash flow ran like lizards. All were burned, and Fairbridge was dangerously burned.

They went into the hover-craft, the seven persons who had not been born on World Abounding. They rose into the smoky volcanic air, and they hovered.

The young people, the World Abounding people, still sat and wined and dined themselves on the scorched Terraces. The hot ash and the fiery liquid shoved in upon them and rose to engulf them. They were encapsuled and preserved in the caking hot ash. Least Lass, at the rivermost edge of the Terraces, was the last of them to be completely covered. She made a happy signal to them in the hover-craft, and her mother Judy signaled back.

Hot ash filled the banquet plate of Least Lass by then, and hot lava filled her cup. Smiling and easy, she ate and drank the living coals to her pleasant death. Then she had disappeared completely under the flow of it, as the rest of them had done.

The Volcano covered them with another two meters of fill. Then he pushed on to have his will with the river.

"It did not happen, it could not have happened, it must not be allowed to have happened," Fairbridge Exendine was mumbling inanely, but Fairbridge was mind out of body now. His mind was at the feet of Least Lass in the merciful ashes of the new topmost Terrace.

"The report will be a difficult one," Hilary hazarded. "Just how are we to explain that a normal human settlement is im-

possible here? How explain that it will always end in such
swift short generations? How explain that every World
Abounding culture is, by its nature, a terminal culture?"
"Why bother?" asked Erma Planda of the still golden body
and emerald eyes. "We will make the entry that several of
the other expeditions have made. Yes, and we will be classed
as such disgraceful failures as they have been. What else to
do?"

She wrote the damning entry quickly.

"We were warned that there would be some necks wrung
if that phrase was used in our report," Rushmore said sourly.

"Wring my neck who can," Erma challenged. "There. It's
done. And they really wouldn't have believed it, you know."

Dream

He was a morning type, so it was unusual that he should feel
depressed in the morning. He tried to account for it, and
could not.

He was a healthy man, so he ate a healthy breakfast. He
was not too depressed for that. And he listened unconsciously
to the dark girl with the musical voice. Often she ate at Cahill's in the mornings with her girl friend.

Grape juice, pineapple juice, orange juice, apple juice . . .
why did people look at him suspiciously just because he took
four or five sorts of juice for breakfast?

"Agnes, it was ghastly. I was built like a sack. A sackful of
skunk cabbage, I swear. And I was a green-brown color and
had hair like a latrine mop. Agnes, I was sick with misery. It
just isn't possible for anybody to feel so low. I can't shake it
at all. And the whole world was like the underside of a log.
It wasn't that, though. It wasn't just one bunch of things. It
was everything. It was a world where things just weren't
worth living. I can't come out of it. . . ."

"Teresa, it was only a dream."

Sausage, only four little links for an order. Did people
think he was a glutton because he had four orders of sausage? It didn't seem like very much.

"My mother was a monster. She was a wart-hoggish animal. And yet she was still recognizable. How could my mother look like a wart hog and still look like my mother? Mama's pretty!"

"Teresa, it was only a dream. Forget it."

The stares a man must suffer just to get a dozen pancakes on his plate! What was the matter with people who called four pancakes a tall stack? And what was odd about ordering a quarter of a pound of butter? It was better than having twenty of those little pats each on its coaster.

"Agnes, we all of us had eyes that bugged out. And we stank! We were bloated, and all the time it rained a dirty green rain that smelled like a four-letter word. Good grief, girl! We had hair all over us where we weren't warts. And we talked like cracked crows. We had crawlers. I itch just from thinking about it. And the dirty parts of the dream I won't even tell you. I've never felt so blue in my life. I just don't know how I'll make the day through."

"Teresa, doll, how could a dream upset you so much?"

There isn't a thing wrong with ordering three eggs sunny-side up, and three over easy, and three poached ever so soft, and six of them scrambled. What law says a man should have all of his eggs fixed alike? Nor is there anything wrong with ordering five cups of coffee. That way the girl doesn't have to keep running over with refills.

Bascomb Swicegood liked to have bacon and waffles after the egg interlude and the earlier courses. But he was nearly at the end of his breakfast when he jumped up.

"What did she say?"

He was surprised at the violence of his own voice.

"What did who say, Mr. Swicegood?"

"The girl that was just here, that just left with the other girl."

"That was Teresa, and the other girl was Agnes. Or else that was Agnes and the other girl was Teresa. It depends on which girl you mean. I don't know what either of them said."

Bascomb ran out into the street.

"Girl, the girl who said it rained dirty green all the time, what's your name?"

"My name is Teresa. You've met me four times. Every morning you look like you never saw me before."

"I'm Agnes," said Agnes.

"What did you mean it rained dirty green all the time? Tell me all about it."

"I will not, Mr. Swicegood. I was just telling a dream I had to Agnes. It isn't any of your business."

"Well, I have to hear all of it. Tell me everything you dreamed."

"I will not. It was a dirty dream. It isn't any of your business. If you weren't a friend of my Uncle Ed Kelly, I'd call a policeman for your bothering me."

"Did you have things like live rats in your stomach to digest for you? Did they—"

"Oh! How did you know? Get away from me. I *will* call a policeman. Mr. McCarty, this man is annoying me."

"The devil he is, Miss Ananias. Old Bascomb just doesn't have it in him any more. There's no more harm in him than a lamppost."

"Did the lampposts have hair on them, Miss Teresa? Did they pant and swell and smell green—"

"Oh! You couldn't know! You awful man!"

"I'm Agnes," said Agnes; but Teresa dragged Agnes away with her.

"What is the lamppost jag, Bascomb?" asked Officer Mossback McCarty.

"Ah—I know what it is like to be in hell, Mossback. I dreamed of it last night."

"And well you should, a man who neglects his Easter duty year after year. But the lamppost jag? If it concerns anything on my beat, I have to know about it."

"It seems that I had the same depressing dream as the young lady, identical in every detail."

Not knowing what dreams are (and we do not know), we should not find it strange that two people might have the same dream. There may not be enough of them to go around, and most dreams are forgotten in the morning.

Bascomb Swicegood had forgotten his dismal dream. He could not account for his state of depression until he heard Teresa Ananias telling pieces of her own dream to Agnes Schoenapfel. Even then it came back to him slowly at first, but afterwards with a rush.

The oddity wasn't that two people should have the same dream, but that they should discover the coincidence, what with the thousands of people running around and most of the dreams forgotten.

Yet, if it were a coincidence, it was a multiplex one. On the night when it was first made manifest it must have been dreamed by quite a number of people in one medium-large city. There was a small piece in an afternoon paper. One

doctor had five different worried patients who had had
dreams of rats in their stomachs, and hair growing on the in-
sides of their mouths. This was the first publication of the
shared-dream phenomenon.

The squib did not mention the foul-green-rain background,
but later investigation uncovered that this and other details
were common to the dreams.

But it was a reporter named Willy Wagoner who really put
the town on the map. Until he did the job, the incidents and
notices had been isolated. Doctor Herome Judas had been
putting together some notes on the Green-rain Syndrome.
Doctor Florenz Appian had been working up his evidence on
the Surex Ventriculus Trauma, and Professor Gideon
Greathouse had come to some learned conclusions on the inner meaning of warts. But it was Willy Wagoner who went to
the people for it, and then gave his conclusions back to the
people.

Willy said that he had interviewed a thousand people at
random. (He hadn't really; he had talked to about twenty. It
takes longer than you might think to interview a thousand
people.) He reported that slightly more than sixty-seven percent had had a dream of the same repulsive world. He reported that more than forty-four percent had had the dream
more than once, thirty-two percent more than twice, twenty-
seven percent more than three times. Many had had it every
damned night. And many refused frostily to answer questions
on the subject at all.

This was ten days after Bascomb Swicegood had heard
Teresa Ananias tell her dream to Agnes.

Willy published the opinions of the three learned gentlemen above, and the theories and comments of many more.
He also appended a hatful of answers he had received that
were sheer levity.

But the phenomenon was not local. Wagoner's article was
the first comprehensive (or at least wordy) treatment of it,
but only by hours. Similar things were in other papers that
very afternoon, and the next day.

It was more than a fad. Those who called it a fad fell
silent after they themselves experienced the dream. The
suicide index rose around the country and the world. The
thing was now international. The cacophonous ditty *Green
Rain* was on all the jukes, as was *The Wart Hog Song*. People began to loath themselves and each other. Women feared
that they would give birth to monsters. There were new per-
versions committed in the name of the thing, and several or-
giastic societies were formed with the stomach rat as a sym-

bol. All entertainment was forgotten, and this was the only
topic.

Nervous disorders took a fearful rise as people tried to
stay awake to avoid the abomination, and as they slept in
spite of themselves and suffered the degradation.

It is no joke to experience the same loathsome dream all
night every night. It had actually come to that. *All* the people
were dreaming it *all* night *every* night. It had passed from
being a joke to being a universal menace. Even the sudden
new millionaires who rushed their cures to the market were
not happy. They also suffered whenever they slept, and they
knew that their cures were not cures.

There were large amounts posted for anyone who could
cure the populace of the wart-hog-people dreams. There was
presidential edict and dictator decree, and military teams attacked the thing as a military problem, but they were not
able to subdue it.

Then one night a nervous lady heard a voice in her
noisome dream. It was one of the repulsive cracked wart-hog
voices. "You are not dreaming," said the voice. "This is the
real world. But when you wake you will be dreaming. That
barefaced world is not a world at all. It is only a dream. This
is the real world." The lady awoke howling. And she had not
howled before, for she was a demure lady.

Nor was she the only one who awoke howling. There were
hundreds, then thousands, then millions. The voice spoke to
all and engendered a doubt. Which was the real world? Almost equal time was now spent in each, for the people had
come to need more sleep and most of them had arrived at
spending a full twelve hours or more in the nightmarish
world.

"It Could Be" was the title of a headlined article on the
subject by the same Professor Greathouse mentioned above.
It could be, he said, that the world on which the green rain
fell incessantly was the real world. It could be that the wart-
hogs were real and the people a dream. It could be that rats
in the stomach were normal, and other methods of digestion
were chimerical.

And then a very great man went on the air in world-wide
broadcast with a speech that was a ringing call for collective
sanity. It was the hour of decision, he said. The decision
would be made. Things were at an exact balance, and the
balance would be tipped.

"But we can decide. One way or the other, we *will* decide.
I implore you all in the name of sanity that you decide right.

One world or the other will be the world of tomorrow. One of them is real and one of them is a dream. Both are with us now, and the favor can go to either. But listen to me here: whichever one wins, the other *will have always been* a dream, a momentary madness soon forgotten. I urge you to the sanity which in a measure I have lost myself. Yet in our darkened dilemma I feel that we yet have a choice. Choose!"

And perhaps that was the turning point.

The mad dream disappeared as suddenly as it had appeared. The world came back to normal with an embarrassed laugh. It was all over. It had lasted from its inception six weeks.

Bascomb Swicegood, a morning type, felt excellent this morning. He breakfasted at Cahill's, and he ordered heavily as always. And he listened with half an ear to the conversation of two girls at the table next to his.

"But I should know you," he said.

"Of course, I'm Teresa."

"I'm Agnes," said Agnes.

"Mr. Swicegood, how could you forget? It was when the dreams first came, and you overheard me telling mine to Agnes. Then you ran after us in the street because you had had the same dream, and I wanted to have you arrested. Weren't they horrible dreams? And have they ever found out what caused them?"

"They were horrible, and they have not found out. They ascribe it to group mania, which is meaningless. And now there are those who say that the dreams never came at all, and soon they will be nearly forgotten. But the horror of them! The loneliness!"

"Yes, we hadn't even pediculi to curry our body hair. We almost hadn't any body hair."

Teresa was an attractive girl. She had a cute trick of popping the smallest rat out of her mouth so it could see what was coming into her stomach. She was bulbous and beautiful. "Like a sackful of skunk cabbage," Bascomb murmured admiringly in his head, and then flushed green at his forwardness of phrase.

Teresa had protuberances upon protuberances and warts on warts, and hair all over her where she wasn't warts and bumps. "Like a latrine mop!" sighed Bascomb with true admiration. The cracked clang of Teresa's voice was music in the early morning.

All was right with the earth again. Gone the hideous nightmare world when people had stood barefaced and lonely, without bodily friends or dependents. Gone that ghastly world of the sick blue sky and the near absence of entrancing odor.

Bascomb attacked manfully his plate of prime carrion. And outside the pungent green rain fell incessantly.

Ride a Tin Can

These are my notes on the very sticky business. They are not in the form of a protest, which would be useless. Holly is gone, and the Shelni will all be gone in the next day or two, if indeed there are any of them left now. This is for the record only.

Holly Harkel and myself, Vincent Vanhoosier, received funds and permission to record the lore of the Shelni through the intercession of that old correlator John Holmberg. This was unexpected. All lorists have counted John as their worst enemy.

"After all, we have been at great expense to record the minutiae of pig grunts and the sound of earthworms," Holmberg told me, "and we have records of squeakings of hundreds of species of orbital rodents. We have veritable libraries of the song and cackle of all birds and pseudo-ornins. Well, let us add the Shelni to our list. I do not believe that their thumping on tree roots or blowing into jug gourds is music. I do not believe that their sing song is speech anymore than the squeaking of doors is speech. We have recorded, by the way, the sound of more than thirty thousand squeaking doors. And we have had worse. Let us have the Shelni, then, if your hearts are set on it. You'll have to hurry. They're about gone.

"And let me say in all compassion that anyone who looks like Miss Holly Harkel deserves her heart's desire. That is no more than simple justice. Besides, the bill will be footed by the Singing Pig Breakfast Food Company. These companies are bitten by the small flea of remorse every now and then and they want to pitch a few coins into some fund for luck. It's never many coins that they want to pitch; the remorse bug that bites them is never a very large one. You may be able to stretch it to cover your project though, Vanhoosier."

So we had our appropriation and our travel, Miss Holly and myself.

Holly Harkel had often been in disrepute for her claims to understand the languages of various creatures. There was

128

special outrage to her claim that she would be able to understand the Shelni. Now that was odd. No disrepute attached to
Captain Charbonnett for his claim to understand the planetary simians, and if there was ever a phony claim it was this.
No disrepute attached to Meyrowitz for his claim of finding
esoteric meanings in the patterns of vole droppings. But there
seemed something incredible in the claim of the goblin faced
Holly Harkel that not only would she be able to understand
the Shelni instantly and completely but that they were not
low scavenger beasts at all, that they were genuine goblin
people who played goblin music and sang goblin songs.

Holly Harkel had a heart and soul too big for her dwarfish
body, and a brain too big for her curious little head. That, I
suppose, is what made her so lumpy everywhere. She was entirely compounded of love and concern and laughter, and
much of it bulged out from her narrow form. Her ugliness
was one of the unusual things and I believe that she enjoyed
giving it to the worlds. She had loved snakes and toads, she
had loved monkeys and misbegottens. She had come to look
weirdly like them when we studied them. She *was* a snake
when we studied them, she was a toad when they were our
subject. She studied every creature from the inside of it. And
here there was an uncommon similarity, even for her.

Holly loved the Shelni instantly. She became a Shelni, and
she hadn't far to go. She moved and scooted and climbed like
a Shelni. She came down trees headfirst like a Shelni or a
squirrel. She had always seemed to me to be a little other
than human. And now she was avid to record the Shelni
things"—before they be gone."

As for the Shelni themselves, some scientists have called
them humanoid, and then braced themselves for the blow
and howl. If they were humanoid they were certainly the
lowest and oddest humanoids ever. But we folklorists knew
intuitively what they were. They were goblins pure and simple—I do not use the adjectives here as cliché. The tallest of
them were less than three feet tall; the oldest of them were
less than seven years old. They were, perhaps, the ugliest
creatures in the universe, and yet of a pleasant ugliness.
There was no evil in them at all. Scientists who have tested
them have insisted that there was no intelligence in them at
all. They were friendly and open. Too friendly, too open, as
it happened, for they were fascinated by all human things, to
their harm. But they were no more human than a fairy or an
ogre is human. Less, less, less than a monkey.

"Here is a den of them," Holly divined that first day (it
was the day before yesterday). "There will be a whole coven

of them down under here and the door is down through the roots of this tree. When I got my doctorate in primitive music I never imagined that I would be visiting Brownies down under tree roots. I should say that I never so much as *hoped* that I would be. There was *so* much that they didn't teach us. There was even one period in my life when I ceased to believe in goblins."

The latter I do not believe.

Suddenly Holly was into a hole in the ground headfirst, like a gopher, like a ground squirrel, like a Shelni. I followed her, letting myself down carefully, and not headfirst. I myself would have to study the Shelni from the outside. I myself would never be able to crawl inside their green goblin skins, never be able to croak or carol with their frog tongues, never feel what made their popeyes pop. I myself would not even have been able to sense out their dens.

And at the bottom of the hole, at the entrance to the den itself, was an encounter which I disbelieved at the time I was seeing and hearing it. There occurred a conversation which I heard with my own ears, they having become transcendent for the moment. It was in the frog-croak Shelni talk between Holly Harkel and the five-year-old Ancient who guarded the coven, and yet it was in a sort of English and I understood it:

"Knockle, knockle." (This from Holly).

"Crows in cockle." (This from the guard).

"Wogs and wollie."

"Who you?" "Holly."

"What's a dinning?"

"Coming inning."

So they let us in. But if you think you can enter a Shelni coven without first riming with the five-year-old Ancient who guards it, then it's plain that you've never been in one of the places. And though the philologists say that the "speech" of the Shelni is meaningless croaking, yet it was never meaningless to Holly, and in flashes it was not meaningless to me. The secret guess of Holly was so.

Holly had insisted that the Shelni spoke English within the limits of their vocal apparatus. And they told her at this very first session that they never had had any language of their own "because no one had ever made one for us"; so they used English as soon as they came to hear it. "We would pay you for the use of it if we had anything to pay you with," they said. It is frog-croak English, but only the pure of ear can understand it.

I started the recorder and Holly started the Shelni. Quite

soon she had them playing on those jug shaped flutes of theirs. Frog music. Ineffably sad *sionnach* skirries. Rook, crow, and daw squabbling melody. They were pleasant, weird little pieces of music that sounded as though they were played underwater. It would be hard to imagine them not played under the ground at least.

The tunes were short just as all tunes of children are short. There was no real orchestration, though that should have been possible with the seven flutes differently jugged and tuned. Yet there was true melody in these: short, complete, closed melody, dwarfed perfection. They were underground fugues full of worms' blood and cool as root cider. They were locust and chaffer and cricket din.

Then Holly got one of the most ancient of the Shelni to tell stories while the jug flutes chortled. Here are the two of them that we recorded that first day. Others who listen to them today say that there is nothing to them but croaking. But I heard them with Holly Harkel, she helped interpret them to me, so I can hear and understand them perfectly in frog-croak English.

Take them, Grisly Posterity! I am not sure that you deserve even this much of the Shelni.

The Shelni Who Lost His Burial Tooth
It is told this way.

There was a Shelni who lost his burial tooth before he died. Every Shelni begins life with six teeth, and he loses one every year. Then, when he is very old and has only one tooth left, he dies. He must give the last tooth to the Skokie burial-person to pay for his burial. But this Shelni had either lost two teeth in one year or else he had lived to too great an age.

He died. And he had no tooth left to pay with.

'I will not bury you if you have no tooth left to pay me with,' said the Skokie burial-person. 'Should I work for nothing?'

'Then I will bury myself,' said the dead Shelni.

'You don't know how,' said the Skokie burial-person. 'You don't know the places that are left. You will find that all the places are full. I have agreement that everybody should tell everybody that all the places are full, so only the burial-person may bury. That is my job.'

Nevertheless, the dead Shelni went to find a place to bury himself. He dug a little hole in the meadow, but wherever he dug he found that it was already full of dead Shelnis or

Skokies or Frogs. And they always made him put all the dirt
back that he had dug.

He dug holes in the valley and it was the same thing. He
dug holes on the hill, and they told him that the hill was full
too. So he went away crying for he could find no place to lie
down.

He asked the *Eanlaith* whether he could stay in their tree.
And they said, no he could not. They would not let any dead
folks live in their tree.

He asked the *Eise* if he could stay in their pond. And they
said, no he could not.

They would not allow any dead folks in their pond.

He asked the *Sionnach* if he could sleep in their den. And
they said, no he could not. They liked him when he was alive,
but a dead person has hardly any friends at all.

So the poor dead Shelni wanders yet and can find no place
to rest his head.

He will wander forever unless he can find another burial
tooth to pay with.

They used to tell it so.

One comment on this burial story: The Shelni do have
careful burial. But the burial crypts are plainly dug, not by
the six fingered Shelni, but by the seven-clawed Skokie. There
must be substance to the Skokie burial-person. Moreover, the
Skokie, though higher on the very low scale than the Shelni,
do not bury their own.

Furthermore, there are no Shelni remains going back more
than about thirty equivalent years. There are no random
lying or fossil Shelni at all, though such remains are common
for every other species here.

The second story (of the first day).

The Shelni Who Turned into a Tree

This is how they tell it.

There was a woman who was neither Shelni nor Skokie
nor Frog. She was Sky Woman. One day she came with her
child and sat down under the Shelni tree. When she got up to
go she left her own child who was asleep and picked up a
Shelni child by mistake. Then the Shelni woman came to get
her own child and she looked at it. She did not know what
was wrong but it was a Sky People child.

'Oh, it has pink skin and flat eyes! How can that be?' the
Shelni woman asked. But she took it home with her and it
still lives with the Shelni and everyone has forgotten the difference.

Nobody knows what the Sky Woman thought when she got the Shelni child home and looked at it. Nevertheless she kept it, and it grew and was more handsome than any of them.

But when the second year came and the young Shelni was grown, it walked in the woods and said 'I do not feel like a Sky People. But if I am not a Sky People, then what am I? I am not a Duck. I am not a Frog. And if I am a Bird, what kind of Bird am I? There is nothing left. It must be that I am a Tree.' There was reason for this. We Shelni do look a little bit like trees and we feel a little bit like trees.

So the Shelni put down roots and grew bark and worked hard at being a tree. He underwent all the hardships that are the life of a tree. He was gnawed by goats and gobniu; he was rough-tongued by cattle and crom; he was infested by slugs and befouled by the nameless animal. Moreover, parts of him were cut away for firewood.

But he kept feeling the jug music creeping up all the way from his undertoes to his hair and he knew that this music was what he had always been looking for. It was the same jug and tine music that you hear even now.

Then a bird told the Shelni that he was not really a tree but that it was too late for him to leave off growing like a tree. He had brothers and sisters and kindred living in the hole down under his roots, the bird said, and they would have no home if he stopped being a tree.

This is the tree that is the roof of our den where we are even now. This tree is our brother who was lost and who forgot that he was a Shelni.

This is the way it has always been told.

On the second day it was remarkable how much Holly had come to look like a Shelni. Ah well, she has come to look like every sort of creature we have ever studied together. Holly insists that the Shelni have intelligence, and I half agree with her. But the paragraph in the basic manual of this world is against us:

"—a tendency to attribute to the Shelni an intelligence which they do not possess, perhaps due to their fancied human resemblance. In maze-running they are definitely inferior to the rodents. In the manipulation of latches and stops they are less adept than the earth racoons or the asteroid rojon. In tool handling and true mimicry they are far from equal to the simians. In simple foraging and the instinct for survival they are far below the hog or the harzl. In *mneme*, the necessary prelude to intelligence, they are about on par with the turtles. Their 'speech' lacks the verisimilitude of the talking birds, and their 'music' is below that of the insects. They make poor watchdogs and inadequate scarecrows. It appears that the move to ban shelniphagi, though perhaps sincere, is ill-advised. After all, as an early spaceman put it, 'What else are they good for?' "

Well, we have to admit that the Shelni are not as intelligent as rats or hogs or harzls. Yet I, surely due to the influence of Holly, feel a stronger affinity to them than to rats or hogs or coons or crows or whatever. But no creature is so helpless as the Shelni.

How do they even get together?

The Shelni have many sorts of songs, but they do not have any romantic songs in our sense. After all, they are small children till they die of old age. Their sexual relationship seems distinguished either by total unawareness or by extreme bashfulness.

"I don't see how they bring it off at all, Vincent," Holly said the second day (which was yesterday). "They are here, so they must have been born. But how do these bashful and scatterbrained three-year-olds ever get together to bring it off? I can't find anything at all in their legends or acting patterns, can you?"

"In their legends, all their children are foundlings. They are born or discovered under a blueberry bush (my translation of *spionam*). Or alternately, and in other cycles, they are found under a quicken tree or in a cucumber patch. In common sense we must assume that the Shelni are placental and viviparous. But should we apply common sense to goblin folk?

"They also have a legend that they are fungoid and spring out of the ground at night like mushrooms. And that if a Shelni woman wishes a child, she must buy a fungoid slip from a Skokie and plant it in the ground. Then she will have her child ready the next morning."

But Holly was depressed yesterday morning. She had seen some copy by our sponsor The Singing Pig Breakfast Food Company and it disturbed her:

"Singing Pig! The Children love it! Nourishing Novelty! Nursery Rime Characters in a can for your convenience! Real Meat from Real Goblins! No fat, no bones. If your can has a lucky number tab, you can receive free a facsimile Shelni jug flute. Be the first on your block to serve Singing Pig, the meat from real Goblins. Cornstarch and natural flavor added."

Oh well, it was only an advertisement that they used back on World. We had our recording to do.

"Vincent, I don't know how they got here," Holly said, "but I know they won't be here very long. Hurry, hurry, we have to get it down! I will make them remembered somehow."

Holly got them to play on the tines that second day (which was yesterday). There had been an impediment the day before, she said. The tines may not be played for one until the second day of acquaintance. The Shelni do not have stringed instruments. Their place is taken by the tines, the vibrating, singing forks. They play these many pronged tuned forks like harps, and in playing them they use the tree roots for sounding boards so that even the leaves in the air above partake a little of the music. The tines, the forks are themselves of wood, of a certain very hard but light wood that is sharp with chert and lime dust. They are wood, I believe, in an early stage of petrifaction. The tine fork music usually follows the jug flute music, and the ballads that are sung to it have a dreamlike sadness of tone that belies the childish simplicity of the texts.

Here are two more of those ballad stories that we recorded on the second day (which was yesterday).

The Skokie Who Lost His Wife

This is the way they tell it.

A Skokie heard a Shelni jug flute jugging one night.

'That is the voice of my wife,' the Skokie said. 'I'd know it anywhere.'

The Skokie came over the moors to find his wife. He went down into the hole in the ground that his wife's voice was coming from. But all he found there was a Shelni playing a jug flute.

'I am looking for my poor lost wife,' the Skokie said. 'I have heard her voice just now coming out of this hole. Where is she?'

'There is nobody here but myself,' the Shelni said. 'I am sitting here alone playing my flute to the moons whose light runs down the walls of my hole.'

'But I heard her here,' said the Skokie, 'and I want her back.'

'How did she sound?' asked the Shelni. 'Like this?' And he jugged some jug music on his flute.

'Yes, that is my wife,' said the Skokie. 'Where have you hidden her? That is her very voice.'

'That is nobody's wife,' the Shelni told the Skokie. 'That is just a little tune that I made up.'

'You play with my wife's voice, so you must have swallowed my wife,' the Skokie said. 'I will have to take you apart and see.'

'If I swallowed anybody's wife I'm sorry,' said the Shelni. 'Go ahead then.'

So the Skokie took the Shelni apart and scattered the pieces all over the hole and some of them on the grass outside. But he could not find any part of his wife.

'I have made a mistake,' said the Skokie. 'Who would have thought that one who had not swallowed my wife could make her voice on the flute!'

'It is all right,' said the Shelni, 'so long as you put me together again. I remember part of the way I go. If you remember the rest of the way, then you can put me together again.'

But neither of them remembered very well the way the Shelni was before he was taken apart. The Skokie put him together all wrong. There were not enough pieces for some parts and too many for others.

'Let me help,' said a Frog who was there. 'I remember where some of the parts go. Besides, I believe it was my own wife he swallowed. That was her voice on the flute. It was not a Skokie voice.'

The frog helped, and they all remembered what they could, but it did not work. Parts of the Shelni could not be found again, and some of the parts would not go into him at all. When they had him finished, the Shelni was in great pain and could hardly move, and he didn't look much like a Shelni.

'I've done all I can,' the Skokie said. 'That's the way you'll have to be. Where is Frog?'

'I'm inside,' said Frog.

'That's where you will have to stay,' the Skokie said. 'I've had enough of both of you. Enough, and these pieces left over. I will just take them with me. Maybe I can make someone else out of them.'

That is the way the Shelni still is, put together all wrong. In his wrong form he walks the country by night, being ashamed to go by day. Some folks are startled when they meet him, not knowing this story. He still plays his jug flute with the lost Skokie Wife's voice and with Frog's voice. Listen, you can hear it now! The Shelni goes in sorrow and pain because nobody knows how to put him together right.

The Skokie never did find his lost wife.

This is how it is told.

And then there was the second story that we recorded yesterday, the last story, though we did not know it then, that we would record of the Shelni:

The Singing Pigs

This is how they say it.

We have the ancient story of the singing pigs who sing so loud that they fly up into the sky on the tail of their own singing. Now we ourselves, if we can sing loud enough, if we can jug the flutes strong enough, if we can tang the tines deep enough, will get to be the Singing Pigs of our own story. Many already have gone away as Singing Pigs.

There come certain bell men with music carts. They play rangle-dangle Sky music. They come for love of us. And if we can hurry fast enough when they come we can go with them, we can ride a tin can over the sky.

Bong! bong! that is the bell man with the music cart now! All the Shelni hurry! This is the day you may get to go. Come all you Shelni from the valley and the stream and jump on the cart for the free ride. Come all the Shelni from the meadows and the woods. Come up from the tree roots and the holes underground. The Skokie don't get to go, the Frogs don't get to go, only the Shelni get to go.

Cry if the cart is too full and you don't get to go today, but don't cry too long. The bell men say that they will come back tomorrow and every day till there are no Shelni left at all.

'Come all you little Singing-Pig-Shelni,' a bell man shouts. 'Come get your free rides in the tin cans all the way to Earth! Hey, Ben, what other animal jumps onto the slaughter wagon when you only ring a bell? Come along little Shelni-Pigs, room for ten more on this wagon. That's all, that's all. We'll have lots more wagons going tomorrow. We'll take all of you, all of you! Hey, Ben, did you ever see little pigs cry when there's no more room for them on the slaughter wagon?' These are the high kind words that a bell man speak for love of us.

Not even have to give a burial tooth or other tooth to pay for the ride. Frogs can't go, Skokies can't go, only the Shelni get to go!

Here are the wonderful things! From the wagon, the Shelni get to go to one room where all their bones are taken out. This does never happen to Shelni before. In another room the Shelni are boiled down to only half their size, little as little-boy Shelni. Then they all get to play the game and crawl into the tin cans. And then they get their free ride in the tin cans all the way to Earth. Ride a tin can!

Wipe off your sticky tears you who miss the music cart to-day. Go to sleep early tonight and rise early tomorrow. Sing your loudest tomorrow so the bell men will know where to come. Jug the flutes very strong tomorrow, tang the tines deep, say *whoop! whoop!* here we are, bell men.

All laugh when they go with the bell men in the music cart. But there is story that someday a Shelni woman will cry instead of laugh when they take her. What can be the matter with this woman that she will cry? She will cry out 'Damn you, it's murder! They're almost people! You can't take them! They're as much people as I am. Double damn you, you can't take *me!* I'm human. I know I look as funny as they do but I'm human. Oh, oh, oh!' This is the funniest thing of the story, the prophecy thing part.

Oh, oh, oh, the woman will say, Oh, oh, oh, the jug flutes will echo it. What will be the matter with the Shelni woman who cries instead of laughs?

This is our last story, wherever it is told. When it is told for the last time, then there will be no more stories here, there will be no more Shelni. Who needs stories and jug flute music who can ride a tin can?

That is how it has been said.

Then we went out (for the last time, as it happened) from the Shelni burrow. And, as always, there was the riming with the five-year-old Ancient who guarded the place:

"What to crowing?"

"Got to going."

"Jinx on Jolly,
Golly, Holly!"

"Were it other,
Bug, my brother!"

"Holly crying.
Sing her flying,
Jugging, shouting."

"Going outing."

Now this was remarkable. Holly Harkel *was* crying when we came out of the burrow for the (as it happened) last time. She was crying great goblin tears. I almost expected them to be green.

Today I keep thinking how amazingly the late Holly Harkel had finally come to look like the Shelni. She *was* a Shelni. "It is all the same with me now," she said this morning. "Would it be love if they should go and I should stay?"

It is a sticky business. I tried to complain, but those people were still ringing that bell and chanting "All you little Pig-Shelni-Singers come jump on the cart. Ride a tin can to Earth! Hey, Ben, look at them jump on the slaughter wagon!"

"It was inexcusable," I said. "Surely you could tell a human from a Shelni."

"Not that one," said a bell ringer. "I tell you they all jumped on the wagon willingly, even the funny looking one who was crying. Sure, you can have her bones, if you can tell which ones they are."

I have Holly's bones. That is all. There was never a creature like her. And now it is over with.

But it is not over!

Singing Pig Breakfast Food Company, beware! There will be vengeance!

It has been told.

Aloys

He had flared up more brightly than anyone in memory. And then he was gone. Yet there was ironic laughter where he had been; and his ghost still walked. That was the oddest thing: to encounter his ghost.

It was like coming suddenly on Halley's Comet drinking beer at the Plugged Nickle Bar, and having it deny that it was a celestial phenomenon at all, that it had ever been beyond the sun.

For he could have been the man of the century, and now it was not even known if he was alive. And if he were alive, it would be very odd if he would be hanging around places like the Plugged Nickel Bar.

This all begins with the award. But before that it begins with the man.

Professor Aloys Foulcault-Oeg was acutely embarrassed and in a state of dread.

"These I have to speak to, all these great men. Is even glory worth the price when it must be paid in such coin?"

Aloys did not have the amenities, the polish, the tact. A child of penury, he had all his life eaten bread that was part sawdust, and worn shoes that were part cardboard. He had an overcoat that had been his father's, and before that his grandfather's, willed for generations to the eldest son.

This coat was no longer handsome, its holes being stuffed and quilted with ancient rags. It was long past its years of greatness, and even when Aloys had inherited it as a young man it was in the afternoon of its life. And yet it was worth more than anything else he owned in the world.

Professor Aloys had become great in spite of—or because of?—his poverty. He had worked out his finest theory, a series of nineteen interlocked equations of cosmic shapeliness and simplicity. He had worked it out on a great piece of butchers' paper soaked with lamb's blood, and had so given it to the world.

And once it was given, it was almost as though nothing else could be added on any subject whatsoever. Any further detailing would be only footnotes to it and all the sciences no more than commentaries.

Naturally this made him famous. But the beauty of it was that it made him famous, not to the commonalty of mankind (this would have been a burden to his sensitively tuned soul), but to a small and scattered class of extremely erudite men (about a score of them in the world). By them his worth was recognized, and their recognition brought him almost complete satisfaction.

But he was not famous in his own street or his own quarter. And it was in this stark conglomerate of dark-souled alleys and roofs that Professor Aloys had lived all his life till just thirty-seven days ago.

When he received the announcement, award, and invitation, he quickly calculated the time. It was not very long to allow for traveling halfway around the world. Being locked out of his rooms, as he often was, he was unencumbered with baggage or furniture, and he left for the ceremony at once.

With the announcement, award, and invitation, there had also been a check; but as he was not overly familiar with the world of finance or with the English language in which the check was drawn, he did not recognize it for what it was. Having used the back of it to write down a formula that had crept into his mind, he shoved the check, forgotten, into one of the pockets of his greatcoat.

For three days he rode the riverboat to the port city hidden and hungry. There he concealed himself on an ocean tramp. That he did not starve on this was due to the caprice of certain lowlifes who discovered him, for they made him stay hidden in a terrible bunker, and every day they passed in a bucket to him. And sometimes this contained food. But sometimes offal.

Then, several ports and many days later, he left the ship like a crippled, dirty animal. And it was in That City and on That Day. For the award was to be that evening.

"All these I have to speak to, all these wonderful men who are higher than grocers, higher even than the butchers. These men get more respect than a policeman, than a canal boat captain. They are wiser than a mayor and more honored than a merchant. They know arts more intricate than a clock-maker's and are virtuous beyond the politicians. More perspicacious than editors, more talented than actors, these are the great men of the world. And I am only Aloys, and now I am too ragged and dirty even to be Aloys anymore. I am no longer a man with a name."

For he was very humble as he walked the great town where even the shop girls dressed like princesses, and all the restaurants were so fine that only the rich people would have dared to go into them at all. Had there been poor people (and there were none) there would have been no place for them to eat. They would have starved.

"But it is to me that they have given the prize. Not to Schellendore and not to Ottleman, not to Francks nor Timiryaseff, not even to Piritim-Kess, the latchet of whose shoe I am not—but why do I say that?—he is not after all very bright—all of them are inadequate in some way—the only one who was ever able to get to the heart of these great things was Aloys Foulcault-Oeg, who happens to be myself. It is a strange thing that they should honor me, and yet I believe they could not have made a better choice."

So pride and fear warred in him, but it was always the pride that lost. For he had only a little bit of pride, undernourished and on quaking ground, and against it were a whole legion of fears, apprehensions, shames, dreads, embarrassments, and nightmarish bashfulnesses.

He begged a little bit when he found a poor part of town. But even here the people were of the rich poor, not of the poor as he had known them.

When he had money in his pocket, he had a meal. Then he went to the Jiffy Quick While You Wait Cleaners Open Day and Night to have his clothes cleaned. He wrapped himself in dignity and a blanket while he waited, as many years before he had had to forego the luxury of underclothes. And as the daylight was coming to an end they brought his clothes back to him.

"We have done all we could do," they told him. "If we had a day or a week or a month we might do a little more, but not much. We have not done anything at all to the greatcoat. The workers were afraid of it. They said it barked at them."

"Yes, sometimes it will do that."

Then he went out into the town, cleaner than he had been in many days, and he walked to the hall of the Commendation and Award. Here he watched all the great men arrive in private cars and taxis: Ergodic Eimer, August Angstrom, Vladimir Vor. He watched them and thought of what he would say to them, and then he realized that he had forgotten his English.

"I remember Sir or Madam as the Case May Be. I remember Dog, that is the first word I ever learned, but what will I say to them about a dog? I remember house and horse and apple and fish. Oh, now I remember the entire language. But what if I forget it again? Would it not be an odd speech if I could only say apple and fish and house and dog? I would be shamed."

He wished he were rich and could dress in fine white like the streetsweepers, or in black leather like the newsboy on the corner. He saw Edward Edelsteim and Christopher Cronin enter and he cowed on the street and knew that he would never be able to talk to those great men.

A fine gentleman came out and walked directly to him.

"You are the great Professor Foulcault-Oeg? I would have known you anywhere. True greatness shines from you. Our city is honored tonight. Come inside and we will go to a little room apart, for I see that you will have to compose yourself first. I am Graf-Doktor Hercule Bienville-Stravroguine."

Why he ever said he was the Graf-Doktor is a mystery, because he was Willy McGilly and the other was just a name that he made up that minute.

Within they went to a small room behind the cloak room. But here, in spite of the smooth kindness of the gracious gentleman, Aloys knew that he would never be able to compose himself. He was an épouvantail, a pugalo, a clown, a ragamuffin. He looked at the nineteen-point outline of the address he was to give. He shuddered and quaked, he gobbled like a turkey. He sniffled and he wiped his nose on his sleeve. He was terrified that the climax of his life's work should find him too craven to accept it. And he discovered that he had forgotten his English again.

"I remember bread and butter, but I don't know which one goes on top. I know pencil and penknife and bed, but I have entirely forgotten the word for maternal uncle. I remember plow, but what in the world will I say to all those great men about a plow? I pray that this cup may pass from me."

Then he disintegrated completely in one abject mass of terror.

Several minutes went by.

But when he emerged from that room he was a different man entirely. Erect, alive, intense, queerly handsome, and now in formal attire, he mounted with the sure grace of a panther to the speaker's platform.

Once only he glanced at the nineteen-point outline of his address. As there is no point in keeping it a secret, it was as follows: 1. Cepheid and Cerium—How long is a Yardstick? 2. Double Trouble—Is Ours a Binary Universe? 3. Cerebrum and Cortex—The Mathematics of Melancholia. 4. Microphysics and Megacyclic Polyneums. 5. *Ego, No, Hemeis*—The Personality of the Subconscious. 6. Linear Convexity and Lateral Intransigence. 7. Betelgeuse Betrayed—The Myth of Magnitude. 8. Mu-Meson, the Secret of the Metamorphosis. 9. Theogony and Tremor—The Mathematics of Seismology. 10. Planck's Constant and Agnesi's Variable. 11. Diencephalon and Di-Gamma—Unconscionable Thoughts About Consciousness. 12. Inverse Squares and the Quintesimal Radicals. 13. The Chain of Error in the Linear-B Translation—Or Where the Cretans Really Came From. 14. Cybernetics—Or a Brain for Every Man. 15. Ogive and Volute—Thoughts of Celestial Curvature. 16. Conic Sections—Small Pieces of Infinity. 17. Eschatology—Medium Thoughts About the End. 18. Hypolarity and Cosmic Hysterisis. 19. The Invisible Quadratic—or This Is All Simpler Than You Think.

You will immediately see the beauty of this skeleton, and yet to flesh it would not be the work of an ordinary man.

He glanced over it with a sure smile of complete confidence. Then he spoke softly to the master of ceremonies in a queer whisper with a rumble in it that could be heard throughout the Hall.

"I am here. I will begin. There is no need for any further introduction. It will be late by the time I finish."

For the next three and a half hours he held that intelligent audience completely spellbound, enchanted. They followed, or seemed to follow, his lightning flashes of metaphor illumining the craggy chasms of his vasty subjects.

They thrilled to the magnetic power of his voice, urbane yet untamed, with its polyglot phrasing and its bare touch of accent so strange as to be baffling; ancient surely and European, and yet from a land beyond the pale. And they quivered with interior pleasure at the glorious unfolding in climax after climax of these before only half-glimpsed vistas.

Here was the world of mystery revealed in all its wildness, and it obeyed and stood still, and he named its name. The nebula and the conch lay down together, and the ultra-galaxies equated themselves with the zeta mesons. Like the rich householder, he brought from his store treasures old and new, and nothing like them had ever been seen or heard before.

At one point Professor Timiryaseff cried out in bafflement and incomprehension, and Doctor Ergodic Eimer buried his face in his hands, for even those most erudite men could not glimpse all the shattering profundity revealed by the fantastic speaker.

And when it was over they were delighted that so much had been made known to them like a great free gift. They had the crown without the cross, and the odd little genius had filled them all with a rich glow.

The rest was perfunctory: commendations and testimonials from all the great men. The trophy, heavy and rich but not flashy, worth the lifetime salary of a professor of mathematics, was accepted almost carelessly. And then the cup was passed quietly, which is to say the tall cool glasses went around as the men lingered and talked with hushed pleasure.

"Gin," said the astonishing orator. "It is the drink of the bums and impoverished scholars, and I am both. Yes, anything at all with it."

Then he spoke to Maecenas, who was at his side, the patron who was footing the bill for all this gracious extravagance.

"The check I have never cashed, having been much in movement since I have received it. And as to me it is a large amount, though perhaps not to others, and as you yourself have signed it, I wonder if you would cash it for me now."

"At once," said Maecenas, "at once. Ten minutes and we shall have the sum here. Ah, you have endorsed it with a formula! Who but the Professor Aloys Foulcault-Oeg could be so droll? Look, he has endorsed it with a formula."

"Look, look, let us copy. Why, this is marvelous. It takes us even beyond his great speech of tonight. The implications of it!"

"Oh, the implications!" they said as they copied it off, and the implications rang in their heads like bells of the future.

Now it has suddenly become very late, and the elated little man with the gold and gemmed trophy under one arm and the packet of bank notes in his pocket disappeared as by magic.

Maecenas went to his villa in the province, which is to say Long Island. And all the Professors, Doctors, and erudite gentlemen went to their homes and lodgings.

But later, and after the excitement had worn off, none of them understood a thing about it at all, not even those who had comprehended part of it before the talk. And this was odd.

They'd been spooked.

Professor Aloys Foulcault-Oeg was not seen again; or, if seen, he was not known, for hardly anyone would have known his face. In fact, when he had painfully released the bonds by which he had been tied in the little room behind the back room, and had removed the shackles from his ankles, he did not pause at all. Not for many blocks did he even remove the gag from his mouth, not realizing in his confusion what it was that obstructed his speech and breathing. But when he got it out it was a pleasant relief.

A kind gentleman took him in hand, the second to do so that night. He was bundled into a kind of taxi and driven to a mysterious quarter called Wreckville. And deep inside a secret building he was given a bath and a bowl of hot soup. And later he gathered with others at the festive board.

Here Willy McGilly was king. As he worked his way into his cups, with the gold trophy in front of him, he expounded and elucidated.

"I was wonderful. I held them in the palm of my hand. Was I not wonderful, Oeg?"

"I could not hear all, for I was on the floor of the little room. But from what I could hear, yes, you were wonderful."

It wasn't supposed that Aloys made that speech, was it? It was stated that when he came out of that room he was a different man entirely. Nobody but Willy McGilly would give a talk like that.

"Only once in my life did I give a better speech," said Willy. "It was the same speech, but it was newer then. That was in Little Dogie, New Mexico, and I was selling a snake-oil derivative whose secret I yet cannot reveal. But I was good tonight and some of them cried. And now what will you do, Oeg? Do you know what we are?"

"*Moshennekov.*"

"Why, so we are!"

"*Schwindlern.*"

"The very word."

"Lowlife con men. And the world you live on is not the one you were born on. I will join you if I may."

"Oeg, you have a talent for going to the core of the apple."

For when a man (however unlikely a man) shows real talent, then the Wreckville bunch have to recruit him. They cannot have uncontrolled talent running loose in the commonalty of mankind.

Entire and Perfect Chrysolite

Having achieved perfection, we feel a slight unease. From our height we feel impelled to look down. We make our own place and there is nothing below us; but in our imagination there are depths and animals below us. To look down breeds cultishness.

There are the cults of the further lands and the further peoples. The Irish and Americans and Africans are respectable, philosophical and industrial parties, but the cultishness is something beyond. Any addition to the world would mar the perfect world which is the perfect thought of the Maker. Were there an Africa indeed, were there an Ireland, were there an America or an Atlantis, were there the Indies, then we would be other than we are. The tripartite unity that is the ecumene would be broken: the habitable world-island, the single eye in the head that is the world-globe would be voided.

There are those who say that our rational and perfect world should steep itself in this great unconscious geography of the under-mind, in the outré fauna and the incredible continents of the tortured imagination and of black legends. They pretend that this would give us depth.

We do not want depth. We want height! Let us seal off the under-things of the under-mind, and exalt ourselves! And our unease will pass.

Exaltation Philosophy—Audifax O'Hanlon

The *True Believer* was sailing offshore in an easterly direction in the latitude of fifteen degrees north and the longitude of twenty-four degrees east. To the north of the coasting ship was the beautiful Cinnamon Coast of Libya with its wonderful beaches and its remarkable hotels tawny in the distance. To the east and south and west were the white-topped waves that went on for ever and ever. The *True Believer* sailed along the southernmost edge of the ecumene, the habitable and inhabited world.

August Shackleton was drinking Roman Bomb out of a potbellied bottle and yelping happily as he handled the wheel of the *True Believer:*

"It's a kids' thing to do," he yipped, "but there were never such beautiful waters to do it in. We try to call in outer spirits. We try to call up inner spirits and lands. It's a children's antic. Why do we do it, Boyle, other than for the fun of it?"

"Should there be another reason, Shackleton? Well, there is; but we go about it awkwardly and without knowing what we're doing. The thing about humans which nobody apparently wishes to notice, is that we're a species which has never had an adult culture. We feel that lack more and more as we become truly adult in other ways. It grows tedious to stretch out a childhood forever. The easy enjoyments, the easy rationality, the easy governments and sciences, are really childish things. We master them while we are yet children, and we look beyond. But there *isn't anything* beyond the childishness, Shackleton. We must find a deeper view somehow. We are looking for that something deeper here."

"What? By going on a lark that is childish even to children, Boyle? I was ashamed in front of my sons when I confessed on what sort of diversion I was going. First there were the séances that we indulged in. If we raised any spirits there, they were certainly childish ones. And now we're on this voyage on the *True Believer*. We're looking for the geographical home of certain collective unconscious images! Why shouldn't the children hoot at us? Ah well, let us not be too ashamed. It's colorful and stimulating fun, but it isn't adult."

The other four members of the party, Sebastian Linter and the three wives, Justina Shackleton, Luna Boyle, and Mintgreen Linter, were swimming in the blue ocean. The *True Believer* was coasting very slowly and the four swimmers were clipped to outrigger towlines.

"There's something wrong with the water!" Justina Shackleton suddenly called up to her husband. "There's weeds in it, and there shouldn't be. There's reeds in it, and swamp grasses. There's mud. And there's green slime!"

"You're out of your lovely head, lovely," Shackleton called back. "It's all clear blue water off a sand coast. I can see fish twenty meters down. It's clear."

"I tell you it's full of green slime!" Justina called back. "It's so thick and heavy that it almost tears me away from the line. And the insects are so fierce that I have to stay submerged."

But they were off the Cinnamon Coast of Libya. They could smell the warm sand, and the watered gardens ashore. There was no mud, there was no slime, there were no insects off the Cinnamon Coast ever. It was all clear and bright as living, moving glass.

Sebastian Linter had been swimming on the seaward side of the ship. Now he came up ropes to the open deck of the ship, and he was bleeding.

"It *is* thick, Shackleton," he panted. "It's full of snags and it's dangerous. And that fanged hog could have killed me. Get the rest of them out of the water!"

"Linter, you can see for yourself that it is clear everywhere. Clear, and of sufficient depth, and serene."

"Sure, I see that it is, Shackleton. Only it isn't. What we are looking for has already begun. The illusion has already happened to all senses except sight. Stuff it, Shackleton! Get them out of the water! The snakes and the crocs will get them. The animals threshing around in the mud will get them. And if they try to climb up into the shore, the beasts there will break them up and tear them to pieces."

"Linter, we're two thousand meters off shore and everything is clear. But you are disturbed. Oof, so am I! The ship just grounded, and it's fifty meters deep here. All right, everyone! I order everybody except my wife to come out of the water! I request that she come out. I am unable to order her to do anything."

The other two women, Luna Boyle and Mintgreen Linter, came out of the water. And Justina Shackleton did not.

"In a while, August, in a while I come," Justina called up to the ship. "I'm in the middle of a puzzle here and I want to study it some more. August, can an hallucination snap you in two? He sure is making the motions."

"I don't know, lovely," August Shackleton called back to her doubtfully.

Luna Boyle and Mintgreen Linter had come out of the ocean up the ropes. Luna was covered with green slime and was bleeding variously. Mintgreen was covered with weeds and mud, and her hands and feet were torn. And she hobbled with pain.

"Is your foot broken, darling?" Sebastian Linter asked her with almost concern, "But, of course, it is all illusion."

"I have the illusion that my foot is broken," Mintgreen sniffled, "and I have the illusion that I am in very great pain. Bleeding blubberfish, I wish it were real! It couldn't really hurt this much."

"Oh, elephant hokey!" Boyle stormed. "These illusions are nonsense. There can't be such an ambient creeping around us. We're not experiencing anything."

"Yes we are, Boyle," Shackleton said nervously. "And your expression is an odd one at this moment. For the elephant was historical in the India that is, was fantastic in the further India that is fantastic, and is still more fanciful in its African contingency. In a moment we will try to conjure up the African elephant which is twice the mass of the historical Indian elephant. The ship is dragging badly now and might even break up if this continues, but the faro shows no physical contact. All right, the five of us on deck will put our heads together for this. You lend us a head too, Justina!"

"Take it, take my head. I'm about to let that jawful snapper have my body anyhow. August, this stuff is real! Don't tell me I imagine that smell," Justina called.

"We will all try to imagine that smell, and other things," August Shackleton stated as he uncorked another bottle of Roman Bomb. In the visible world there was still the Cinnamon Coast of Libya, and the blue ocean going on forever. But in another visible world, completely unrelated to the first and occupying absolutely a different space (but both occupying total space), were the green swamps of Africa, the sedgy shores going sometimes back into rain forests and sometimes into savannas, the moon mountains rising behind them, the air sometimes heavy with mist and sometimes clear with scalding light, the fifth levels of noises, the hundred levels of colors.

"The ambient is forming nicely even before we start," Shackleton purred. Some of them drank Roman Bomb and some of them Green Canary as they readied themselves for the psychic adventure.

"We begin the conjure," Shackleton said, "and the conjure begins with words. Our little group has been involved in several sorts of investigations, foolish ones perhaps, to discover whether there are (or more importantly, to be sure that there are not) physical areas and creatures beyond those of the closed ecumene. We have gone on knob-knockers, we have held séances. The séances in particular were grotesque, and I believe we were all uneasy and guilty about them. Our Faith forbids us to evoke spirits. But where does it forbid us to evoke geographies?"

"Ease up a little on the evoking!" Justina shrilled up at

them. "The snapper just took me off at the left ankle. I pray he doesn't like my taste."

"It has been a mystery for centuries," said August (somewhat disturbed by his wife's vulgar outburst from the ocean), "that out of the folk unconscious there should well up ideas of continents that are not in the world, continents with highly imaginary flora and fauna, continents with highly imaginary people. It is a further mystery that these psychic continents and islands should be given bearings, and that apparently sane persons have claimed to visit them. The deepest mystery of all is Africa. Africa, in Roman days, was a subdivision of Mauretania, which was a subdivision of Libya, one of the three parts of the world. And yet the entire coast of Libya has been mapped correctly for three thousand years, and there is no Africa beyond, either appended or separate. We prove the nonsense of it by sailing in clear ocean through the middle of that pretended continent."

"We prove the nonsense further by getting our ship mired in a swamp in the middle of the imaginary continent and seeing that continent begin to form about us," said Boyle. His Green Canary tasted funny to him. There was a squalling pungency in the air and something hair-raisingly foreign in the taste of the drink.

"This is all like something out of Carlo Forte," Linter laughed unsteadily.

"The continental ambient forms about us," said Shackleton. "Now we will evoke the creatures. First let us conjure the great animals: the rhinoceros, the lion, the leopard, the elephant, which all have Asian counterparts; but these of the contingent Africa are to be half again or twice the size, and incomparably fierce."

"We conjure them, we conjure them," they all chanted, and the conjured creatures appeared mistily.

"We conjure the hippopotamus, the water behemoth, with its great comical bulk, its muzzle like a scoop shovel, and its eyes standing up like big balls—"

"Stop it, August!" Justina Shackleton shrieked from the water. "I don't know whether the hippo is playful or not, but he's going to crush me in a minute."

"Come out of the water, Justina!" August ordered sternly.

"I will not. There isn't any ship left for me to come to. You're all sitting on a big, slippery, broken tree out over the water, and the snappers and boas are coming very near your legs and necks."

"Yes, I suppose so, one way of looking at it," August said. "Now everybody conjure the animals that are compounded out of grisly humor, the giraffe with a neck alone that is longer than a horse, and the zebra which is a horse in a clown suit."

"We conjure them, we conjure them," they all chanted.

"The zebra isn't as funny as I thought it would be," Boyle complained. "Nothing is as funny as I thought it would be."

"Conjure the great snake that is a thousand times heavier than other snakes, that can swallow a wild ass," Shackleton gave them the lead.

"We conjure it, we conjure it," they all chanted.

"August, it's over your head, reaching down out of the giant mimosa tree," Justina screamed warning from the swamp. "There's ten meters of it reaching down for you."

"Conjure the crocodile," Shackleton intoned. "Not the little crocodile of the River of Egypt, but the big crocodile of deeper Africa that can swallow a cow."

"We conjure it, we imagine it, we evoke it, and the swamps and estuaries in which it lives," they all chanted.

"Easy on that one," Justina shrilled. "He's been taking me by little pieces. Now he's taking me by big pieces."

"Conjure the ostrich," Shackleton intoned, "the bird that is a thousand times as heavy as other birds, that stands a meter taller than man, that kicks like a mule, the bird that is too heavy to fly. I wonder what delirium first invented such a wildlife as Africa's, anyhow?"

"We conjure it, we conjure it," they chanted.

"Conjure the great walking monkey that is three times as heavy as a man," August intoned. "Conjure a somewhat smaller one, two-thirds the size of man, that grins and gibbers and understands speech, that could speak if he wished."

"We conjure them, we conjure them."

"Conjure the third of the large monkeys that is dog-faced and purple of arse."

"We conjure it, we conjure it, but it belongs in a comic strip."

"Conjure the gentle monster, the okapi that is made out of pieces of the antelope and camel and contingent giraffe, and which likewise wears a clown suit."

"We conjure it, we conjure it."

"Conjure the multitudinous antelopes, koodoo, nyala, hartebeest, oryx, bongo, klipspringer, gemsbok, all so out of keeping with a warm country, all such grotesque takeoffs of the little alpine antelope."

"We conjure them, we conjure them."

"Conjure the buffalo that is greater than all other buffalo or cattle, that has horns as wide as a shield. Conjure the quagga. I forget its pretended appearance, but it cannot be ordinary."

"We conjure it, we conjure it."

"We come to the top of it all! Conjure the most anthropomorphic group in the entire unconsciousness: men who are men indeed, but who are as black as midnight in a hazel grove, who are long of ankle and metatarsus and lower limb so they can run and leap uncommonly, who have crumpled hair and are massive of feature. Conjure another variety that are only half as tall as men. Conjure a third sort that are short of stature and prodigious of hips."

"We conjure them, we conjure them," they all chanted. "They are the caricatures from the beginning."

"But can all these animals appear at one time?" Boyle protested. "Even on a contingent continent dredged out of the folk unconsciousness there would be varieties of climates and land-form. All would not be together."

"This is rhapsody, this is panorama, this is Africa," said Luna Boyle.

And they were all totally in the middle of Africa, on a slippery bole of a broken tree that teetered over a green swamp. And the animals were around them in the rain forests and the savannas, on the shore, and in the green swamp. And a man black as midnight was there, his face broken with emotion.

Justina Shackleton screamed horribly as the crocodile sliced her in two. She still screamed from inside the gulping beast as one might scream under water.

2

The Ecumene, the world island, has the shape of an egg 110° from East to West and 45° from North to South. It is scored into three parts, Europa, Asia, and Libya. It is scored by the incursing seas, Europa from Asia by the Pontus and the Hyrcanum Seas, Asia from Libya by the Persian Sea, and Libya from Europa by the Tyrrhenian and Ionian Seas (the Mediterranean Complex). The most westerly part of the world is Coruna in Iberia or Spain, the most northerly is Kharkovsk in Scythia or Russia, the most easterly is Sining in Han or China, the most southerly is the Cinnamon Coast of Libya.

The first chart of the world, that of Eratosthenes, was thus, and it was perfect. Whether he had it from primitive revelation or from early exploration, it was correct except in minor detail. Though Britain seems to have been charted as

*an Island rather than a Peninsula, this may be an error of an
early copyist. A Britain unjoined to the Main would shrivel,
as a branch hewed from a tree will shrivel and die. There are
no viable islands.*

*All islands fade and drift and disappear. Sometimes they
reappear briefly, but there is no life in them. The juice of life
flows through the continent only. It is the One Land, the Living and Holy Land, the Entire and Perfect Jewel.*

*Thus, Ireland is seen sometimes, or Hy-Brasil, or the
American rock-lands: but they are not always seen in the
same places, and they do not always have the same appearances. They have neither life nor reality.*

*The secret geographies and histories of the American Soci-
ety and the Atlantis Society and such are esoteric lodge-
group things, symbolic and murky, forms for the initiated;
they contain analogs and not realities.*

*The ecumene must grow, of course, but it grows inwardly
in intensity and meaning; its form cannot change. The form
is determined from the beginning, just as the form of a man
is determined before he is born. A man does not grow by add-
ing more limbs or heads. That the ecumene should grow ap-
pendages would be as grotesque as a man growing a tail.*
       World as Perfection—Diogenes Pontifex.

August Shackleton guffawed nervously when his wife was
sliced in two and the half of her swallowed by the crocodile;
and his hand that held the Roman Bomb trembled. Indeed,
there was something unnerving about the whole thing. That
cutoff screaming of Justina Shackleton had something shock-
ing and unpleasant about it.

Justina had once gone hysterical at a séance when the
ghosts and appearances had been more or less conventional,
but August was never sure just how sincere her hysteria was.
Another time she had disappeared for several days from a
séance, from a locked room, and had come back with a
roguish story about being in spirit land. She was a high-
strung clown with a sense of the outrageous, and this present
business of being chopped in two was typical of her creations.

And suddenly they were all explosively creative, each one's
subjective patterns intermingling with those of the other to
produce howling chaos. What had been the ship the *True Believer,* what had been the slippery overhanging bole, had now
come dangerously down into the swamp. They all wanted a
closer look.

There was screaming and trumpeting, there was color and
surge and threshing mass. The crocodile bellowed as a bull

might, not at all as Shackleton believed that a croc should
sound. But someone there had the idea that a crocodile
should bellow like that, and that someone had imposed his
ideate on the others. Unhorselike creatures whinnied, and
vivid animals sobbed and gurgled.

"Go back up, go back up!" the black man was bleating.
"You will all be killed here."

His face was a true Mummers-Night black-man mask. One
of the party was imagining strongly in that stereotyped form.
But the incongruous thing about the black man was that he
was gibbering at them in French, in bad French as though it
were his weak second language. Which one of them was
linguist enough to invent such a black French on the edge of
the moment? Luna Boyle, of course. But why had she put
grotesque French into the mouth of a black man in contingent Africa?

"Go back up, go back up," the black man cried. He had
an old rifle from the last century and he was shooting the
crocodile with it.

"Hey, he's shooting Justina too," Mintgreen giggled too
gaily. "Half of her is in the dragon thing. Oh, she will have
some stories to tell about this! She has the best imagination
of all of us."

"Let's get her out and together again," Linter suggested.
They were all shouting too loudly and too nervously. "She's
missing the best part of it."

"Here, here, black man," Shackleton called. "Can you get
the half of my wife out of that thing and put her together
again?"

"Oh, white people, white people, this is real and this is
death," the black man moaned in agony. "This is a closed
wild area. You should not be here at all. However you have
come here, whatever is the real form of that balk or tree on
which you stand so dangerously, be gone from here if you
can do it. You do not know how to live in this. White people,
be gone! It is your lives!"

"One can command a fantasy," said August Shackleton.
"Black man fantasy, I command that you get the half of my
wife out of that dying creature and put her together again."

"Oh, white people on dope, I cannot do this," the black
man moaned. "She is dead. And you joke and drink Green
Bird and Bomb, and hoot like demented children in a
dream."

"We are in a dream, and you are of the dream," Shackleton said easily. "And we may experiment with our dream
creatures. That is our purpose here. Here, catch a bottle of

Roman Bomb!" and he threw it to the black man, who caught it.

"Drink it," said Shackleton. "I am interested in seeing whether a dream figure can make incursion on physical substance."

"Oh, white people on dope," the black man moaned. "The watering place is no place for you to be. You excite the animals, and then they kill. When they are excited it is danger to me also who usually move among them easily. I have to kill the crocodile who is my friend. I do not want to kill others. I do not want more of you to be killed."

The black man was booted and jacketed quite in the manner of a hunting store outfitting, this possibly by the careful imagining of Boyle who loved hunting rig. The black Mummers-Night mask was contorted in agony and apprehension, but the black man did drink the Roman Bomb nervously the while he begged them to be gone from that place.

"You will notice that the skull form is quite human and the bearing completely erect," Linter said. "You will notice also that he is less hairy than we are and is thick of lip, while the great ape is more hairy and thin of lip. I had imagined them to be the same creature differently interpreted."

"No, you imagine them to be as they appear," Shackleton said. "It is your imagining of these two creatures that we are watching."

"But notice the configuration of the tempora and the mandible shape," Linter protested, "—not what I expected."

"You are the only one of us who knows about tempora and mandible shape," said Shackleton. "I tell you that it *is* your own imagery. He is structured by you, given the conventional Mummers-Night black-mask by all of us, clothed by Boyle, and speeched by Luna Boyle. His production is our joint effort. Watch it, everyone! It becomes dangerous now, even explosive! Man, I'm getting as hysterical as my wife! The dream is so vivid that it has its hooks in me. Ah, it's a great investigative experience, but I doubt if I'll want to return to this particular experience again. Green perdition! But it does become dangerous! Watch out, everyone!"

Ah, it *had* become wild: a hooting and screaming and bawling wild Africa bedlam, a green and tawny dazzle of fast-moving color, pungent animal stench of fear and murder, acrid smell of human fear.

A lion defiled the watering place, striking down a horned buck in the muddy shallows and going muzzle-deep into the hot-colored gore. A hippo erupted out of the water, a behemoth from the depths. Giraffes erected like crazily articulated derricks and galloped ungainly through the boscage.

"Enough of this!" cried Mintgreen Linter. Frightened, she took the lead, incanting:

"That the noon-time nightmare pass! The crocodile-dragon and the behemoth."

"We abjure them, we abjure them," they all chanted in various voices.

"That the black man and the black ape pass, and all black things of the black-green land."

"We abjure them, we abjure them," they chanted. But the black man was already down under the feet and horns of a buffalo creature, dead, and his last rifle shot still echoing. He had tried to prevent the buffalo from upsetting the teetering bole and dumping all the white people into the murder swamp. The great ape was also gone, terrified, back to his high-grass savannas. Many of the other creatures had disappeared or become faint, and there was again the tang of salt water and of distant hot-sand beaches.

"That the lion be gone who roars by day," Luna Boyle took up the incantation, "and the leopard who is Pan-Ther, the all-animal of grisly mythology. That the crushing snakes be gone, and the giant ostrich, and the horse in the clown suit."

"We abjure them all, we abjure them all," everybody chanted.

"That the *True Believer* form again beneath our feet in the structure we can see and know," August Shackleton incanted.

"We conjure it up, we conjure it up," they chanted, and the *True Believer* rose again barely above the threshold of the senses.

"That the illicit continents fade, and all the baleful islands of our writhing under-minds!" Boyle blurted in some trepidation.

"We abjure them, we abjure them," they all chanted contritely. And the illicit Africa had now become quite fragile, while the Cinnamon Coast of South Libya started to form as if behind green glass.

"Let us finish it! It lingers unhealthily!" Shackleton spoke loudly with resolve. "Let us drop our reservations! That we dabble no more in this particular illicitness! That we go no more hungering after strange geographies that are not of proper world! That we seal off the unsettling things inside us!"

"We seal them off, we seal them off," they chanted.

And it was finished.

They were on the *True Believer*, sailing in an easterly direction off the Cinnamon Coast of Libya. To the north was that lovely coast with its wonderful beaches and remarkable hotels. To the south and east were the white-topped waves that went on for ever and ever. It was over with, but the incantation had shaken them all with the sheer psychic power of it.

"Justina isn't with us," Luna Boyle said nervously. "She isn't on the *True Believer* anywhere. Do you think something has happened to her? Will she come back?"

"Of course she'll come back," August Shackleton purred. "She was truant from a séance for two days once. Oh, she'll have some good ones to tell when she does come back, and I'll rather enjoy the vacation from her. I love her, but a man married to an *outré* wife needs a rest from it sometimes."

"But look, look!" Luna Boyle cried. "Oh, she's impossible! She always did carry an antic too far. That's in bad taste."

The severed lower half of Justina Shackleton floated in the clear blue water beside the *True Believer*. It was bloodied and gruesome and was being attacked by slashing fishes.

"Oh, stop it, Justina!" August Shackleton called angrily. "What a woman! Ah, I see it now. We turn to land."

It was the opening to the Yacht Basin, the channel through the beach shallows to the fine harbor behind. They tacked, they turned, they nosed in towards the Cinnamon Coast of Libya.

The world was intact again, one whole and perfect jewel, lying wonderful to the north of them. And south was only great ocean and great equator and empty places of the under-mind. The *True Believer* came to port passage with the perfect bright noon-time on all things.

Incased in Ancient Rind

1

The eye is robbed of impetus
By Fogs that stand and shout:
And swiftness all goes out from us
And all the stars go out.

Lost Skies——O'Hanlon

"Wear a mask or die," the alarmists had been saying louder and louder; and now they were saying "Wear a mask and die anyhow." And why do we so often hold the alarmists in contempt? It isn't always a false alarm they sound, and this one wasn't. The pollution of air and water and land had nearly brought the world to a death halt, and crisis was at hand as the stifling poison neared critical mass.

"Aw, dog dirt, not another air pollution piece," you say.

Oh, come off of it. You know us better than that. This is not such an account as you might suppose. It will not be stereotype, though it may be stereopticon.

"The lights are burning very brightly," said Harry Baldachin, "this club room is sealed off as tightly as science can seal it, the air conditioning labors faithfully, the filters are the latest perfection, this is the clearest day in a week (likely a clearer day than any that will ever follow), yet we have great difficulty in seeing each other's face across the table. And we are in Mountain Top Club out in the high windy country beyond the cities. It is quite bad in the towns, they say. Suffocation victims are still lying unburied in heaps."

"There's a curious thing about that though," Clement Flood said. "The people are making much progress on the unburied heaps. People aren't dying as fast as they were even a month ago. Why aren't they?"

"Don't be so truculent about it, Clement," Harry said. "The people will die soon enough. All the weaker ones have already died, I believe, and the strong ones linger awhile; but I don't see how any of us can have lungs left. There'll be another wave of deaths, and then another and another. And all of us will go with it."

"I won't," said Sally Strumpet. "I will live forever. It doesn't bother me very much at all: just makes my nose and eyes itch a little bit. What worries me, though, is that I don't test fertile yet. Do you suppose that the pollution has anything to do with my not being fertile?"

"What are you chattering about, little girl?" Charles Broadman asked. "Well, it is something to think about. Gathering disasters usually increase fertility, as did the pollution disaster at first. It has always been as though some cosmic wisdom was saying 'Fast and heavy fruit now for the fruitless days ahead.' But now it seems as if the cosmic wisdom is saying 'Forget it, this is too overmuch.' But fertility now is not so much inhibited as delayed," Broadman continued almost as if he knew what he was talking about.

Sally Strumpet was a bright-eyed (presently red-eyed) seventeen-year-old actress, and that was her stage name only. Her real name was Joan Struthio, and she was met for club dinner with Harry Baldachin, Clement Flood, and Charles Broadman, all outstanding in the mentality set, because she had a publicity man who arranged such things. Sally herself belonged to the mentality set by natural right, but not many suspected this fact: only Charles Broadman of those present, only one in a hundred of those who were entranced by Sally's rather lively simpering, hardly any of the mucous-lunged people.

"This may be the last of our weekly dinners that I am able to attend," Harry Baldachin coughed. "I'd have taken to my bed long ago except that I can't breathe at all lying down any more. I'm a dying man now, as are all of us."

"I'm not, neither the one nor the other," Sally said.

"Neither is Harry," Charles Broadman smiled snakishly, "not the first, surely, and popular doubt has been cast on the second. You're not dying, Harry. You'll live till you're sick of it."

"I'm sick of it now. By my voice you know that I'm dying."

"By your voice I know that there's a thickening of the pharynx," Charles said. "By your swollen hands I know that there is already a thickening of the metacarpals and phalanges, not to mention the carpals themselves. Your eyes seem unnaturally deep-set now as though they had decided to withdraw into some interior cave. But I believe that it is the thickening of your brow ridges that makes them seem so, and the new bulbosity of your nose. You've been gaining weight, have you not?"

"I have, yes, Broadman. Every pound of poison that I take in adds a pound to my weight. I'm dying, and we're all dying."

"Why Harry, you're coming along amazingly well. I thought I would be the first of us to show the new signs, and instead it is yourself. No, you will be a very, very long time dying."

"The whole face of the earth is dying," Harry Baldachin maintained.

"Not dying. Thickening and changing," said Charles Broadman.

"There's a mortal poison on everything," Clement Flood moaned. "When last was a lake fish seen not floating belly upward? The cattle are poisoned and all the plants, all dying."

"Not dying. Growing larger and weirder," said Broadman.

"I am like a dish that is broken," said the Psalmist, "my strength has failed through affliction, and my bones are consumed. I am forgotten like the unremembered dead."

"Your dish is made thicker and grosser, but it is not broken," Broadman insisted. "Your bones are not consumed but altered. And you are forgotten only if you forget."

"Poor Psalmist," said Sally. This was startling, for the Psalmist had always been a private joke of Charles Broadman, but now Sally was aware of him also. "Why, your strength hasn't failed at all," she said. "You come on pretty strong to me. But my own nose is always itching, that's the only bad part of it. I feel as though I were growing a new nose. When can I come to another club supper with you gentlemen?"

"There will be no more," Harry Baldachin hacked through his thickened pharynx. "We'll all likely be dead by next week. This is the last of our meetings."

"Yes, we had better call our dinners off," Clement Flood choked. "We surely can't hold them every week now."

"Not every week," said Charles Broadman, "but we will still hold them. This all happened before, you know."

"I want to come however often they are," Sally insisted.

"How often will we hold them, dreamer, and we all near dead?" Harry asked. "You say that this has happened before, Broadman? Well then, didn't we all die with it before?"

"No. We lived an immeasurably long time with it before," Charles Broadman stated. "What, can you not read the signs in the soot yet, Harry?"

"Just how often would you suggest that we meet then, Charles?" Clement Flood asked with weary sarcasm.

"Oh, how about once every hundred years, gentlemen and Sally. Would that be too often?"

"Fool," Harry Baldachin wheezed and peered out from under his thickening orbital ridges.

"Idiot," Clement Flood growled from his thickening throat.

"Why, I think a hundred years from today would be perfect," Sally cried. "That will be a Wednesday, will it not?"

"That was fast," Broadman admired. "Yes, it will be a Wednesday, Sally. Do be here, Sally, and we will talk some more of these matters. Interesting things will have happened in the meanwhile. And you two gentlemen will be here?"

"No, don't refuse," Sally cut in. "You are so unimaginative about all this. Mr. Baldachin, say that you will dine with us here one hundred years from today if you are alive and well."

"By the emphyseman God that afflicts us, and me dying and gone, yes, I will be here one hundred years from today if I am alive and well," Harry Baldachin said angrily. "But I will not be alive this time next week."

"And you say it also, Mr. Flood," Sally insisted.

"Oh, stop putting fools' words in peoples' mouths, little girl. Let me die in my own phlegm."

"Say it, Mr. Flood," Sally insisted again, "say that you will dine with us all here one hundred years from this evening if you are alive and well."

"Oh, all right," Clement Flood mumbled as he bled from his rheumy eyes. "Under those improbable conditions I will be here."

But only Sally and Charles Broadman had the quick wisdom to understand that the thing was possible.

Fog, smog, and grog, and the people perished. And the more stubborn ones took a longer time about perishing than the others. But a lethal mantle wrapped the whole globe now. It was poison utterly compounded, and no life could stand against it. There was no possibility of improvement, there was no hope of anything. It could only get worse. Something drastic had to happen.

And of course it got worse. And of course something drastic happened. The carbon pollution on earth reached trigger mass. But it didn't work out quite as some had supposed that it might.

2

We shamble through our longish terms
Of Levallosian mind
Till we be ponderous Pachyderms
Incased in ancient rind.

Lost Skies——O'Hanlon

Oh, for one thing, no rain, or almost no rain fell on the earth for that next hundred years. It was not missed. Moisture was the one thing that was in abounding plenty.

"But a mist rose from the earth and watered all the surface of the ground."

Rainless rain forests grew and grew. Ten million cubic miles of seawater rose to the new forming canopy and hung there in a covering world-cloud no more than twenty miles up. Naturally the sun and moon and stars were seen no more on the earth for that hundred years; and the light that did come down through the canopy seemed unnatural. But plants turned into giant plants and spread over the whole earth, gobbling the carbon dioxide with an almost audible gnashing.

So there was more land, now, and wetter land. There was a near equipoise of temperature everywhere under the canopy. The winds were all gathered up again into that old leather bag and they blew no more on the earth. Beneath the canopy it was warm and humid and stifling from pole to pole and to the utmost reaches of the earth.

It was a great change and everything felt it. Foot-long saurians slid out of their rocks that were warm and moist again: and gobbled and grew, and gobbled and grew, and gobbled and grew. Old buried fossil suns had been intruded into the earth air for a long time, and now the effect of their carbon and heat was made manifest. Six-foot-diameter turtles, having been ready to die, now postponed that event: and in another hundred years, in two hundred, they would be ten-foot-diameter turtles, thirteen-foot-diameter turtles.

The canopy, the new lowering copper-colored sky, shut out the direct sun and the remembered blue sky, and it shut out other things that had formerly trickled down: hard radiation, excessive ultraviolet rays and all the actinic rays, and triatomic oxygen. These things had been the carriers of the short and happy life, or the quick and early death; and these things were no longer carried down.

There was a thickening of bone and plate on all boned creatures everywhere, as growth continued for added years. There were new inhibitors and new stimulants; new bodies for old—no, no—older bodies for old. Certain teeth in cerain beasts had always grown for all the beast life. Now the beast life was longer, and the saber-tooths appeared again.

It was murky under the new canopy, though. It took a long time to get used to it—and a long time was provided. It was a world filled with fogs, and foggy phrases.

'A very ancient and fish-like smell.'

'Just to keep her from the foggy foggy dew.'

'There were giants on the earth in those days.'

'When Enos was ninety years old, he became the father of Cainan. Enos lived eight hundred and fifteen years after the birth of Cainan, and had other sons and daughters.'

'Behold now Behemoth, which I have made with thee.'

'And beauty and length of days.'

'There Leviathan ... stretched like a promotory sleeps or swims.'

'I will restore to you the years that the locust has eaten.'

"A land where the light is as darkness," said Job.

"Poor Job," said Sally Strumpet.

"This is my sorrow, that the right hand of the Most High is changed," said the Psalmist.

"Poor Psalmist," said Sally Strumpet.

The world that was under the canopy of the lowering sky was very like a world that was under water. Everything was incomparably aged and giantized and slow. Bears grew great. Lizards lengthened. Human people broadened and grew in their bones, and lengthened in their years.

"I suppose that we are luckier than those who come before or after," Harry Baldachin said. "We had our youths, we had much of our proper lives, and then we had this."

This was a hundred years to a day (a Wednesday, was it not?) since that last club dinner, and the four of them, Harry Baldachin, Clement Flood, Charles Broadman, and Sally Strumpet were met once more in the Mountain Top Club. Two of them, it will be remembered, hadn't expected to be there.

"What I miss most in these last nine or ten decades is colors," Clement Flood mused. "Really, we haven't colors, not colors as we had when I was young. Too much of the sun is intercepted now. Such aviators as still go up (the blue-sky hobbyists and such) say that there are still true colors above the canopy, that very ordinary objects may be taken up there and examined, and that they will be in full color as in ancient times. I believe that the loss of full color was understood by earlier psychologists and myth makers. In my youth, in my pre-canopy youth, I made some studies of very ancient photography. It was in black and white and gray only, just as most dreams were then in black and white and gray only. It is strange that these two things nearly anticipated the present world: we are so poor in color that we nearly fall back to the old predictions. No person under a hundred years old, unless he has flown above the canopy, has ever seen real color. But I will remember it."

"I remember wind and storm," said Harry Baldachin, "and these cannot now be found in their real old form even by going above the canopy. I remember frost and snow, and these are very rare everywhere on earth now. I remember rain, that most inefficient thing ever—but it's pleasant in memory."

"I remember lightning," said Charles Broadman, "and thunder. Ah, thunder."

"Well, it's more than made up for in amplitude," Clement smiled. "There is so much more of the earth that is land now, and all the land is gray and growing—I had almost used the old phrase 'green and growing,' but the color green can be seen now only by those who ascend above the canopy. But the world is warm and moist from pole to pole now, and filled with giant plants and giant animals and giant food. The canopy above, and the greenhouse diffusion effect below, it makes all the world akin. And the oceans are so much more fertile now—one can almost walk on the backs of the fish. There is such a lot more carbon in the carbon cycle than there used to be, such a lot more life on the earth. And more and more carbon is being put into the cycle every year."

"That's true," said Harry Baldachin. "That's about the only industrialism that is still being carried out, the only industrialism that is still needed: burning coal and petroleum to add carbon to the cycle, burning it by the tens of thousands of cubic miles. Certain catastrophes of the past had buried great amounts of this carbon, had taken it out of the cycle, and the world was so much poorer for it. It was as if the fruit of whole suns had been buried uselessly in the earth. Now, in the hundred years since the forming or the reforming of the canopy, and to a lesser extent during the two hundred years before its forming, these buried suns have been dug up and put to use again."

"The digging up of buried suns has caused all manner of mischief," Charles Broadman said.

"You are an old fogy, Charles," Clement Flood told him. "A hundred years of amplitude have made no change at all in you."

The hundred years had really made substantial changes in all of them. They hadn't aged exactly, not in the old way of aging. They had gone on growing in a new, or a very old way. They had thickened in face and body. They had become more sturdy, more solid, more everlasting. Triatomic oxygen, that old killer, was dense in the world canopy, shutting out the other killers; but it was very rare at ground level, a perfect arrangement. There was no wind under the canopy, and things held their levels well. How long persons might live now could only be guessed. It might be up to a thousand years.

"And how is the—ah—younger generation?" Harry Baldachin asked. "How are you, Sally? We have not seen you for a good round century."

"I am wonderful, and I thought you'd never ask. People take so much longer to get to the point now, you know. The most wonderful news is that I now test fertile. When I was seventeen I worried that I didn't test out. The new times had already affected me, I believe. But now my term has come around, and about time I'd say. I'm a hundred and seventeen and there are cases of girls no more than a hundred who are ready. I will marry this very week and will have sons and daughters. I will marry one of the last of the aviators who goes above the canopy. I myself have gone above the canopy and seen true colors and felt the thin wind."

"It's not a very wise thing to do," said Harry. "They are going to put a stop to flights above the canopy, I understand. They serve no purpose; and they are unsettling."

"Oh, but I want to be unsettled," Sally cried.

"You should be old enough not to want any such thing, Sally," Clement Flood advised. "We are given length of days now, and with them wisdom should come to us."

"Well, *has* wisdom come?" Charles Broadman asked reasonably. "No, not really. Only slowness has come to us."

"Yes, wisdom, we have it now," Harry Baldachin insisted. "We enter the age of true wisdom. Long wisdom. Slow wisdom."

"You are wrong, and unwise," Charles Broadman said out of his thickened and almost everlasting face. "There is not, there has never been any such name or thing as unqualified Wisdom. And there surely are not such things as Long Wisdom or Slow Wisdom."

"But there *is* a thing named Swift Wisdom," Sally stated with great eagerness.

"There was once, there is not now, we lost it," Charles Broadman said sadly.

"We almost come to disagreement," Baldachin protested, "and that is not seemly for persons of the ample age. Ah well, we have lingered five hours over the walnuts and the wine, and perhaps it were the part of wisdom that we leave each other now. Shall we make these dinners a regular affair?"

"I want to," Sally said.

"Yes, I'd rather like to continue the meetings at regular intervals," Clement Flood agreed.

"Fine, fine," Charles Broadman murmured. "We will meet here again one hundred years from this evening."

3

And some forget to leave or let
And some forget to die:
But may my right hand wither yet
If I forget the sky.

Lost Skies———O'Hanlon

We are not so simple as to say that the Baluchitherium returned. The Baluchitherium was of an earlier age of the earth

and flourished under an earlier canopy. Something that
looked very like the Baluchitherium did appear, however. It
was not even of the rhinoceros family. It was a horse grown
giant and gangly. Horses of course, being artificial animals
like dogs, are quite plastic and adaptable. A certain upper-
lippiness quickly appeared when this new giant animal had
turned into a giant leaf eater and sedge eater ("true" grass
had about disappeared: how could it compete with the richer
and fuller plants that flourished under the canopy?); a certain
spreading of the hoofs, a dividedness more of appearance
than of fact, was apparent after this animal had become a
swamp romper. Well, it was a giant horse and a mighty suc-
culent horse, but it looked like the Baluchitherium of old.

We are not so naive as to accept that the brontosaurus
came back. No. But there was a small flatfooted lizard that
quickly became a large flatfooted lizard and came to look
more and more like the brontosaurus. It came to look like
this without changing anything except its size and its general
attitude towards the world. Put a canopy over any creature
and it will look different without much intrinsic change.

We surely are not gullible enough to believe that the
crinoid plants returned to the ponds and the slack water
pools. Well, but certain conventional long-stemmed water
plants had come to look and behave very like the crinoids.

All creatures and plants had made their peace with the canopy, or they had perished. The canopy, in its two hundredth
year, was a going thing; and the blue-sky days had ended
forever.

There was still vestigial organic nostalgia for the blue-sky
days, however. Most land animals still possessed eyes that
would have been able to see full colors if there were such
colors to be seen; man himself still possessed such eyes. Most
food browsers still possessed enough crown to their teeth to
have grazed grass if such an inefficient thing as grass had remained. Many human minds would still have been able to
master the mathematics of stellar movements and positions,
if ease and the disappearance of the stellar content had not
robbed them of the inclination and opportunity for such
things.

(There was, up to about two hundred years ago, a rather
cranky pseudo-science named astronomy.)

There were other vestiges that hung like words in the fog
and rank dew of the world.

'And the name of the star is called Wormwood.'

'In the brightness of the saints, before the day-star."

'It was the star-eater who came, and then the sky-eater.'

"And the stars are not clear in his sight," said Job.

"Poor Job," said Sally.

The second hundred years had gone by, and the diners had met at Mountain Top Club again. And an extra diner was with them.

"Poor Sally," said Harry Baldachin. "You are still a giddy child, and you have already had sons and daughters. But you should not have brought your husband to this dinner without making arrangements. You could have proposed it this time, and had him here the next time. After all, it would only be a hundred years."

We are not so soft-headed as to say that the Neanderthal Men had returned. But the diners at Mountain Top Club, with that thickening of their faces and bones and bodies that only age will bring, had come to look very like Neanderthals—even Sally a little.

"But I wanted him here this time," Sally said. "Who knows what may happen in a hundred years?"

"How could anything happen in a hundred years?" Harry Baldachin asked.

"Besides, your husband is in ill repute," Clement Flood said with some irritation. "He's said to be an outlaw flyer. I believe that a pickup order for his arrest was put out some six years ago, so he may be picked up at any time. In the blue-sky days he would have been picked up within twenty-four hours, but we move more graciously and slowly under the canopy."

"It's true that there's a pickup order out for me," said the husband. "It's true that I still fly above the canopy, which is now illegal. I doubt if I'll be able to do it much longer. I might be able to get my old craft up one more time, but I don't believe I would be able to get it down. I'll leave if you want me to."

"You will stay," Charles Broadman said. "You are a member of the banquet now, and you and I and Sally have them outnumbered."

The husband of Sally was a slim man. He did not seem to be properly thickened to joint and bone. It was difficult to see how he could live a thousand years with so slight a body. Even now he showed a certain nervousness and anxiety, and that did not bode a long life.

"Why should anyone want to go above the canopy?" Harry Baldachin asked crossly. "Or rather, why should anyone want to claim to do it, since it is now assumed that the canopy is endless and no one could go above it?"

"But we do go above it," Sally stated. "We go for the sun and the stars; for the thin wind there which is a type of the old wind; for the rain even—do you know that there is sometimes rain passing between one part of the canopy and another?—for the rainbow—do you know that we have actually seen a rainbow?"

"I know that the rainbow is a sour myth," Baldachin said.

"No, no, it's real," Sally swore. "Do you recall the lines of the old Vachel Lindsay: 'When my hands and my hair and my feet you kissed/When you cried with your love's new pain/What was my name in the dragon mist/In the rings of rainbowed rain?' Is that not wonderful?"

Harry Baldachin pondered it a moment.

"I give it up, Sally," he said then. "I can't deduce it. Well, what's the answer to the old riddle? What is the cryptic name that we are supposed to guess?"

"Forgive him," Charles Broadman murmured to the husband and to Sally. "We have all of us been fog-bound for too long a time below the canopy."

"It is now believed that the canopy has always been there," Baldachin said stiffly.

"Almost always, Harry, but not always," Charles Broadman answered him. "It was first put there very early, on the second day, as a matter of fact. You likely do not remember that the second day is the one that God did not call good. It was surely a transient and temporary backdrop that was put there to be pierced at the proper times by early death and by grace. One of the instants it was pierced was just before this present time. It had been breached here and there for short ages. Then came the clear instant, which has been called glaciation or flood or catastrophe, when it was shattered completely and the blue sky was seen supreme. It was quite a short instant, some say it was not more than ten thousand years, some say it was double that. It happened, and now it is gone. But are we expected to forget that bright instant?"

"The law expects you to forget that instant, Broadman, since it never happened, and it is forbidden to say that it happened," Baldachin stated stubbornly. "And you, man, the outlaw flyer, it is rumored that you have your craft hidden somewhere on this very mountain. Ah, I must leave you all for a moment."

They sat for some five hours over the walnuts and wine. It is the custom to sit for a long time after eating the heavy steaks of any of the neo-saurians. Baldachin returned and left several times, as did Flood. They seemed to have something going between them. They might even have been in a hurry about it if hurry were possible to them. But mostly the five persons spent the after-dinner hours in near congenial talk.

"The short and happy life, that is the forgotten thing," the husband of Sally was saying. "The blue-sky interval—do you know what that was? It was the bright death sword coming down in a beam of light. Do you know that in the blue-sky days hardly one man in ten lived to be even a hundred years old? But do you know that in the blue-sky days it wasn't sealed off? The sword stroke was a cutting of the bonds. It was a release and an invitation to higher travel. Are you not tired of living in this prison for even two hundred years or three hundred?"

"You are mad," Harry Baldachin said.

Well of course the young man was mad. Broadman looked into the young man's eyes (this man was probably no older than Sally, he likely was no more than two hundred and twenty) and was startled by the secret he discovered there. The color could not be seen under the canopy, of course; the eyes were gray to the canopy world. But if he were above the canopy, Broadman knew, in the blue-sky region where the full colors could be seen, the young man's eyes would have been sky-blue.

"For the short and happy life again, and for the infinite release," Sally's husband was saying. "For those under the canopy there is no release. The short and happy life and scorching heat and paralyzing cold. Hunger and disease and fever and poverty, all the wonderful things! How have we lost them? These are not idle dreams. We have them by the promise—the Bow in the Clouds and the Promise that we be no more destroyed. But you destroy yourselves under the canopy."

"Mad, mad. Oh, but they are idle dreams, young man, and now they are over." Harry Baldachin smiled an old saurian smile. And the room was full of ponderous guards.

"Take the two young ones," Clement Flood said to the thickened guards.

But the laughter of Sally Strumpet shivered their ears and got under their thick skins.

"Take us?" she hooted. "How would they ever take us?"

"Girl, there are twenty of them, they will take you easily," Baldachin said slowly. But the husband of Sally was also laughing.

"Will twenty creeping turtles be able to catch two soaring birds on the high wing?" he laughed. "Would two hundred of them be able to? But your rumor is right, Baldachin, I do have my craft hidden somewhere on this very mountain. Ah, I believe I will be able to get the old thing up one more time."

"But we'll never be able to get it down again," Sally whooped. "Coming, Charles?"

"Yes," Charles Broadman cried eagerly. And he meant it, he meant it.

Those guards were powerful and ponderous, but they were just too slow. Twenty creeping turtles were no way able to catch those two soaring birds in their high flight. Crashing through windows with a swift tinkle of glass, then through the uncolored dark of the canopy world, to the rickety craft named Swift Wisdom that would go up one more time but would never be able to come down again, the last two flyers escaped through the pachydermous canopy.

"Mad," said Harry Baldachin.

"Insane," said Clement Flood.

"No," Charles Broadman said sadly. "No." And he sank back into his chair once more. He had wanted to go with them and he couldn't. The spirit was willing but the flesh was thickened and ponderous.

Two tears ran down his heavy cheeks but they ran very slowly, hardly an inch a minute. How should things move faster on the world under the canopy?

The Ugly Sea

"The sea is ugly," said Sour John, "and it's peculiar that I'm the only one who ever noticed it. There have been millions of words written on the sea, but nobody has written this. For a time I thought it was just my imagination, that it was only ugly to me. Then I analyzed it and found that it really is ugly.

"It is foul. It is dirtier than a cesspool; yet men who would not willingly bathe in a cesspool will bathe in it. It has the aroma of an open sewer; yet those who would not make a pilgrimage to a sewer will do so to the sea. It is untidy; it is possibly the most untidy thing in the world. And I doubt if there is any practical way to improve it. It cannot be drained; it cannot be covered up; it can only be ignored.

"Everything about it is ignoble. Its animals are baser than those of the land. Its plant life is rootless and protean. It contaminates and wastes the shores. It is an open grave where the living lie down with dead."

"It *does* smell a little, Sour John, and it *is* untidy. But I don't think it's ugly. You cannot deny that sometimes it is really beautiful."

"I do deny it. It has no visual beauty. It is monotonous, with only four or five faces, and all of them coarse. The sun and the sky over it may be beautiful; the land that it borders may be fair; but the old sewer itself is ugly."

"Then why are you the only one who thinks so?"

"There could be several reasons. One, that I've long suspected, is that I'm smarter than other people. And another is that mankind has just decided to deny this ugliness for subconscious reasons, which is to say for no reason at all. The sea is a lot like the subconscious. It may even *be* the subconscious; that was the teaching of the Thalassalogians. The Peoples of the Plains dreamed of the Sea before they visited it. They were guilty dreams. They knew the sea was there, and they were ashamed of it. The Serpent in the Garden was a Hydra, a water snake. He ascended the river to its source to prove that nothing was beyond his reach. That is the secret we have always to live with: that even the rivers of Paradise flow finally into that evil grave. We are in rhythm with the old ocean: it rises irregularly twice in twenty-four hours, and then repents of rising; and so largely do we."

"Sour John, I will still love the sea though you say it is ugly."

"So will I. I did not say I did not love it. I only said it was ugly. It is an open secret that God was less pleased with the sea than with anything else he made. His own people, at least, have always shunned it.

"O, they use it, and several times they have nearly owned it. But they do not go to sea as seamen. In all history there have been only three Jewish seamen. One was in Solomon's navy; he filled a required berth, and was unhappy. One served a Caliph in the tenth century; why I do not know. And the third was Moysha Uferwohner."

"Then let us hear about Moysha."

"Moysha was quite a good man. That is what makes it sad. And the oddest thing is what attracted him to the evil sea. You could not guess it in ten years."

"Not unless it was a waterfront woman."

"That is fantastic. Of all unlikely things that would seem the most unlikely. And yet it's the truth and you hit it at once. Not a woman in being, however, but in potential (as the philosophers have it); which is to say, quite a young girl. "Likely you have run across her. So I will tell it all."

This begins ten years ago. Moysha was then a little short of his majority, and was working with his father in an honorable trade not directly connected with the sea, that of the loan shark. But they often loaned money to seamen, a perilous business, for which reason the rates were a little higher than you might expect.

Moysha was making collections and picking up a little new trade. This took him to the smell of the sea, which was painful to him, as to any sensible man. And it took him to the Blue Fish, a water front cafe, bar, and lodging house.

A twelve-year-old girl, a cripple, the daughter of the proprietor, was playing the piano. It was not for some time, due to the primacy of other matters, that Moysha realized that she was playing atrociously. Then he attempted to correct it. "Young lady, one should play well or not at all. Please play better, or stop. That is acutely painful."

She looked as though she were going to cry, and this disconcerted Moysha, though he did not know why it did. Half an hour later the fact intruded itself on his consciousness that she was still playing, and still playing badly; but now with a stilted sort of badness.

"Young lady, this is past all bearing. I suggest that you stop playing the damned thing and go to your bed. Or go anywhere and do anything. But this is hideous. Stop it!"

The little girl really did cry then. And as a result of it Moysha got into an altercation, got his head bloodied, and was put out of the place; the first time that such a thing had ever happened to him. Then he realized that the seamen liked the little girl, and liked the way she played the piano.

This does not seem like a good beginning for either a tender love or a great passion. But it had to be the beginning; that was the first time they ever saw each other.

For the next three days Moysha was restless. A serpent was eating at his liver and he could not identify it. He began to take a drink in the middle of the day (it had not been his custom); and on the third day he asked for rum. There was a taste in his mouth and he was trying to match it. And in the inner windings of his head there was an awful smell, and it made him lonesome.

By the evening of the third day the terrible truth came to him: he had to go down for another whiff of that damned sea; and he possibly could not live through another night unless he heard that pretty little girl play the piano again.

Bonny *was* pretty. She had a wise way with her, and a willful look. It was as though she had just decided not to do something very mean, and was a little sorry that she hadn't.

She didn't really play badly; just out of tune and as nobody else had ever played, with a great amount of ringing in the ballad tunes and a sudden muting, then a sort of clashing and chiming. But she stopped playing when she saw that Moysha was in the room.

Moysha did not get on well at the Blue Fish. He didn't know how to break into the conversation of the seamen, and in his embarrassment he ordered drink after drink. When finally he became quarrelsome (as he had never been before) they put him out of the place again.

Moysha lay on a dirty tarp out on a T head and listened while Bonny played the piano again. Then she stopped. She had probably been sent to bed.

But instead she came out to the T head where he was.

"You old toad, you give me the creeps."

"I do, little girl?"

"Sure you do. And papa says 'Don't let that Yehude in the place again, he makes everybody nervous, if someone wants to borrow money from him let them borrow it somewhere else.' Even the dogs growl at you down here."

"I know it."

"Then why do you come here?"

"Tonight is the only time I ever did come except on business."

"Tonight is what I am talking about."

"I came down to see you."

"I know you did, dear. O, I didn't mean to call you that. I call everybody that."

"Do you want to take it back?"

"No, I don't want to take it back. You old toad, why aren't you a seaman like everybody else?"

"Is everybody else a seaman?"

"Everybody that comes to the Blue Fish. How will you come to the Fish now when Papa won't let you in the place?"

"I don't know."

"If you give me one of your cards I'll call you up."

"Here."

"And if you give me two dollars and a half I'll pay you back three dollars and a quarter Saturday."

"Here."

"I can't play the piano any other way. If you were a seaman I bet you'd like the way I play the piano. Good night, you old toad."

"Good night, Bonny."

And it was then that the dismal thought first came to Moysha: "What if I should be a seaman after all?"

Now this was the most terrible thing he could have done. He could have become a Christian, he could have married a tramp, he could have been convicted of embezzlement. But to leave his old life for the sea would be more than he could stand and more than his family could stand.

And there was no reason for it: only that a twelve-year-old girl looked at him less kindly than if he had been a seaman. It is a terrible and empty thing to go to sea: all order is broken up and there are only periods of debauchery and boredom and work and grinding idleness, and the sickening old pond and its dirty borders. It was for such reasons that Moysha hesitated for three months.

Bonny came to see him for possibly the tenth time. She was now paying him interest of sixty cents a week on an old debt which, in the normal state of affairs, she would never be able to clear.

"Bonny, I wish there was something that I could say to you."

"You can say anything you want to me."

"O Bonny, you don't know what I mean."

"You want to bet I don't?"

"Bonny, what will you be doing in four years?"

"I'll be getting married to a seaman if I can find one to take me."

"Why shouldn't one take you?"

"For a seaman it is bad luck to marry a crippled woman."

So on the first day of summer Moysha went off to sea as a lowly wiper. It broke his heart and shamed his family. He woke and slept in misery for the foulness of the life. He ate goy food and sinned in the ports in attempting to be a salty dog. And it was nine weeks before he was back to his home port; and he went to the Blue Fish with some other seamen.

It was afternoon, and Bonny went for a walk with him across the peninsula and down to the beach.

"Well, I'm thunderstruck is all I can say. Why in the world would a sensible man want to go to sea?"

"I thought you liked seamen, Bonny."

"I do. But how is a man going to turn into a seaman if he isn't one to start with? A dog could turn into a fish easier. That's the dumbest thing anyone ever did. I had an idea when you came to the place today that you turned into a seaman just for me. Did you?"

"Yes."

"I could be coy and say 'Why Moysha, I'm only twelve years old,' but I already knew how you felt. I will tell you something. I never did a mean thing, and I never saw anybody I wanted to be mean to till I met you. But I could be mean to you. It would be fun to ruin you. We aren't good for each other. You oughtn't to see me ever again."

"I have to."

"Then maybe I have to be mean to you. It's for both of us that I ask you not to see me again. I don't want to ruin you, and I don't want to be a mean woman; but I will be if you keep coming around."

"Well, I can't stay away."

"Very well, then I'll be perverse. I'll shock you every time I open my mouth. I'll tell you that I do filthy things, and you won't know whether I'm lying or not. You won't know what I mean, and you'll be afraid to find out. You'll never be able to stay away from me if you don't stay away now. I'll have husbands and still keep you on a string. You'll stand outside in the dark and look at the light in my window, and you'll eat your own heart. Please go away. I don't want to turn mean."

"But Bonny, it doesn't have to be that way."

"I hope it doesn't, but it scares me every time I see you. Now I'll make a bargain with you. If you try to stay away I'll try to stay good. But if you come back again I won't be responsible. You ought to go back uptown and not try to be a seaman any more."

After that the little girl went back to the Blue Fish.

Moysha did not go back uptown. He returned to the sea, and he did not visit that port again for a year. And there was a change in him. From closer acquaintance he no longer noticed that the sea was foul. Once at sunset, for a moment, he found something pleasant about it. He no longer sinned excessively in the ports. Ashore he traveled beyond the waterfront bars and visited the countries behind and met the wonderful people. He got the feel of the rough old globe in his head. In a *pension* in Holland he played chess with another twelve-year-old girl, who was not precocious, and who did not dread turning into a mean woman. In a pub in Denmark he learned to take snuff like the saltiest seaman of them all. At an inn in Brittany he was told that the sea is the heritage of the poor who cannot afford the land. It was in Brittany that he first noticed that he now walked like an old salt.

After a year he went back to his home port and to the Blue Fish.

"In a way I'm glad to see you," said Bonny. "I've been

feeling contrary lately and you'll give me an excuse. Every morning I wake up and say 'This day I'm going to raise hell.' Then I can't find anyone to raise hell with. All those water rats I like so well that I can't be mean to them. But I bet I know how to be mean to you. Well go get a room and tell me where it is, and I'll come to you tonight."

"But you're only a little girl, and besides you don't mean it."

"Then you're going to find out if I mean it. I intend to come. If you think you love me because I'm pretty and good, then I'll make you love me for a devil. There's things you don't even know about, and you've been a seaman for a year. I'll make you torture me, and it'll be a lot worse torture to you. I'll show you what unnatural really means. You're going to be mighty sorry you came back."

"Bonny, your humor is cruel."

"When did I ever have any humor? And you don't know if I'm kidding, and you never will know. Would you rather I did these things with someone else than with you?"

"No."

"Well I will. If you don't tell me where your room is, I'll go to someone else's room tonight. I'll do things so filthy you wouldn't believe it. And even if I don't go to somebody, I'll tell you tomorrow that I did."

But Moysha would not tell her where his room was. So late that night when he left the Blue Fish she followed him. It was fantastic for a grown man to walk faster and faster to escape a thirteen-year-old crippled girl, and finally to turn in panic through the dark streets. But when finally she lost him she cried out with surprising kindness: "Goodnight Moysha, I'm sorry I was mean."

But she wasn't very sorry, for the next night she was still mean.

"You see that old man with the hair in his ears? He's filthy and we don't even understand each other's language. But he understood what I wanted well enough. He's the one I spent last night with."

"Bonny, that's a lie, and it isn't funny."

"I know it isn't funny. But can you be sure that it's a lie? I only lie part of the time, and you never know when. Now tonight, if you don't tell me where your room is, I'm going to take either that old red-faced slobberer or that black man. And you can follow me, since you run away when I follow you, and see that I go with one of them. And you can stand out in the street and look up at our light. I always leave the light on."

"Bonny, why are you mean?"

"I wish I knew, Moysha, I wish I knew."

After a week of this he went to sea again, and did not come back to his home port for two years. He learned of the sea-leaning giants.

"I do not know the name of this tree," said Sour John, "though once I knew it. This is the time of a story where one usually says it's time for a drink. However, for a long time I have been worried about my parasites who are to me almost like my own children, and this constant diet of rum and red-eye cannot be good for them. I believe if the young lady would fry me a platter of eggs it would please my small associates, and do me more good than harm."

He learned, Moysha did, of the sea-leaning giants. They are massive trees of the islands and the more fragmentary mainlands, and they grow almost horizontal out toward the sea. They are not influenced by the wind; from the time they are little whips the wind is always blowing in from the sea, and they grow against it and against all reason. They have, some of them, trunks nine feet thick, but they always lean out over the sea. Moysha began to understand why they did, though most people would never understand it.

He acquired a talking bird of great versatility. He acquired also a ring-tailed monkey and a snake that he carried around inside his shirt, for Moysha was now a very salty seaman.

He was prosperous, for he had never forsaken the trade of the moneylender, and he was always a shrewd buyer of novelties and merchandise. He turned them over as he went from port to port, and always at a profit.

He became a cool student of the ceaseless carnage of the ocean, and loved to muse on the ascending and descending corpses and their fragments in the old watery grave.

He spent seven months on a certain Chinese puzzle, and he worked it, the only Occidental who ever had patience enough to do so.

When she was fifteen Bonny married a seaman, and he was not Moysha. This happened just one week before Moysha came back to port and to the Blue Fish. The man she married was named Oglesby Ogburn; and if you think that's a funny name, you should have heard the handles of some of them that she turned down.

The very day that Moysha came to the Blue Fish was the day that Oglesby left; for the honeymoon was over, and he had to go back to sea. Bonny was now all kindness to every-one. But she still put the old needle into Moysha.

"I've had a husband for a week now, so I won't be able to get along without a man. You stay with me while you're in town; and after that I'll get another, and then another and another. And by that time Oglesby will be back for a week."

"Don't talk like that, Bonny, even if I know you're joking."

"But you don't know that I'm joking. You never know for sure."

"How can anyone who looks so like an angel talk like that?"

"It does provide a contrast. Don't you think it makes me more interesting? I didn't know you were the kind who chased married women."

"I'm not. But O Bonny! What am I to do?"

"Well I've certainly offered you everything. I don't know how I can offer you any more."

And a few days later when Moysha was leaving port they talked again.

"You haven't even given me a wedding present or wished me luck. And we do need it. It's always bad luck for a seaman to marry a crippled woman. What are you going to give me for a wedding present?"

"The only thing I will give you is the serpent from my bo-som."

"O don't talk so flowery."

Then he took the snake out of his shirt.

"O, I didn't know you had a real snake. Is he for me? That's the nicest present anyone ever gave me. What do you call him?"

"Why, just a snake. Ular, that is, he's a foreign snake."

So he went back to sea and left the little girl there with the snake in her hands.

Bonny was a widow when she was sixteen, as everyone had known she would be. It's no joke about it being bad luck for a seaman to marry a cripple. They seldom lose much time in perishing after they do it. Oglesby died at sea, as all the Ogburns did; and it was from a trifling illness from which he was hardly sick at all. It was many weeks later that Moysha heard the news, and then he hurried back to his home port.

He was too late. Bonny had married again.

"I thought you'd probably come, and I kind of wanted it to be you. But you waited so long, and the summer was half over, that I decided to marry Polycarp Melish. I'm halfway sorry I did. He wouldn't let Ular sleep with us, and he killed him just because he bit him on the thumb.

"But I tell you what you do. What with the bad luck and all, Polycarp won't last many months. Come around earlier next year. I like to get married in the springtime. I'll be a double widow then."

"Bonny, that's a terrible way to talk even when kidding."

"I'm not kidding at all. I even have an idea how we can beat the jinx. I'll tell you about it after we get married next year. Maybe a crippled girl gets to keep her third husband."

"Do you want Polycarp to die?"

"Of course I don't. I love him. I love all my husbands, just like I'll love you after I marry you. I can't help it if I'm bad luck. I told him, and he said he already knew it; but he wanted to do it anyhow. Will you bring me another snake the next time you're in port?"

"Yes. And you can keep the monkey in place of it till I come back. But you can't have the bird yet. I have to keep someone to talk to."

"All right. Please come in the spring. Don't wait till summer again or it'll be too late and I'll already be married to someone else. But whether we get married or not, I'm never going to be mean again. I'm getting too old for that."

So he went to sea again happier than he ever had before.

When she was seventeen Bonny was a widow again as everyone had known she would be. Polycarp had been mangled and chopped to pieces in an unusual accident in the engine room of his ship.

Moysha heard of it very soon, before it could have been heard of at home. And he took council with his talking bird, and with one other, technically more human.

"This other," said Sour John, "was myself. It was very early spring, and Moysha was wondering if it were really best to hurry home and marry Bonny.

" 'I am not at all superstitious,' he said. 'I do not believe that a crippled woman is necessarily bad luck to seamen. But I believe that Bonny may be bad luck to everyone, including herself.'

"We were on a chocolate island of a French flavor and a French name. On it were girls as pretty as Bonny, and without her reputation for bad luck: girls who would never be either wives or widows. And there is a way to go clear around the world from one such place to another.

" 'The Blue Fish is not necessarily the center of the earth,' I told him. 'I have always believed it to be a little left of center. And Bonny may not be the queen. But if you think that she is, then for you she is so. Nine months, or even a year is not very long to live, and you will be at sea most of the time.

But if you think a few weeks with the little girl is enough, then it is enough for you. A lot of others who will not have even that will be dead by next Easter.' I said this to cheer him up. I was always the cheerful type.

" 'And what do you think?' Moysha asked the talking bird.

" 'Sampah,' said the bird in his own tongue. This means rubbish. But whether he meant that the superstition was rubbish, or the idea of marrying with a consequent early death was rubbish, is something that is still locked up in his little green head."

Moysha hurried home to marry Bonny. He brought a brother of Ular for a present, and he went at once to the Blue Fish.

"Well you're just in time. I was going to have the banns read for me and somebody tomorrow, and if you'd been an hour later it wouldn't have been you."

"I was halfway afraid to come."

"You needn't have been afraid. I told you I knew a way to beat the jinx. I'm selling the Blue Fish. I wrote you that Papa was dead. And we're going to take a house uptown and forget the sea."

"Forget the sea? How could anyone forget the sea?"

"Why, you're only a toy seaman. You weren't raised to it. When you go away from it you won't be a seaman at all. And crippled women are only bad luck to seamen, not to other men."

"But what would I do? The sea is all I know."

"Don't be a child, Moysha. You hate the sea, remember? You always told me that you did. You only went to sea because you thought I liked seamen. You know a hundred ways to make a dollar, and you don't have to go near the sea for any of them."

So they were married. And they were happy. Moysha discovered that Bonny was really an angel. Her devil talk had been a stunt.

It was worth all five dark years at sea to have her. She was now even more lovely than the first night he had seen her. They lived in a house uptown in the heart of the city, and were an urbane and civilized couple. And three years went by.

Then one day Bonny said that they ought to get rid of the snake, and maybe even the monkey. She was afraid they would bite one of the children, or one of the children would bite them.

The talking bird said that if his friends left he would leave, too.

"But Bonny," said Moysha, "these three are all that I have to remind me of the years when I was a seaman."

"You have me, also. But why do you want to be reminded of those awful days?"

"I know what we could do, Bonny. We could buy the Blue Fish again. It isn't doing well. We could live there and run it. And we could have a place there for the snake and the monkey and the bird."

"Yes, we could have a place for them all, but not for the children. That is no place to raise children. I know, and I was raised there. Now my love, don't be difficult. Take the three creatures and dispose of them. And remember that for us the sea isn't even there any more."

But it was still there when he went down to the Blue Fish to try to sell the three creatures to the seaman. An old friend of his was present and was looking for an engineer first class to ship out that very night. And there was a great difficulty in selling the creatures.

He could not sell them unless he put a price on them, and he was damned if he'd do that. That was worse than putting a price on his own children. He had had them longer than his children, and they were more peculiarly his own. He could not sell them. And he could not go home and tell his wife that he could not sell them.

"He went out and sat on the horns of the dilemma and looked at the sea. And then his old friend (who coincidentally was myself)," said Sour John, "came out and said that he sure did need an engineer first class to leave that very night.

"And then what do you think that Moysha did?"

"O, he signed on and went back to sea."

Sour John was thunderstruck.

"How did you know that? You've hit it again. I never will know how you do it. Well, that's what he did. In the face of everything he left his beautiful wife and children, and his clean life, and went to the filthy sea again. It's incredible."

"And how is he doing now?"

"God knows. I mean it literally. Naturally he's dead. That's been a year. You don't expect a seaman married to a crippled woman to live forever do you?"

"And how is Bonny?"

"I went to see her this afternoon; for this is the port where it all happened. She had out an atlas and a pencil and piece of string. She was trying to measure out what town in the whole country is furthest from the sea.

"She is lonely and grieves for Moysha, more than for either of her other husbands. But O she is lovely! She supports herself and her brood by giving piano lessons."

"Is there a moral to this?"

"No. It is an immoral story. And it's a mystery to me. A man will not normally leave a clean home to dwell in an open grave, nor abandon children to descend into a sewer, nor forswear a lovely and loving wife to go faring on a cesspool, knowing that he will shortly die there as a part of the bargain.

"But that is what he did."

Cliffs that Laughed

"Between ten and ten-thirty of the morning of October 1, 1945, on an island that is sometimes called Pulau Petir and sometimes Willy Jones Island (neither of them its map name), three American soldiers disappeared and have not been seen since.

"I'm going back there, I tell you! It was worth it. The limbs that laughed! Let them kill me! I'll get there! Oh, here, here, I've got to get hold of myself.

"The three soldiers were Sergeant Charles Santee of Orange, Texas; Corporal Robert Casper of Gobey, Tennessee; and PFC Timothy Lorrigan of Boston which is in one of the eastern states. I was one of those three soldiers.

"I'm going back there if it takes me another twenty years!"

No, no, no! That's the wrong story. It happened on Willy Jones Island also, but it's a different account entirely. That's the one the fellow told me in a bar years later, just the other night, after the usual "Didn't I used to know you in the Islands?"

"One often makes these little mistakes and false starts," Galli said. "It is a trick that is used in the trade. One exasperates people and pretends to be embarrassed. And then one hooks them."

Galli was an hereditary storyteller of the Indies. "There is only one story in the world," he said, "and it pulls two ways. There is the reason part that says 'Hell, it can't be' and there is the wonder part that says 'Hell, maybe it is.'" He was the storyteller, and he offered to teach me the art.

For we ourselves had a hook into Galli. We had something he wanted.

"We used the same stories for a thousand years," he said. "Now, however, we have a new source, the American Comic Books. My grandfather began to use these in another place and time, and I use them now. I steal them from your orderly tents, and I have a box full of them. I have *Space Comics* and *Commander Midnight;* I have *Galactic Gob* and *Mighty Mouse* and the *Green Hornet* and the *Masked Jetter*. My grandfather also had copies of some of these, but drawn by older hands. But I do not have *Wonder Woman,* not a single copy. I would trade three-for-one for copies of her. I would pay a premium. I can link her in with an island legend to create a whole new cycle of stories, and I need new stuff all the time. Have you a *Wonder Woman?*"

When Galli said this, I knew that I had him. I didn't have a *Wonder Woman,* but I knew where I could steal one. I believe, though I am no longer sure, that it was *Wonder Woman Meets the Space Magicians.*

I stole it for him. And in gratitude Galli not only taught me the storyteller's art, but he also told me the following story:

"Imagine about flute notes ascending," said Galli. "I haven't my flute with me, but a story should begin so to set the mood. Imagine about ships coming out of the Arabian Ocean, and finally to Jilolo Island, and still more finally to the very island on which we now stand. Imagine about waves and trees that were the great-great-grandfathers of the waves and trees we now have."

It was about the year 1620, Galli is telling it, in the late afternoon of the high piracy. These Moluccas had already been the rich Spice Islands for three hundred years. Moreover, they were on the road of the Manila galleons coming from Mexico and the Isthmus. Arabian, Hindu, and Chinese piracy had decayed shamefully. The English were crude at the business. In trade the Dutch had become dominant in the Islands and the Portuguese had faded. There was no limit to the opportunities for a courageous and dedicated raider in the Indies.

They came. And not the least of these new raiding men was Willy Jones.

It was said that Willy Jones was a Welshman. You can believe it or not as you like. The same thing has been said about the Devil. Willy was twenty-five years old when he finally possessed his own ship with a mixed crew. The ship was built like a humpbacked bird, with a lateen sail and suddenly-appearing rows of winglike oars. On its prow was a swooping bird that had been carved in Muskat. It was named the *Flying Serpent,* or the *Feathered Snake,* depending on what language you use.

"Pause a moment,' said Galli. 'Set the mood. Imagine about dead men variously. We come to the bloody stuff at once."

One early morning, the *Feathered Snake* overtook a tall Dutchman. The ships were grappled together, and the men from the *Snake* boarded the Dutch ship. The men on the Dutchman were armed, but they had never seen such sudden-ness and savagery as shown by the dark men from the *Snake.* There was slippery blood on the decks, and the croaking of men being killed.

'I forgot to tell you that this was in the passage between the Molucca Sea and the Banda,' Galli said.

The *Snake* took a rich small cargo from the Dutch ship, a few ablebodied Malay seamen, some gold specie, some pa-pers of record, and a dark Dutch girl named Margaret. These latter things Willy Jones preempted for himself. Then the *Snake* devoured that tall Dutchman and left only a few of its burning bones floating in the ocean.

'I forgot to tell you that the tall Dutch ship was named the *Luchtkastell,*' Galli said.

Willy Jones watched the *Luchtkastell* disappearing under the water. He examined the papers of record, and the dark Dutch girl Margaret. He made a sudden decision: He would cash his winnings and lay up for a season.

He had learned about an island in the papers of record. It was a rich island, belonging to the richest of the Dutch spice men who had gone to the bottom with the *Luchtkastell.* The fighting crew would help Willy Jones secure the island for himself; and in exchange, he would give them his ship and the whole raiding territory and the routes he had worked out.

Willy Jones captured the island and ruled it. From the ship he kept only the gold, the dark Dutch girl Margaret, and three golems which had once been ransom from a Jew in Oman.

'I forgot to tell you that Margaret was the daughter of the Dutch spice man who had owned the island and the tall ship and who was killed by Willy,' Galli said, 'and the island really belonged to Margaret now as the daughter of her father.'

For one year Willy Jones ruled the small settlement, drove the three golems and the men who already lived there, had the spices gathered and baled and stored (they were worth their weight in silver), and built the Big House. And for one year he courted the dark Dutch girl Margaret, having been unable to board her as he had all other girls.

She refused him because he had killed her father, because he had destroyed the *Luchtkastell* which was Family and Nation to her, and because he had stolen her island.

This Margaret, though she was pretty and trim as a *kuching*, had during the affair of the *Feathered Snake* and the *Luchtkastell* twirled three seamen in the air like pinwheels at one time and thrown them all into the ocean. She had eyes that twinkled like the compounded eyes of the devil-fly; they could glint laughter and fury at the same time.

"Those girls were like volcanoes," the man said. "Slim, strong mountains, and we climbed them like mountains. Man, the uplift on them! The shoulders were cliffs that laughed. The swaying—"

No, no! Belay that last paragraph! That's from the ramble of the fellow in the bar, and it keeps intruding.

'I forgot to tell you that she reminds me of *Wonder Woman*,' Galli said.

Willy Jones believed that Margaret was worth winning unbroken, as he was not at all sure that he could break her. He courted her as well as he could, and he used to advantage the background of the golden-green spicery on which they lived.

'Imagine about the Permata bird that nests on the moon,' Galli said, 'and which is the most passionate as well as the noblest-singing of the birds. Imagine about flute notes soaring.'

Willy Jones made this tune to Margaret:

The Nutmeg Moon is the third moon of the year.
The Tides come in like loose Silk all its Nights.
The Ground is animated by the bare Feet of Margaret
Who is like the *Pelepah* of the *Ko-eng* Flower.

Willy made this tune in the Malaya language in which all the words end in *ang*.

'Imagine about water leaping down rocky hills,' Galli said. 'Imagine about red birds romping in green groves.'

Willy Jones made another tune to Margaret:

A Woman with Shoulders so strong that a Man
    might ride upon them
The while she is still the little Girl watching for the
    black Ship
Of the Hero who is the same age as the Sky,
But she does not realize that I am already here.

Willy made this tune in the Dutch language in which all the words end in *lijk*.

'Imagine about another flute joining the first one, and their notes scamper like birds,' Galli said.

Willy Jones made a last tune to Margaret:
> Damnation! That is enough of Moonlight and
>   Tomorrows!
> Now there are mats to plait, and *kain* to sew.
> Even the smallest crab knows to build herself a
>   house in the sand.
> Margaret should be raking the oven coals and
>   baking a *roti*.
> I wonder why she is so slow in seeing this.

Willy made this tune in the Welsh language in which all the words end in *gwbl*.

When the one year was finished, they were mated. There was still the chilliness there as though she would never forgive him for killing her father and stealing her island; but they began to be in accord.

'Here pause five minutes to indicate an idyllic interlude,' Galli said. 'We sing the song *Bagang Kali Berjumpa* if you know the tune. We flute, if I have my flute.'

The idyllic interlude passed.

Then Willy's old ship, the *Feathered Snake*, came back to the Island. She was in a pitiful state of misuse. She reeked of old and new blood, and there were none left on her but nine sick men. These nine men begged Willy Jones to become their captain again to set everything right.

Willy washed the nine living skeletons and fed them up for three days. They were fat and able by then. And the three golems had refitted the ship.

"All she needs is a strong hand at the helm again," said Willy Jones. "I will sail her again for a week and a day. I will impress a new crew, and once more make her the terror of the Spice Islands. Then I will return to my island, knowing that I have done a good deed in restoring the *Snake* to the bloody work for which she was born."

"If you go, Willy Jones, you will be gone for many years," said the dark Dutch Margaret.

"Only one at the most," said Willy.

"And I will be in my grave when you return."

"There is no grave could hold you, Margaret."

"Aye, it may not hold me. I'll out of it and confront you when you come back. But it gives one a weirdness to be in the grave for only a few years. I will not own you for my husband when you do come back. You will not even know whether I am the same woman that you left, and you will never know. I am a volcano, but I banked my hatred and accepted you. But if you leave me now, I will erupt against you forever."

But Willy Jones went away in the *Flying Serpent* and left her there. He took two of the golems with him, and he left one of them to serve Margaret.

What with one thing and another, he was gone for twenty years.

"We were off that morning to satisfy our curiosity about the Big House," the fellow said, "since we would soon be leaving the island forever. You know about the Big House. You were on Willy Jones Island too. The Jilolos call it the House of Skulls, and the Malaya and Indonesia people will not speak about it at all.

"We approached the Big House that was not more than a mile beyond our perimeter. It was a large decayed building, but we had the sudden feeling that it was still inhabited. And it wasn't supposed to be. Then we saw the two of them, the mother and the daughter. We shook like we were unhinged, and we ran to them.

"They were so alike that we couldn't tell them apart. Their eyes twinkled like the compounded eyes of a creature that eats her mate. Noonday lightning! How it struck! Arms that swept you off your feet and set your bones to singing! We knew that they were not twins, or even sisters. We knew that they were mother and daughter.

"I have never encountered anything like them in my life! Whatever happened to the other two soldiers, I know it was worth it to them. Whatever happened, I don't care if they kill me! They were perfect, those two women, even though we weren't with them for five minutes."

"Then it was the Badger."

No, no, no! That's the wrong story again. That's not the story Galli told me. That's part of the story the fellow told me in the bar. His confused account keeps interposing itself, possibly because I knew him slightly when we were both soldiers on Willy Jones Island. But he had turned queer, that fellow. "It is the earthquake belt around the world that is the same as the legend belt," he said, "and the Middleworld underlies it all. That's why I was able to walk it." It was as though he had been keel-hauled around the world. I hadn't known him well. I didn't know which of the three soldiers he was. I had heard that they were all dead. "Imagine about conspiracy stuff now," said Galli. "Imagine about a whispering in a pinang grove before the sun is up."

"How can I spook that man?" Margaret asked her golem shortly after she had been abandoned by Willy Jones. "But I am afraid that a mechanical man would not be able to tell me how."

"I will tell you a secret," said the golem. "We are not mechanical men. Certain wise and secret men believe that they made us, but they are wrong. They have made houses for us to live in, no more. There are many of us unhoused spirits, and we take shelter in such bodies as we find. That being so, I know something of the houseless spirits in the depth of every man. I will select one of them, and we will spook Willy Jones with that one. Willy is a Welshman who has become by adoption a Dutchman and a Malayan and a Jilolo man. There is one old spook running through them all. I will call it up when it is time."

"I forgot to tell you that the name of Margaret's golem was Meshuarat," Galli said.

After twenty years of high piracy, Willy Jones returned to his Island. And there was the dark Dutch Margaret standing as young and as smouldering as when he had left. He leapt to embrace her, and found himself stretched flat on the sand by a thunderous blow.

He was not surprised, and was not (as he had at first believed) decapitated. Almost he was not displeased. Margaret had often been violent in her love-making.

"But I will have you," Willy swore as he tasted his own blood delightfully in his mouth and pulled himself up onto hands and knees. "I have ridden the Margaret-tiger before."

"You will never ride my loins, you lecherous old goat," she rang at him like a bell. "I am not your wife. I am the daughter that you left here in the womb. My mother is in the grave on the hill."

Willy Jones sorrowed terribly, and he went to the grave.

But Margaret came up behind him and drove in the cruel lance. "I told you that when you came back you would not know whether I was the same woman you had left," she chortled, "and you will never know!"

"Margaret, you are my wife!" Willy Jones gasped.

"Am I of an age to be your wife?" she jibed. "Regard me! Of what age do I seem to be?"

"Of the same age as when I left," said Willy. "But perhaps you have eaten of the besok nut and so do not change your appearance."

"I forgot to tell you about the besok nut," said Galli. "If one eats the nut of the besok tree, the tomorrow tree, the time tree, that one will not age. But this is always accompanied by a chilling unhappiness."

"Perhaps I did eat it," said Margaret. "But that is my

grave there, and I have lain in it many years, as has she. You are prohibited from touching either of us."

"Are you the mother or the daughter, Witch?"

"You will never know. You will see us both, for we take turns, and you will not be able to tell us apart. See, the grave is always disturbed, and the entrance is easy."

"I'll have the truth from the golem who served you while I was gone," Willy swore.

'A golem is an artificial man,' said Galli. 'They were made by the Jews and Arabs in earlier ages, but now they say that they have forgotten how to make them. I wonder that you do not make them yourselves, for you have advanced techniques. You tell them and you picture them in your own heroic literature' (he patted the comic books under his arm), 'but you do not have them in actuality."

The golem told Willy Jones that the affair was thus:

A daughter had indeed been born to Margaret. She had slain the child, and had then put it into the middle state. Thereafter, the child stayed sometimes in the grave, and sometimes she walked about the island. And she grew as any other child would. And Margaret herself had eaten the besok nut so that she would not age.

When mother and daughter had come to the same age and appearance (and it had only been the very day before that, the day before Willy Jones had returned), then the daughter had also eaten the besok nut. Now the mother and daughter would be of the same appearance forever, and not even a golem could tell them apart.

Willy Jones came furiously onto the woman again.

"I was sure before, and now I am even more sure that you are Margaret," he said, "and now I will have you in my fury."

"We both be Margaret," she said. "But I am not the same one you apprehended earlier. We changed places while you talked to the golem. And we are both in the middle state, and we have both been dead in the grave, and you dare not touch either of us ever. A Welshman turned Dutchman turned Malayan turned Jilolo has this spook in him four times over. The Devil himself will not touch his own daughters."

The last part was a lie, but Willy Jones did not know it.

"We be in confrontation forever then," said Willy Jones. "I will make my Big House a house of hate and a house of skulls. You cannot escape from its environs, neither can any visitor. I'll kill them all and pile their skulls up high for a monument to you."

Then Willy Jones ate a piece of bitter bark from the pokok ru.

'I forgot to tell you that when a person eats bark from the pokok ru in anger, his anger will sustain itself forever,' Galli said.

"If it's visitors you want for the killing, I and my mother-daughter will provide them in numbers," said Margaret. "Men will be attracted here forever with no heed for danger. I will eat a telor tuntong of the special sort, and all men will be attracted here even to their death."

'I forgot to tell you that if a female eats the telor tuntong of the special sort, all males will be attracted irresistibly,' Galli said. 'Ah, you smile as though you doubted that the be-sok nut or the bark of the pokok ru or the telor tuntong of the special sort could have such effects. But yourselves come now to wonder drugs like little boys. In these islands they are all around you and you too blind to see. It is no ignorant man who tells you this. I have read the booklets from your orderly tents: *Physics without Mathematics, Cosmology without Chaos, Psychology without Brains.* It is myself, the master of all sciences and disciplines, who tells you that these things do work. Besides hard science, there is soft science, the science of shadow areas and story areas, and you do wrong to deny it the name.

'I believe that you yourself can see what had to follow, from the dispositions of the Margarets and Willy Jones," Galli said. "For hundreds of years, men from everywhere came to the Margarets who could not be resisted. And Willy Jones killed them all and piled up their skulls. It became, in a very savage form, what you call the Badger Game."

Galli was a good-natured and unhandsome brown man. He worked around the army base as translator, knowing (besides his native Jilolo), the Malayan, Dutch, Japanese and English languages, and (as every storyteller must) the Arabian. His English was whatever he wanted it to be, and he burlesqued the speech of the American soldiers to the Australians, and the Australians to the Americans.

"Man, it was a Badger!" the man said. "It was a grizzle-haired, glare-eyed, flat-headed, underslung, pigeon-toed, hook-clawed, clam-jawed Badger from Badger Game Corner! They moved in on us, but I'd take my chances and go back and do it again. We hadn't frolicked with the girls for five minutes when the Things moved in on us. I say Things; I don't know whether they were men or not. If they were, they

were the coldest three men I ever saw. But they were directed by a man who made up for it. He was livid, hopping with
hatred. They moved in on us and began to kill us."

*No, No, that isn't part of Galli's story. That's some more
of the ramble that the fellow told me in the bar the other
evening.*

It has been three hundred years, and the confrontation
continues. There are skulls of Malayan men and Jilolo men
piled up there; and of Dutchmen and Englishmen and of Portuguese men; of Chinamen and Philippinos and Goanese; of
Japanese, and of the men from the United States and Aus-
tralia.

'Only this morning there were added the skulls of two
United States men, and there should have been three of
them," Galli said. "They came, as have all others, because
the Margarets ate the telor tuntong of the special sort. It is a
fact that with a species (whether insect or shelled thing or
other) where the male gives his life in the mating, the female
has always eaten of this telor tuntong. You'd never talk the
males into such a thing with words alone."

'How is it that there were only two United States skulls
this morning, and there should have been three?' I asked him.

'One of them escaped,' Galli explained, 'and that was unusual. He fell through a hole to the middle land, that third
one of them. But the way back from the middle land to one's
own country is long, and it must be walked. It takes at least
twenty years, wherever one's own country is; and the joke
thing about it is that the man is always wanting to go the
other way.

'That is the end of the story, but let it not end abruptly,'
Galli said. 'Sing the song *Chari Yang Besar* if you remember
the tune. Imagine about flute notes lingering in the air.'

"I was lost for more than twenty years, and that's a fact,"
the man said. He gripped the bar with the most knotted
hands I ever saw, and laughed with a merriment so deep that
it seemed to be his bones laughing. "Did you know that
there's another world just under this world, or just around
the corner from it? I walked all day every day. I was in a
torture, for I suspected that I was going the wrong way, and
I could go no other. And I sometimes suspected that the middle land through which I traveled was in my head, a derange-
ment from the terrible blow that one of the Things gave me
as he came in to kill me. And yet there are correlates that
convince me it was a real place.

"I wasn't trying to get home. I was trying to get back to those girls even if it killed me. There weren't any colors in that world, all gray tones, but otherwise it wasn't much different from this one. There were even bars there a little like the Red Rooster."

(I forgot to tell you that it was in the Red Rooster bar that the soldier from the islands told me the parts of his story.)

"I've got to get back there. I think I know the way now, and how to get on the road. I have to travel it through the middle land, you know. They'll kill me, of course, and I won't even get to jazz those girls for five minutes; but I've got to get back there. Going to take me another twenty years, though. That sure is a weary walk."

I never knew him well, and I don't remember which of the names was his. But a man from Orange, Texas, or from Gobey, Tennessee, or from Boston, in one of the eastern states, is on a twenty-year walk through the middle land to find the dark Dutch Margarets, and death.

I looked up a couple of things yesterday. There was Revel's recent work on Moluccan Narcotics. He tells of the Besok Nut which *does* seem to inhibit aging but which induces internal distraction and hypersexuality. There is the Pokok Ru whose bitter bark impels even the most gentle to violent anger. There is one sort of Telor Tuntong which sets up an inexplicable aura about a woman eater and draws all males overpoweringly to her. There is much research still to be done on these narcotics, Revel writes.

I dipped into Mandrago's *Earthquake* and *Legend and the Middle World*. He states that the earthquake belt around the world is also the legend belt, and that one of the underlying legends is of the underlying land, the middle world below this world where one can wander lost forever.

And I went down to the Red Rooster again the next evening, which was last evening, to ask about the man and to see if he could give me a more cogent account. For I had re-remembered Galli's old story in the meanwhile.

"No, he was just passing through town," the barman said. "Had a long trip ahead of him. He was sort of a nutty fellow. I've often said the same thing about you."

That is the end of the other story, but let it not end suddenly. Pause for a moment to savor it. Sing the song *Itu Masa Dahulu* if you remember the tune.

Imagine about flute notes falling. I don't have a flute, but a story should end so.